PROLOGUE

WHO CARES? A MEMOIR BY JULIAN GRIGGS

Introduction

Many of you will know me as the victim of a terrible crime. On a dark November night, someone broke into my Edinburgh home and murdered my beautiful wife, Helen. Smothered her with a pillow as she slept. The crime attracted nationwide coverage. Many of you sent me heartfelt messages of support, and I know you shared my disbelief that anyone could harm such a vulnerable woman. A woman who, in her forty-two years of life, had already suffered so much misfortune.

Ten years before Helen's death, we were involved in a car accident. The spinal injury she sustained paralysed her lower body. Her head injuries left her with brain damage – her cognitive abilities severely impaired and her impulse control almost eradicated. But despite these traumas, she still had the same feisty personality, and she endured her merciless suffering with all the dignity she was capable of.

When I finally brought Helen home after months of hospitalisation, I had no idea of the difficulties that lay ahead. Like many people in similar situations, we lost everything. Our jobs, our home, our independence. Forced to live on benefits, we struggled through life, but, as I often pointed out to Helen, at least we had each other. Hard as it may be to believe, the accident made the bond between us stronger than ever.

As I write this memoir, sitting with my laptop in a fashionable café not far from my London home, it is difficult to accept that, to this day, her murder remains unsolved. It is an apparently motiveless crime. Money and jewellery were stolen from our ransacked home, and the police still believe a random stranger broke in, intending to burgle us. A stranger who ended up killing Helen in the process. Thoughts of this individual often keep me awake me at night. I cannot help wondering what could have driven him or her to commit such a seemingly pointless act. In all honesty, I am still amazed that despite a thorough investigation, the police have been unable to find any leads or produce a suspect. This lack of closure has left questions that may never be resolved: who killed my wife and why?

THE PERFECT HOLIDAY

T. J. EMERSON

First published in Great Britain in 2022 by Boldwood Books Ltd.

Copyright © T.J. Emerson, 2022

Cover Design by Head Design Ltd

Cover Photography: Shutterstock

Every effort has been made to obtain the necessary permissions with reference to copyright material, both illustrative and quoted. We apologise for any omissions in this respect and will be pleased to make the appropriate acknowledgements in any future edition.

A CIP catalogue record for this book is available from the British Library.

Paperback ISBN 978-1-80415-163-1

Large Print ISBN 978-1-80415-159-4

Hardback ISBN 978-1-80415-158-7

Ebook ISBN 978-1-80415-156-3

Kindle ISBN 978-1-80415-157-0

Audio CD ISBN 978-1-80415-164-8

MP3 CD ISBN 978-1-80415-161-7

Digital audio download ISBN 978-1-80415-155-6

Boldwood Books Ltd
23 Bowerdean Street
London SW6 3TN
www.boldwoodbooks.com

AFTER

1

Julian Griggs woke at dawn. His bleary eyes took in the dark wooden beam in the ceiling above him and the rotating fan blades suspended from it. Turning his head, he saw a pair of green shutters outlined by the golden glow of the Mallorcan sun.

Olivia stirred beside him and snuggled her warm, solid body against his.

'Happy birthday,' he said.

'What time is it?' she asked in her raspy voice.

'About six.'

'I'm not ready to be fifty-four,' she said. 'Go back to sleep, little mouse.' Little mouse because she said he rubbed his beard against his pillow when he slept, and the rustling sound reminded her of mice.

He shut his eyes and dozed until his aching bladder forced him awake. Untangling himself from his wife, he clambered out of bed and padded across the cold terracotta tiles. On his way to the en suite bathroom, he picked up Olivia's black kaftan from the floor and draped it over the chair beside the wardrobe. He paused to inspect himself in the long, thin mirror on the wardrobe door. Not bad for a man of forty-nine. Streaks of grey had colonised his dark brown hair, but, although it had thinned at the temples, he still had plenty on top. A neat, grey goatee had replaced his once scruffy beard, and these days, his dark brown eyes were no longer blood-shot and dull from lack of sleep.

Almost four years had passed since Helen's death, and he'd worked on his appearance a lot in that time. His body had grown stronger and more muscular thanks to regular gym visits and the training he'd endured for his fundraising marathon last year. His stomach had developed a slight paunch since then. Julian pinched this excess flesh as he looked at himself in the mirror. With his height, he could carry a few extra pounds, but he didn't want to let himself go again.

In the bathroom, he opened the small window set into the thick white wall behind the toilet and gazed out as he emptied himself in short, noisy spurts. Last night, they'd arrived from London in the dark, and he hadn't had a chance to enjoy the view from the villa. The sun had yet to rise over the top of the Teix mountain, and the lower flanks of the Serra de Tramuntana range were in shadow. In the distance, he could see the terracotta-tiled rooftops of Deià village. Beautiful. The air he drew into his lungs was cool, but the blue Mallorcan sky promised a hot day to come.

He spotted a large bird circling high overhead, wings outspread. The slow majesty with which it rode the currents identified it as a bird of prey. A hawk, he thought, or an eagle. Breath held, he watched the bird, compelled by its grace and menace.

When he returned to the bedroom, he found Olivia lying on her back, a pale, freckled calf sticking out from beneath the sheet. Standing beside the bed, he had the unsettling notion he might still be asleep. He feared his new reality might be a dream. A precarious dream that could be shattered at any moment.

He climbed in beside his wife, intending to rest his head on her heavy breasts, but she reached between his legs and took hold of him with her large dry palm.

'Come here, little mouse,' she said.

2

After Julian finished having pleasant, unadventurous sex with his wife, he rolled off her and lay spent in her arms, her heartbeat racing beneath his left ear.

'Fifty-four,' Olivia said. 'Where do the years go?'

He refrained from insisting she looked younger than her age. She didn't, and she couldn't bear flattery. He admired her lack of vanity, one of her many good qualities. She'd given up dying her cropped auburn hair, content to let the grey take over. She had a long broad nose and heavy-lidded grey eyes, but she radiated a warmth Julian found comforting.

'I think you're a very attractive woman, Olivia Pearson,' he said.

She kissed the top of his head. 'And you, Julian Griggs, are a truly good man.'

The pumping of her heart made him suddenly uncomfortable, and he had to sit up. 'How about we get the birthday girl some breakfast?'

'I'll drive into Deià and pick up some pastries.'

'Good idea. I'll come with you.'

'No, you have your swim. I know how much you've been looking forward to it.'

True. He'd promised himself a swim before breakfast every morning.

'What about your morning walk?' he asked.

'I'll start tomorrow.'

Olivia took a shower, emerging after only three minutes. She didn't approve of wasting water. Even if she had, the villa's ancient, fickle boiler system wouldn't have allowed her to linger. She gave her body a vigorous dry before dropping her towel on the floor. Julian watched his naked wife's beauty routine through half-closed eyes – a brush pulled at speed through wet hair, a cursory smear of cheap moisturiser over her face.

'Right.' She picked up the black kaftan from the chair and slipped it on. 'Won't be long.' She pushed her feet into black Birkenstock sandals and blew Julian a kiss. As she exited the room, the soles of her shoes slapped against the tiles, a sound Julian found reassuring. The soundtrack to his new life. Even at home, in their Bloomsbury townhouse, Olivia wore either sandals or clogs, and he could always hear her clopping about the place. He traced her passage along the hall and her descent of the staircase.

As soon as their hired Fiat 500 started up in the courtyard below, Julian hauled himself out of bed and put on the new swimming shorts he'd purchased from a fashionable shop in Covent Garden. The same store where he'd treated himself to the tortoiseshell Ray-Ban sunglasses he now perched on top of his head.

After grabbing a towel from the bathroom, he walked barefoot out of the bedroom and onto the terracotta tiles of the hallway. He passed another bedroom, the main bathroom and the upstairs sitting room with its cream sofas and colourful rugs. His feet trod the smooth dark wood of the staircase to the ground floor, where they met white marbled ceramic. He scampered across these icy tiles, past the guest room and turned left into another narrow hallway that led to the kitchen, a large room boasting traditional features – a rectangular stone sink and cupboards made from the same dark wood as the villa's doors and window frames. From here, a set of steps led down into a shady dining room with a round oak table and a set of patio doors that Julian pulled open.

He stepped out onto the terrace. The terracotta tiles beneath his feet, smaller than the ones indoors, were already giving off heat. Overhead, a canopy of gnarled vines wound around a metal frame to create shelter from the sun. Only the first week of July, but he could already sense the heat as a separate entity he would have to share his holiday with.

He gazed at the view he could not believe was his to enjoy. The sky, vast and cloudless. The Mediterranean, stretching into the distance like a big blue dream. At a recent drinks party held by one of Olivia's London friends, Julian had overheard his wife saying, 'We'll be in Mallorca this summer. We have a villa there.'

We.

Blue ceramic pots filled with succulents and herbs decorated the edges of the tiled terrace. Julian stepped beyond the hardy plants, onto a strip of yellow grass bordered by geraniums and Mediterranean daisies. With the dry blades scratching the soles of his feet, he walked to where two lemon trees formed a low canopy over a set of rocky steps. He stopped to touch the waxy, puckered skin of a ripe lemon, dazzled by its actual, growing presence.

He climbed down the steps that led to the pool terrace, pausing on the third step from the bottom to brush away a stray pebble that had lodged in the ball of his right foot. Bougainvillea, luscious and pink, surrounded him. It smothered the long wall that ran along one side of the pool terrace. Through a gap in the blooms, he could see four wooden sun loungers with navy cushions and, nearby, a round, wrought-iron table and four matching chairs.

When he stepped out onto the terrace, the villa's twenty-metre pool greeted him, a burst of breeze rippling the pale green water. Two dragonflies chased each other across it. Fighting or flirting; he couldn't tell which.

He laid his towel over the back of one of the wrought-iron chairs and looked out to sea. At the edge of the terrace, the land descended in a series of further scrubby terraces, populated by olive and carob trees. Somewhere down there lay a trail that joined up with the nearby coastal path that ran from Deià to Sóller. Olivia liked to walk part of the trail as her pre-breakfast exercise, and they'd agreed to take a few longer hikes along the coastal path together when the weather wasn't too hot.

As he sauntered around to the deep end of the pool, he noted that part of the nearby rockery had collapsed. Grey and yellow rocks had tumbled onto the flagstones. Maybe they should get someone from Casa Feliz, the property management agency in Palma, to come and fix it?

Shaded by a cluster of tall Aleppo pines, Julian stood and swung his arms back and forth for a moment before diving into the pool. The icy water made his breath catch in his chest. He surfaced with a gasp and, seconds later, let out an exhilarated howl. His height allowed him to stand at the deep end with his head well above the water and he bounced up and down, letting himself adjust to the temperature before pushing off from the side and settling into a rhythmical breaststroke. Kick, pull, breathe. Kick, pull, breathe. His limbs loose and free, his body weightless in the water. In less than three weeks, he would turn fifty, but he felt fitter than ever. Now he led a less stressful life, he no longer even needed his blood pressure medication.

He swam fifteen lengths before taking a break. Clinging to the side of the pool, he gazed up at the traditional Mallorcan villa that had once belonged to his wife's parents and now belonged to her.

Villa Soledad. He admired the thick walls clad with pink and honey-coloured stones from the nearby mountains, the paned windows with their green shutters and the sloping terracotta roof. A dream property, he thought with a smile.

'Darling.' Olivia's voice drifted down from the villa. 'I'm back.'

'Jesus.' He ducked his head as a huge insect darted at him. It had the body shape of a wasp, the black-blue hide of a beetle and it emitted a heavy drone that made it sound twice as large. He had to swat it away three times before it lost interest.

'Julian.'

He hauled himself out of the water. 'Coming.'

3

IN SICKNESS AND IN HEALTH

At the end of each writing day, as I walk the short distance from my favourite café to the townhouse in Bloomsbury where I now reside, I am painfully aware that my new, privileged existence is a far cry from the difficult life Helen and I were forced into after the accident. We started married life with such high hopes, and at times it is hard to accept the hand fate dealt us.

At least life had prepared me for our trying circumstances. From the age of eight, I cared for my father, who had to give up his army career after he was diagnosed with multiple sclerosis. He'd served as a drill sergeant at the Shorncliffe Army Camp in Folkestone, and we remained in the seaside town after his discharge. Many of you may wonder how I coped with such responsibility at such a young age, but life as a carer was all I knew. As a sensitive child who loved books, I dreamt of one day studying English Literature at university, but my dad's poor health disrupted my education. Hard as it may be to believe, I have never resented him for that. How could I?

Sometimes he would go through a good spell, leaving me free to attend school every day, but often, when his vision and mobility failed him, he needed me home for weeks at a time. Life is hard enough for child carers nowadays, even with the increased awareness and support services. Back then, I just had to get on with it, my caring duties a cause for pity from my teachers and ridicule from my classmates. I left school at sixteen with four O levels and had to get part-time work to supplement Dad's benefits and army pension. I found employment at the Imperial Hotel on Folkestone Leas, starting as a dishwasher. My father, a strict disciplinarian with traditional values, had instilled in me the importance of hard work, and it didn't take me long to make my way up from dishwasher to receptionist.

I was thirty-four when my father died. I was relieved the terrible suffering had ended, but I was also a little lost. Caring for him had been the focus of my life for so long. Soon after his death, I met Helen. She was attending a wedding reception at the Imperial, and I knew instantly that this strong, capable woman was the one for me. Like me, she had no family. She'd lost her mother to breast cancer a year before we met, and her estranged father to a heart attack long before that.

We married six months after that first meeting. A simple, no-fuss ceremony at Folkestone Town Hall. We exchanged the standard vows, minus 'obey', of course. When we promised to love each other in sickness and in health, neither of us could have imagined how binding that vow would turn out to be.

Not long after our wedding, we moved to Edinburgh, where Helen had secured a job as marketing manager for Hame, a homeless charity. I soon found work in a second-hand bookshop near the University of Edinburgh. It didn't pay much, but I had no issues with my talented wife being the main earner and was happy to support her career in any way I could. I also signed up for an access course at the university, in the hope of doing an English Literature degree there, and we decided to wait a few years before starting a family.

With a small inheritance from her mother, Helen was able to put a deposit on a flat in the Bruntsfield area of the city. A beautiful property with high corniced ceilings, large, light windows and stripped wooden floors. You can imagine the pain I felt at having to sell it after the accident. I hung on for as long as I could, but with me caring for Helen full-time and no income, I had little choice.

The council provided us with a bungalow on Shawfair Street, in the Fountainbridge area of the city. At times, I found myself feeling isolated. In the immediate aftermath of Helen's accident, friends and former colleagues helped us as much as they could but, as time passed, they drifted away. Some moved to other cities, some started families, some simply couldn't cope with Helen's complex needs.

I must confess I didn't always find my caring duties easy. Every morning and evening, agency carers would come for an hour to help me get Helen in and out of bed and to shower her, but everything else I had to do myself. Yet no matter how hard things got, my wife kept me going. Her needs always came first. I abandoned my university access course and my dreams of studying, but what did that matter? In comparison to Helen's suffering, my former aspirations appeared trivial. At least my wife was alive, I kept telling myself. At least we were still together. As I'm sure many of you will understand, it was impossible for me to imagine life without her.

4

After Julian had showered and changed into a pair of shorts and a T-shirt, he and Olivia prepared breakfast together, accompanied by hits of the eighties coming from an old transistor radio on the kitchen worktop. Olivia sang along to Duran Duran's 'Rio' in her gravelly voice. She sounded as if she still smoked twenty cigarettes a day, a habit she'd given up years ago.

'These Spanish stations are quite something,' Julian said.

'Aren't they just?' Olivia's fleshy arm forced half an orange onto a glass juicer and twisted it, releasing a citrusy tang that mingled with the scent of the coffee percolating in the espresso pot. The gas hob the pot sat on belonged to an old freestanding cooker in dire need of updating. Julian suspected the fridge-freezer that hummed and shuddered next to it wouldn't last much longer. He loved the quirkiness of it all, the deliberate effort Olivia said her parents had made to keep the place basic. They'd purchased it when Olivia was five years old, as a retreat from their busy, outwardly respectable lives. According to Olivia, her father had also used it as a place to get away with his numerous mistresses. The faded photograph hanging next to the fridge showed Mrs Pearson on her knees in the villa's garden, trowel in hand and a wide-brimmed straw hat flopping over her long hair. Her husband stood behind her in white shorts, his broad chest bare, his thick fingers gripping a spade. The multimillionaire commercial property heir and his equally wealthy, upper-class wife. Julian often wondered what they'd have made of him, had they been alive.

Olivia bustled past and retrieved a glass jug from the wooden dresser. 'Can you get the yoghurt out?'

'Si, señorita.'

'Señora.'

'Si, señora.'

Olivia smiled. 'We'll make a local of you yet.'

He fetched the yoghurt from the fridge and chose a small blue bowl from the dresser to put it in.

'Not that one,' Olivia said. 'That's for olives.'

'Oh, right. Sorry.' He followed her instructions and selected a yellow bowl instead. At least he could get to know the villa properly during this visit. Last Easter, after they'd married in a low-key civil ceremony at Tavistock House in Bloomsbury, they'd come to the villa for a four-night honeymoon. Olivia had, by her own admission, neglected the place in recent years. After her divorce from Lars, her second husband, she'd found the place riddled with painful memories of him. All that had changed now, she'd assured Julian. They would create fresh memories together. Happy ones.

He told her about the rockery down at the pool. 'I thought Casa Feliz might be able to send someone to fix it. A gardener, maybe.'

'Good plan. I'll be giving them a ring this week anyway. See if we can sort out a regular cleaner while we're here.'

Julian placed the bowl of yoghurt on the large wooden tray Olivia had laid out, next to the jug of orange juice and the plate of pastries.

'Nearly there,' Olivia said, hacking the head off a strawberry.

As he waited for her to finish, he browsed the photographs cluttering the walls. Polaroids of Olivia and her elder brother, Charles, playing in the villa's garden. Charles was now a successful property developer in Hong Kong. Julian had only met him once, at his son Daniel's wedding in Canterbury last Christmas. He'd found Charles pleasant but aloof and could see why Olivia didn't feel close to her sibling. Unlike her, Charles had no intention of doing anything charitable with his inheritance. Olivia did, however, love her nephews, Daniel and Alex, and many of the photographs showed her with them at various ages. Others captured her with her numerous godchildren. They had names like Max and Sienna and Lawrence, and Julian couldn't keep track of them all. Olivia's first marriage, to a wealthy investment banker called William, had ended after she'd discovered she couldn't have children, a misfortune she spoke of with her usual stoicism and no trace of bitterness. Lars, ten years her junior, had assured her he didn't want children. After six years of marriage, he'd left her and procreated with a woman ten years younger than him.

'All done.' Olivia placed the strawberries on the tray and lifted it up. Julian picked up the coffee pot and followed her through the dining room and onto the terrace, where she placed the tray on the long white table set with yellow plates and bowls and white coffee cups. She liked to set a proper table.

He poured them both a strong coffee and savoured his first fortifying sip. They helped themselves to strawberries and yoghurt and ate sitting side by side in comfortable silence, absorbing the view. Soledad, the name of the villa, was the Spanish word for solitude. They were far enough from the winding mountain road to protect them from traffic noise, and they had no neighbours close enough to disturb them. The nearest villa jutted out from the cliff some way below, and the tall cypress trees that bordered it ensured both properties maintained their privacy.

'These ensaïmades are incredible,' Julian said when Olivia urged him to have one of the soft, round pastries. 'Greasy and light at the same time.'

'I know.' Olivia dabbed icing sugar from her chin with her napkin.

'Let's have them every day.'

Olivia laughed. 'Why not? We're on holiday. We can do what we bloody well like.'

* * *

After they'd finished eating and had cleared away, they returned to the terrace with a fresh pot of coffee and their mobile phones.

'I vote we do nothing and lounge by the pool,' Olivia said, putting on her oval blue-rimmed reading glasses. 'I picked up a few supplies in Deià so we can rustle up something simple for dinner.'

'Don't you want to go out tonight? It is your birthday.'

She shook her head. 'A quiet night in with you would be perfect.'

'You're sure? I could book us a table at Sa Vinya.' He was certain the owner of Olivia's favourite restaurant in Deià would find room for them.

'Let's go there for your birthday instead. Fifty deserves a proper celebration.'

'Whatever you say.'

'Right.' Olivia picked up her phone. 'Better get to it.' They'd agreed to only check their emails twice a day and to only respond to urgent messages.

'How about we throw our phones in the sea?' Julian said.

Olivia smiled. 'I know you don't mean that. We're so lucky to do something we love, aren't we? It's such a privilege.'

Julian nodded but secretly thought it would be nice to have a complete break. To not have to think about other people's difficult lives for a while. He reminded himself to be grateful. Helen hadn't died in vain. So much good had come from it.

Olivia looked at her phone and frowned.

'David?' Julian said. Olivia nodded and tapped out a reply. Julian couldn't remember a week going by without his wife's accountant sending on forms for her to sign or arranging a meeting to discuss the management of her considerable fortune. Money is a full-time job, she often told him. Almost every day, David got in touch to discuss some aspect of her personal finances or the running of the Pearson Foundation. With these responsibilities and her duties as a board member of several other charities, his wife was a busy woman.

'And Arnold's sent on some dreary forms for me to read through,' she said.

'Nothing new there,' Julian said with a forced smile. Olivia was also in constant contact with her lawyer. Soft-spoken, serious Arnold with his mustard waistcoats and manicured nails. Arnold would be turning up at the end of the month for a week's stay at the villa with his dull, horsey wife, Cynthia.

'He does say they can't wait to join us,' Olivia said.

'That's nice.'

'He and Cynthia like to do a lot of walking when they're here. They often come with me before breakfast and then carry on along the coastal path. Sometimes they don't get back until after lunch.'

'Good for them.' Julian scrolled through his own emails. The black rectangular frames of his reading glasses sat heavy on the bridge of his nose. He'd seen similar glasses on the trendy patrons of the cafés where he'd written his memoir.

'Anything interesting?' Olivia asked.

'Just Mike.' Mike, the part-time office manager for the Helen Griggs Awards, had forwarded an email from Islington College, asking if Julian would give a speech at their careers fair in September. Julian showed Olivia the request. 'I could talk about becoming a male carer. See if I can get the youth interested.'

'If anyone can get young men passionate about caring, it's you.'

'I'll take my memoir along. Read them an extract from it.'

'Good idea.'

He was glad to have Olivia as a trustee of his charity. She'd wanted to donate money to him from her foundation but, to avoid a conflict of interests, they'd decided against it. He also didn't want people thinking he was a kept man. Instead, he had her expertise and valuable contacts, some of whom had already made generous donations.

After typing a brief reply to Mike, he checked the Twitter feed for @TheHelenGriggsAwards and clicked 'like' on a few of the responses to his latest tweet about the effects of austerity on unpaid carers. The account had nearly 30,000 followers. His winning appearance on the Heart of the Nation Awards almost two years ago had a lot to do with that. Polly Dawson, the beloved co-anchor of *Wake Up Britain*, had presented him with his award and praised him for his work on behalf of unpaid carers.

He composed a new tweet, informing his followers he was taking a holiday and added a link to his latest article for the *Caring World* magazine. Since becoming a trustee of the Caring World charity, he'd volunteered to do a regular blog for them and this one emphasised the importance of self-care for carers and the need for regular breaks.

Even if you can't afford a holiday, see if you can arrange to take a day trip somewhere nearby, or visit a tourist attraction in your own town. Perhaps you can snatch half an hour for a walk, or ten minutes to sit quietly by yourself and replenish. You don't need to travel far to find respite.

He posted the tweet. Seconds later, a reply pinged in. @Brian59
wrote:

After wot you've been thru, u deserve a break. UR an inspiration.
#triumphovertragedy

He shared the reply with Olivia.

'You are an inspiration,' she said and kissed his cheek.

'I couldn't do any of it without you.' He pushed back his chair.
'Which is why I've got you something special for your birthday.'

'That's naughty. I said no presents.'

'I've left it upstairs. I'll go and fetch it.'

When he returned clutching two envelopes, she wagged a finger
at him. 'You are a rogue,' she said.

He sat down and passed her the first envelope. 'Happy
birthday.'

She opened it to find a certificate for the £200 he'd donated in
her name to Shelter, one of the charities she made regular generous
contributions to. 'How perfect.'

He handed over her birthday card. A large silver heart on the
front, his message inside.

*Birthday wishes to my incredible wife. Here's to a great year
ahead.*

'Darling.' A radiant smile lit up Olivia's face. 'You are
wonderful.'

Something tickled Julian's right thigh. He looked down and saw
a small white feather perched on his bare skin.

'Someone's got a guardian angel,' Olivia said.

'Really?' A tremor ran through him. Fear or excitement; he
couldn't tell which.

'My mother used to say a white feather was a sign an angel was watching over you.'

He picked up the feather and caressed it between his thumb and forefinger. 'I never used to believe in angels.'

Olivia's attention had returned to her birthday card. 'We are going to have a wonderful year,' she said. 'I know it.'

'We will, my love.' He released the feather and watched it float to the floor. 'I promise you.'

5

WINNING?

Not many people have the humbling experience of being nominated for a Heart of the Nation Award, fewer still know what it is like to win one. My nomination came nearly two years after Helen's death, when I was still struggling to make sense of what had happened.

I travelled overnight by coach to London for the award ceremony and stayed in a bed and breakfast near King's Cross station. At that point, my main income came from my job as a care worker for an agency in Edinburgh. I spent two evenings volunteering for Caring World's emergency helpline, and my occasional appearances on TV debates and radio shows rarely paid a fee.

The tuxedo I wore for the award ceremony came from a charity shop. I attended the event alone and, despite the friendliness of my fellow nominees, I had never missed Helen more. She would have loved the grandeur of the Dorchester Hotel and the glamour of the TV cameras everywhere. Despite my sadness and my nerves, I tried to take in every detail for her sake. It is strange, looking back, to think that my future wife, Olivia, was sitting in that very room. I had no idea we would meet that night. No idea she would be so moved by my acceptance speech she would seek me out after the ceremony and tell me how rare it was to meet a man capable of such devotion. After Helen's death, I never expected to love again, but then Olivia came into my life. Her warmth and compassion have helped me begin the process of healing and self-forgiveness, and her experience as a philanthropist has been vital to the continuing success of the Helen Griggs Awards.

When I first arrived at the Dorchester, I found myself at a table with the other nominees. Our category – Best Charitable Initiative – came towards the end of the evening. The host, Polly Dawson, read out the nominations, and we all watched a short film clip of each nominee's charity work. I had tears in my eyes during the segment about the Helen Griggs Awards. To know that some of the money I'd received from the Criminal Injuries Compensation Authority had enabled the Carers First Centre to restart their volunteer sitter service meant so much to me. Not long after Helen's death, the wonderful woman assigned to me from Victim Support Services had encouraged me to apply for compensation. It seemed absurd I should receive money for the fatal injuries my wife sustained, but I took the advice and applied. When I used the £11,000 payout to set up the Helen Griggs Awards, I had no idea my initiative would receive this kind of acclaim. What else could I have done with the money? How could I in all good conscience have acted otherwise?

I never expected to win. Derek Burnside, the man sitting next to me at the table, had raised over £100,000 for research into secondary breast cancer. My recent sponsored walk of the West Highland Way had raised nothing like that, but, as Polly pointed out before announcing my name: 'This award goes to a man who has triumphed over tragedy. A man who fought evil with good.'

Derek and the other nominees cheered and shook my hand

when Polly declared me the winner. We were all winners, as far I was concerned, and I felt uncomfortable at being singled out.

The table wasn't far from the stage, but the walk towards it felt like the longest trek of my life. My legs were trembling as I climbed the stairs towards Polly. How could I ever speak to all the people sitting before me, as well as the millions of viewers at home?

When Polly handed me the heavy glass heart that was my reward, I felt an overwhelming relief. As if the award finally confirmed to the world that I was a caring man who could never have killed his wife. While no one had ever accused me directly of the crime, I'd had to endure questioning from the police, as well as several spurious news articles that hinted I might not be as innocent as I appeared. Yet I knew I had always done my best for Helen and had only ever wanted to alleviate her suffering. I also had a solid alibi for the night of the murder.

My acceptance speech received a standing ovation. The applause was so loud, the lights so bright. All eyes were on me. Attention I had never sought and didn't feel I deserved. I couldn't help thinking about Helen's killer. The man, or woman, who had evaded detection could be watching me on television at that very moment.

I must confess, for a split second I thought about running away.

6

On the third day of the holiday, a Tuesday, Julian and Olivia left the villa after breakfast to visit the nearby market town of Sóller. They drove along precipitous mountain roads, Olivia guiding the white Fiat 500 around the punishing bends.

'Sorry I can't help with the driving,' he said.

'Don't be silly.'

Olivia understood his reluctance to drive. His nervousness behind the wheel. He gave her thigh an affectionate rub through her grey linen smock.

'I practically learned to drive on these roads.' Olivia turned up the air-conditioning. Twenty-six degrees outside already. Thirty degrees by noon, according to the weather report.

'Nice shirt,' Olivia said, 'goes well with the beige chinos. Is it new?'

'Yes.' He'd purchased the short-sleeved shirt – red roses on a navy background – from the Paul Smith store in Covent Garden. 'Found it in a second-hand shop in Notting Hill.' He didn't know why he'd lied. Olivia never begrudged him anything, even though she considered designer clothing a waste of good money. He'd paid

for the shirt himself, out of the manager's salary given to him by the
Helen Griggs Awards. Only £22,000 a year but it provided some
independent income. Olivia's money paid for almost everything
they owned and spent. He would have liked to put a small amount
aside each month into a savings account, but Olivia had persuaded
him to pay into a private pension. As a small rebellion, he'd
accepted the offer of a credit card from his bank without her knowl-
edge. Olivia had the luxury of boycotting credit cards and their
obscene interest rates, but his card only had a low limit and he'd
told himself it was only for emergencies.

The car in front braked suddenly as it approached a bend.
Olivia beeped her horn.

'Bloody tourists.' She gestured to the line of cars snaking ahead
at slow speed. 'There's far too many of them. The whole industry's
run by the Mafia, that's the problem.'

'Really?'

'Not like it used to be, but there's precious little the Mafia aren't
involved with on this island.' Olivia pushed her oversized cat-eye
sunglasses further up the bridge of her nose. 'And the police here
aren't renowned for their efficiency. Daddy always said they were
riddled with corruption.'

The view soon opened out to reveal a valley surrounded by
grey-green hills, the town of Sóller sprawled across its centre. On
the dusty valley floor, they drove past groves of lemon and orange
trees and soon met the town's unattractive outskirts. Supermarkets,
garages, a huge gelato factory. A left turn near the Botanic Gardens
took them to the narrow, labyrinthine streets of the old town.

'Beautiful,' Julian said, admiring the historic town houses in
ochre, pink and orange.

'Isn't it?' Olivia turned right into a side street. 'A touch
provincial, but I adore it.'

They parked, and Julian stepped out of the car. A welcome gust of wind greeted him. He took his white Panama hat from the back seat and put it on. Olivia rummaged in the boot and emerged with her floppy, wide-brimmed straw hat and a sturdy woven shopping bag.

'Right,' she said. 'To market.'

* * *

They started in the small square by the train station. Two lines of stalls stood beneath the towering plane trees – one side selling summer holiday attire, the other fruit and vegetables.

Olivia steered him to a nearby grocery stall displaying boxes of plump red cherries and the island's ever-abundant oranges. Hefty courgettes and giant gleaming peppers. A young man in jeans and a vest top came to serve them.

'Hola,' said Julian. Before coming away, he'd spent ten minutes a day practising basic Spanish phrases with a language app.

'Hello,' the man said in accented English. 'How are you?'

This had happened to Julian in the bakery in Deià yesterday. What was it about his pronunciation that gave him away?

'Hola,' Olivia said, and the man launched into a rapid stream of Spanish. Julian gave up and let Olivia order and pay. She handed him the shopping basket, and he piled the bulging brown paper bags into it. As he followed his wife past stalls selling kitchen items carved from olive wood, the heavy basket, embroidered with pink and red butterflies, smacked against his legs.

They arrived at the main square, the Plaça de la Constitució. Tourists and locals packed out the cafés. Squealing children chased each other around the pink granite fountain. Julian and Olivia browsed the stalls in front of the town hall, purchasing several different varieties of olives before moving on to a busy cheese stall.

In the queue, a group of elderly Spanish women gave Julian's basket a disparaging look. When Olivia passed him one wax-paper parcel of cheese after another and instructed him how to pack them, one of the women muttered something in Spanish and the others stared at Julian and smirked. He dismissed their mockery; such women wouldn't be used to an enlightened man like him. A man happy for his wife to take charge now and again.

Shopping done, he hauled the cumbersome basket back to the car while Olivia went in search of an empty table at one of the busy cafés in the square. He packed the perishables into the cool box in the Fiat's boot and hurried back to his wife, the navy deck shoes she'd bought him for the holiday rubbing at his heels.

He found her beneath the awning of one of the cafés. He sank into a chair, glad of the shade. Olivia poured him a glass of the sparkling water she'd ordered. Julian took a welcome gulp.

'You need to drink a lot in this heat,' she said, 'you mustn't forget.'

An attractive dark-eyed waitress arrived with their order. 'Dos cafés con leche,' she said. The top three buttons of her white shirt were undone, and, as she leaned over to place Julian's coffee in front of him, he couldn't help glancing at the exposed dip of her cleavage.

'Gracias,' he said.

'You're welcome,' she replied.

Julian and Olivia sipped their coffees and gazed out at the crowded square. Julian noted the time from the clock on the front of the town hall building. He'd stopped wearing a watch the day after Helen's death.

'Isn't the church wonderful?' Olivia pointed to the ornate, modernist façade of the Església de Saint Bartomeu. 'It was restored in the early twentieth century by a disciple of Gaudi.' She sipped her coffee. 'We'll pop in for a look after this.'

A long blast of a high-pitched horn as the tram from the nearby Port de Sóller lurched into the square. The tram lines bisected the Plaça de la Constitució, and the people in the vicinity scattered either side of them as the wooden carriages approached. Children waved from the tram as it passed. Julian and Olivia waved back.

As the last wooden carriage disappeared from view, tinny music floated through the air – a dance beat pulsing beneath infectious drumming. Julian watched three barefoot young men cross the square. One of the black men sported short dreads, the other a shaved head. The white man had his blonde hair in a topknot and a boombox perched on his shoulder. At the centre of the square, they stopped. The blonde man put the boombox down and turned up the volume. When they took off their white T-shirts, the onlookers clapped and whistled.

'Capoeira,' Olivia said. 'I saw a lot of this when I was travelling in Brazil.'

Julian nodded, his eyes fixed on the men in their white drawstring trousers. They were muscular but not bulky, their neat waists making a perfect V with their strong shoulders. They beckoned their audience closer, encouraging them to clap along in time to the drums.

'It's a martial art disguised as a dance,' Olivia said. 'It's very clever.'

The men embarked on a series of complex moves. Spinning kicks and low squats. Handstands, forward and backward flips and, finally, a series of spectacular somersaults that had the crowd cheering.

Olivia let out a loud wolf-whistle as the performance ended. 'Amazing,' she said.

Julian fanned his face with his Panama. When the blonde-haired man approached the café with a wooden bowl, he removed a twenty-euro note from his wallet and held it up. The man skipped over and accepted the money with a gracious bow. Julian's eyes followed his retreat, captivated by the movement of his high, taut buttocks beneath the white trousers.

'Julian?'

He turned to find a solemn expression on his wife's face. 'What's wrong?'

'I was saying there's something I need to ask you.'

Anxiety fluttered in his stomach. 'What?'

She took a deep breath, as though steeling herself. 'I've given it a lot of thought and I've discussed it with Arnold too.'

'Discussed what?'

'I want you to become a trustee of the Pearson Foundation.'

'Oh. Right.' His anxiety subsided. 'Wow. I—'

'We'd really value your input.'

'Arnold said that?'

Julian had always thought Arnold held him in low regard. Before marrying Olivia, Julian had signed a pre-nuptial agreement drawn up by the lawyer. The document ensured Julian would receive nothing if the marriage failed and, as Arnold pointed out, most judges would respect it should Julian ever try to get money through the courts. He'd then muttered something about 'that idiot Lars' learning that the hard way. Julian had signed the document without hesitation, keen to prove he had no interest in Olivia's fortune. Keen to disprove the scepticism he'd sensed from Arnold. A scepticism he still picked up during the monthly board meetings for the Helen Griggs Awards. Arnold had joined the board of trustees at Olivia's suggestion, along with David, her accountant.

'He knows we're a good team.' Olivia reached for Julian's hand. 'You understand how important the foundation is to me. If anything were to happen to me, I'd want you to be able to carry on with the work.'

'Don't talk like that.'

'I know it's hard, especially after everything that happened with Helen, but we need to discuss these things.'

'I couldn't bear the thought of losing you.'

'I'm not planning on going anywhere. But I have a responsibility to the foundation. I have to set the right things in place.' She squeezed his hand. 'Almost everything I have is tied up in trusts and would be used to fund the charity work.'

'Olivia. Really, I—'

'But I want you to know you would be looked after. I've structured my will so you—'

'I don't care about that,' Julian said. A small brown bird landed on the table in search of crumbs.

'The house in London would be yours. And I've put aside—'

'Please. I don't want to know.' The distress in his voice frightened the scavenging bird away.

'We're a partnership,' Olivia said. 'It's only fair I look after you.'

Julian gazed into his wife's eyes and found nothing but love and sincerity there. All his life he had taken care of others, and now he had someone to take care of him. Surely he would not be here now, with this good woman, if he hadn't made the right choices? He must deserve his luck?

'We'll look after each other,' he said.

'The money's not even really mine. I didn't make it. I see myself as its guardian, and I know you can help me do that job better.'

He raised her hand to his lips and kissed it. 'We'll spend the rest of our lives doing great things together. I'm sure of it.'

* * *

On their way back to the car, they stopped in at the church.

'You'll find little hints of the gothic in here,' Olivia said, pushing open the heavy, wooden door, 'but it's mostly a baroque affair.'

Julian nodded, as though well acquainted with eras of European architecture.

As soon as he stepped into the church's cool, gloomy interior and removed his sunglasses, he could see his wife was right. It was impressive. The high, vaulted ceiling, painted ochre and terracotta. The supporting ribs decorated with gilded fleur de lys. The kaleidoscopic rose window above the main entrance, and the stained-glass windows set into both sides of the building. Sombre paintings of biblical scenes hung on the walls. The display in the Sanctuary, behind the altar, gleamed with gold leaf.

He took off his Panama. 'There's so much gold everywhere.' He found the effect both gaudy and earnest.

'Tremendous, isn't it? No one does a Catholic church quite like the Spanish.'

A short, wide woman in a black shirt wandered over and gave Julian an information leaflet written in English.

'Thank you,' he said.

When she offered Olivia a leaflet, the two of them started a conversation in Spanish. Julian wandered off to look at the chapels on the right-hand side of the nave. His deck shoes squeaked on the smooth black and white tiles. The first chapel he came to contained a pious statue of the Virgin Mary, flanked by golden columns. A beautiful piece, but Julian could focus only on the angels. Cherubs with sprouts of golden wings clung to the columns and gazed in adoration at Mary. In the painting above the Virgin's head, a pale angel with translucent wings held out a large key. The key to the eternal kingdom?

Heart thudding, Julian moved to the next chapel but found no sanctuary there. Male angels in pink robes sat on golden thrones, their wings curving inwards to frame stern faces. They glared at him with reproachful eyes, forcing him on to the next chapel, where curvaceous female angels flaunted their silver wings and thought him unfit to look at, their bulging eyes transfixed on the heavens.

He stumbled back to the central aisle and found himself facing the altar. The three-tier display in the Sanctuary behind it dazzled him. Gold classical columns, gold cherubs darting here and there, statues of saints with golden halos. On top of them all, looking down on everything, an angel the size of a man. Muscular arms and legs and dark bobbed hair. His wings a dirty khaki colour and his tunic muddy brown. In one hand he held what looked like a scythe, and one of his sturdy feet pressed down on the prostrate figure beneath him.

Julian stepped closer. He couldn't tell if the figure beneath the angel was male or female. Blood covered the naked torso, and the figure held one arm aloft as though begging for mercy. Its withered legs were wrapped one around the other, a twist of mangled limbs, its feet facing in opposite directions.

'Gabriel,' a voice said next to him.

Julian clutched his chest.

'Are you all right, darling?' Olivia stood by his side, looking at him with concern.

'Fine.' He smoothed down his shirt.

'Did I frighten you?'

'I'm fine.'

'He is frightful.' Olivia pointed up at the angel. 'Gabriel slaying a demon. He doesn't look very angelic, does he?'

'No.' Something hot and frantic gathered in Julian's throat.

Olivia strolled away to inspect the altar. Julian swallowed the hot, frantic thing.

'Gabriel,' he said. The word sounded like an incantation, and he did not repeat it.

7

REGRETS

Truth is, I will never forgive myself for leaving my wife alone that night. Many of you may not understand how I could have done this. I hope you never do. I hope your circumstances are never as trying as mine were at that time.

I will never forget walking into the press conference that took place a few days after Helen's death. The police had asked me to appeal for information that might aid their investigation, but I hadn't rehearsed what I was going to say. When I stepped into that room packed with journalists and cameramen, I sensed both sympathy and hostility in the air. Even though the police had treated me with courtesy and respect, I was aware they would be forced to rule out my involvement in my wife's death. Those closest to a murder victim are always under suspicion. My Family Liaison Officer had already asked if I would volunteer my laptop and mobile phone for inspection. I handed over both items at once. I had nothing to hide on either device.

I knew many of the journalists at the press conference would speculate about my part in the tragedy, but at that point, all I cared about was finding my wife's killer. DS Kirsty Briscoe, the officer in charge of the investigation, had made it clear that success in the early stages was crucial. With the right information early on, they would stand more chance of solving the case. I couldn't help wondering if an attack of conscience might lead the killer to confess at the nearest police station. Thoughts like this often kept me awake until dawn.

At first, I thought I wouldn't find the right words to address the waiting cameras, but when I opened my mouth, I spoke as if in a trance. An unwitting vessel for a greater message. Until I watched the news that night, I had no memory of what came out of my mouth. No memory of breaking down in tears. I certainly had no idea the footage would go viral. Many of you were moved by my claim that everyone was culpable for Helen's murder. Her killer, myself, the government and society as a whole. We were all complicit in creating the circumstances that had led to my wife's death. Some months later, I was invited to appear on Radio Scotland, to contribute to a debate about the state of adult care provision. Other media appearances followed. I began to gain a profile I had not asked for and had no desire to profit from, but with time I came to see I could use the tragedy of my wife's passing to do good in the world. A mission had been thrust upon me, and I would have to accept it.

To have the chance to effect genuine change for carers everywhere is a privilege I do not take lightly. Whether it is through my charitable initiatives, or by sharing my story in this memoir, I am determined to do all I can to find new ways to help those who care for their loved ones. I can only hope Helen would approve of everything I have done in her name.

8

The morning after their trip to Sóller, Olivia suggested they visit the nearby beach at Cala de Deià. Julian packed their beach bag and umbrella into the Fiat and before long they were turning onto the steep, winding road that led down to the sea. Olivia managed to find a space in the busy car park at the bottom of the road and, after Julian had loaded himself up with the bag and umbrella, they followed the track to the beach.

'Wow,' he said when they reached the end of the track. 'It's even better than I remember.' The small bay, enclosed by cliffs, contained some of the clearest water he'd ever seen. Smooth, seaweed-mottled rocks nestled in the jade shallows, like giant eggs waiting to hatch. Further out, the sun highlighted dazzling patches of aqua.

'Stunning, isn't it?' Olivia said.

Ca's Patró March, the fish restaurant built into the left-hand side of the bay, was quiet now, but Julian could see the staff bustling around inside, preparing for lunch. Beside the restaurant lay the rusting slipway once used to launch fishermen's boats and next to it a sloping concrete ramp occupied by girls in bikinis, who lay stretched out on towels like offerings to the sun.

'Good to get down early, before it gets too hot,' Olivia said.

Julian could already feel the sun penetrating his T-shirt and shorts. He suspected he'd only last a couple of hours.

They stepped onto the beach described in guidebooks as shingle. Julian thought the white, grey and pink rocks beneath his feet far too large for that description. They looked more like the shattered vertebrae of some giant creature. He hobbled over them, the beach bag slapping against his right hip and the umbrella wedged against his left. Ahead of him, Olivia made wobbly progress in her Birkenstocks.

'Careful,' he said, 'take your time.'

The scent of frying fish drifted across as they passed Can Lluc, the beach's other restaurant. It sat on a rocky platform, and in the small strip of shade offered by the platform wall, a line of elderly beachgoers sheltered – men with skinny legs and pot bellies and women with leathery cleavages.

They set up base near a large knot of driftwood. The uneven rocks made lying flat impossible, but some had surfaces smooth enough to sit on. Julian slotted the umbrella into a hole in the wood and opened it, providing them with a small radius of shade.

'Perfect,' Olivia said.

He slid the beach bag off his shoulder and sat on one of the smoother rocks to catch his breath. Sweat soaked the back of his T-shirt. He could smell the coconut scent of the suntan lotion he and Olivia had slathered over themselves before leaving the villa. He removed his Panama and fanned his face. 'It's already so hot.'

'You'll cool down when we've had a swim.'

Julian gazed at the inviting water. A cluster of people stood in the shallows talking. Further out, swimmers with masks and snorkel pipes bobbed along with the current, gathering near the large rocks on the right-hand side of the bay. In the cliffs above the rocks were caves once used by fishermen, wooden planks framing their primitive doorways. At the mouth of the bay, someone had moored a large yacht. 'How the other half live,' he said, before remembering his wife was the other half and that now, by association, so was he.

Olivia removed her sunglasses. 'Poor Arnold and Cynthia. They love this beach.'

Last night, Arnold had called to say he and Cynthia wouldn't be able to come to the villa after all. Cynthia's father, who was currently battling bladder cancer, had taken a turn for the worse.

'Yes, it's a shame,' Julian said. He'd found the news of the cancellation a relief.

'I love having people to stay. The villa really comes to life with guests around.' Olivia pulled her kaftan over her head. Her navy swimming costume strained to contain her breasts. 'Let's go in,' she said.

Julian stripped down to his swimming shorts, and the two of them embarked on an awkward odyssey across the rocks. Olivia guided him to a sandy patch on the shore that extended into the sea and would allow them to enter safely. She waded through the shallows and lowered her body into the water.

'Is it warm?' Julian said, still hovering on the shore.

'It's lovely.'

When he entered the water, the cold made him screech.

Olivia laughed. 'It's not that bad. Just plunge in.'

'I'm fine here for the moment.'

Olivia pushed off onto her back. Shivering, Julian tried to adjust to the beautiful but unwelcoming water. He looked towards the tall outcrop of rock on the right-hand side of the bay. The rock's flat summit jutted out over the sea. Teenagers and young travellers hung out there, smoking and sunbathing. As Julian watched, a young woman jumped from the rock into the water below.

'Let's swim out,' Olivia said.

'You go. I'm fine here.'

'Chicken.' Olivia turned onto her front and struck up a strong breaststroke. Julian returned to shore and made his way back to the driftwood with hesitant steps. He dried off his legs, put his hat and sunglasses on and took out the historical novel he was reading from the beach bag. He arranged his towel over a large rock that had another behind it he could lean back on. A surprisingly comfortable seat. He checked on Olivia, who had made it out as far as the snorkellers.

A few pages into his book, he glanced up again and spotted his wife treading water. He watched as she dived beneath the surface, her white legs flicking into the air before the sea swallowed them. He waited for her to emerge. After almost a minute, a dark fear uncoiled in him. Where was she? If anything happened to her, he'd never reach her in time.

She burst from the water and shook her head from side to side. Shielding her eyes with her hand, she sought Julian out and waved. No need to worry, he thought as he waved back. His wife was a strong swimmer. More than capable of looking after herself.

He returned to his reading. The sun soaked into his bones, making him hot and drowsy. He rested his book on his stomach and closed his eyes. Murmured conversations drifted over to him, along with the splashes of swimmers entering the water and the hollers of the daredevils throwing themselves from the rock. His mind slipped deeper. I'm falling asleep, he thought, and did so within seconds.

* * *

The cold dragged him into semi-consciousness. Cold water dripping onto his shins. How could Olivia be so thoughtless? Surely she could get to the towels without leaning over him?

Through slitted eyes, he saw two golden-brown feet straddling his pale legs. Feet belonging to tanned, shapely calves. Black board shorts, soaking wet, clung to lean but muscular thighs.

Julian's eyes shot open. The sun formed a bright golden halo around the head of the man hovering over him.

'Hey, big guy,' the man said, 'it's me. It's Gabriel.'

9

'Sorry, man.' Water leaked from the crotch of Gabriel's board shorts onto Julian's thighs. 'Didn't mean to startle you.'

'Jesus.' Julian sat up in a flurry, losing his hat and sunglasses in the process. He looked up and saw his stunned expression reflected in Gabriel's mirrored aviator glasses. When Gabriel extended a hand, he found himself reaching for it.

The younger man hauled him to his feet. Julian snatched his hand away. His heart stuttered as he took in the familiar shoulder-length tumble of Gabriel's blonde hair. The first hint of that slow smile at the corners of his mouth.

'Bring it in, buddy.' Gabriel opened his arms wide, and Julian, dazed, watched his reflection step into the bare-chested embrace. As Gabriel's arms encircled him, he waited for a signal from his body – a shudder of revulsion, some deep inner recoil. He felt only the cool, damp surface of Gabriel's skin. The younger man's hairless chest crushed the greying hair on his.

'Let's do this Spanish style.' Gabriel released him and kissed him on both cheeks, grazing him with his fine blonde stubble. 'I love the way men kiss each other here,' Gabriel said. 'Don't you love that?'

'Julian?' Olivia appeared behind Gabriel, water dripping from her gooseflesh. 'Everything okay?'

Julian nodded, unable to speak.

'I'm Gabriel.' When Gabriel turned to extend a hand to Olivia, Julian recognised at once the black angel wings tattooed across his back.

Olivia placed her left hand in his. 'You're over here from America?'

'I'm from the States, but I've been on the road for a while.'

'Can I detect a bit of the mid-west in your accent?' Olivia said.

'You sure can.' Gabriel kept hold of Olivia's hand. 'I moved around a lot as a kid, though, so I've got a bit of everything in there. Guess I'm a bit of a mongrel.' He examined the gold band on her ring finger. 'Get you, man,' he said, looking at Julian. 'Finding happiness again, after everything you've been through. You have no idea how that makes me feel.'

Julian, who could see nothing of Gabriel's eyes behind the glasses, did not.

'That's sweet,' Olivia said, removing her hand from Gabriel's.

'Man, I was gutted to read about Helen in the papers,' Gabriel said. 'I wanted to contact you, Julian, like really wanted to, but I figured you'd have enough going on, with the cops and everything.'

A chill descended on Julian. 'Yes,' he said. 'The investigation did keep me busy.'

They all shared a moment's silence.

'Poor Helen,' Olivia said.

'What an awesome human you must be, Olivia.' Gabriel opened his arms. 'Come on, let's hug it out.' He wrapped his arms around her. 'I'm a hugger, lady. Can't help myself.'

Olivia emerged from the embrace with blushing cheeks. Her

breasts had almost escaped from her swimming costume. She rearranged her wide straps and imprisoned them again.

'You're cold,' Gabriel said. 'That water gets into your bones, right?' He picked up Julian's towel from the rocks and passed it to Olivia.

'Thank you,' she said, wrapping it around her shoulders.

'And you, my friend,' Gabriel said, bending down and retrieving Julian's hat, 'could do with a little shade for that head of yours.' He placed the Panama on Julian's head with a firm pat. 'Don't wanna get sunstroke.'

Julian did feel dizzy, but he knew the sun was not to blame.

'He's right, darling,' Olivia said. 'You are a bit pink.'

'I'm fine,' Julian said, ignoring the sting of excess sun on his face and chest. He put his hands on his hips and sucked in his stomach.

'Don't forget these.' Gabriel picked up Julian's sunglasses and brushed the sand from the lenses. 'Here.'

'Thanks.' Julian put the Ray-Bans on, grateful for the chance to hide his eyes.

'I can't believe we bumped into each other like this.' Gabriel shook his head. 'It's crazy. Julian Griggs, after all this time. I always hoped I'd see you again.'

'I never thought I would.' Julian's words had an apologetic tone he hadn't intended.

'Are you here on holiday, Gabriel?' Olivia asked.

'Sure am.'

Olivia wiped her face with the towel. 'Where are you staying?'

'Been doing a little wild camping, sleeping out under the stars and stuff. Hanging out with my buddy, Kai.' Gabriel waved at a short, skinny man standing on top of the tall rock. The man shaded his eyes with his hand but didn't wave back. 'We're heading to Pollença soon to get some kite-surfing in.'

'Well, what a lovely coincidence this is for you both,' Olivia said.

Julian lifted one foot from the hot rocks, then the other.

'I know, right?' said Gabriel.

Olivia laughed her throaty laugh. 'A touch of Mallorcan serendipity.'

'Oh, me and this guy know all about serendipity.' Gabriel draped an arm over Julian's shoulder. 'We are well acquainted with serendipitous meetings.'

Nausea unfurled in Julian's stomach as his shocked brain processed what was happening. This encounter was no coincidence. How had Gabriel known where to find him?

'How do you two know each other?' Olivia said.

'This guy saved my ass back in the day. Truly. Real Good Samaritan style.'

Julian resisted the urge to shrug off Gabriel's arm. 'It was nothing.'

'It wasn't nothing.' Gabriel's words lingered between them as his fingertips brushed Julian's collarbone.

'Do you know each other from Scotland?' Olivia asked.

'That's where we met. Right, big guy? Some village in the middle of nowhere. What was it called?'

'I really can't remember.' The lie set Julian's pulse racing.

'I adore Scotland,' Olivia said.

'I was pretty messed up, but this guy here took pity on me. Listened to my hard luck story, treated me nice.'

'That sounds like my husband,' Olivia said.

A high-pitched scream made them all turn towards the water, where a lithe, topless Spanish girl was mock-wrestling with her boyfriend in the shallows. Julian used the diversion to slip free of Gabriel, move over to his wife and put an arm around her waist.

'How long are you on the island for?' Olivia asked Gabriel.

He shrugged. 'Not sure. I got some work lined up in Ibiza soon.'

'The two of you should swap phone numbers,' she said. 'Catch up for a drink.'

A rollercoaster drop in Julian's guts.

'I don't have a phone.' Gabriel removed his glasses. 'I find that kind of technology intrusive, you know? Like, spiritually toxic.'

Olivia smiled. 'One of my nephews is exactly the same. He's never done lecturing me about the dangers of it all.'

'It doesn't matter,' Julian said, 'I'm sure Gabriel's far too busy to—'

'Come for dinner at ours,' Olivia said. 'You must, Gabriel. We can't let a coincidence like this pass by uncelebrated.'

'Really?' A smile twitched on Gabriel's lips. 'I don't wanna put you guys out.'

Julian cast Gabriel a pleading look but found himself mesmerised by the young man's wide blue eyes.

'Yes, come.' Olivia squeezed Julian close. 'It'd be fun to have a guest over.'

'Tomorrow?' Gabriel said. 'Would that work? You don't need to go to any effort for me, Olivia. I'm like the world's easiest guest. Seriously.'

'Tomorrow would be perfect,' Olivia said. 'Wouldn't it, Julian?'

BEFORE

10

A month before his wife's murder, Julian Griggs drove from his home in Edinburgh to Loch Earn in Perthshire. A journey north that took him almost two hours. When he arrived at Loch Earn, he followed the directions he'd been given. A short journey along the south Loch Earn road brought him to a secluded spot by the side of the water. There, surrounded by ancient, twisted oak trees and towering silver birches, stood a dilapidated static caravan.

He parked his Peugeot Horizon. When he hauled his weary body out of the car, autumn leaves yielded to his boots with a dry whisper. He paused to admire the russet-brown pelt of the hills on both sides of the loch and their reflections in the water's surface. It was a cold, clear October day, but a dark mass of cloud lurked at the loch's western end.

He found the key to the caravan in the key safe beside the front door, just as the owner had promised. When he stepped inside, the musty air suggested he might be the first occupant for some time. He turned on the tap over the small kitchen sink. After a moment's gurgling hesitation, water gushed out. The gas fire beside the bedroom door billowed into life when he switched it on. Everything in working order.

It didn't take him long to unpack his clothes and the few food supplies he'd brought with him. The caravan's kitchen was basic but adequate – a small fridge, kettle, microwave and two-ring hob. Julian found a large bottle of Bell's whisky in one of the cupboards, a few drams short of fullness.

As well as a bedroom, the caravan had a small bathroom with a toilet and shower. When Julian switched on the strip-light above the narrow mirror, his reflection made him shudder. He looked drained and exhausted. A ghost of a man. Forty-six years of age, but he felt older. His beard was uneven and ragged. He never had time to trim it after tending to Helen's needs, and he never had time for a proper shave. His fingertips touched the dark, puffy skin beneath his tired eyes. Helen used to say his eyes were his best feature. Soulful, she'd called them. No such compliments came his way nowadays.

* * *

The large window at the far end of the caravan's living area looked out onto the loch. Above the window stretched a shelf of tattered books and, below it, a table surrounded on three sides by pink, cushioned benches. The caravan's décor had a dated feel – grubby woodchip wallpaper decorated with horse brasses.

Still, Julian thought, as he made himself a strong cup of tea, the caravan was peaceful and secluded. Ideal for his purposes.

He sat at the table with his tea and gazed at the loch and the rocky foreshore. If Helen were here, the old Helen, she would have left him to unpack while she went exploring. She would be on the beach already, removing shoes and socks and rolling up her jeans for a paddle in the icy water. He saw her turning to wave at him, petite and pixieish, sunlight glinting off the sleek black hair that hung down to her waist. The image stirred a familiar sadness. The old Helen had died a long time ago, but he had never stopped grieving her. He wondered if he ever would.

11

RESPITE

Newspaper reports at the time of the murder highlighted my fragile mental state, with one of our regular agency carers telling prying journalists about my recent dishevelled appearance and depressed demeanour. Many of you will understand how easy it is for a carer to succumb to despair. How easy it is for exhaustion and hopelessness to take hold.

About a month before my wife's death, I made an appointment to see my GP, Dr Fiona Hamilton. As always, she checked my blood pressure. I had been on medication for hypertension for seven years. She declared my reading higher than ever and said she would have to prescribe me an increased dosage of Eprosartan.

When she asked after Helen's health, I filled her in on my wife's latest difficulties. At the end of August, Helen had developed a cough that mutated into a chest infection with complications, resulting in a two-week hospital stay. I slept in the chair beside her bed each night to keep her company and to ensure her sudden mood swings and challenging behaviour didn't inconvenience the nurses. During the month's convalescence that followed her discharge from hospital, I hardly left the house. I gained weight due to comfort eating and my fitness levels dropped due to lack of exercise.

Dr Hamilton was as sympathetic to my plight as always. She suggested I take a short holiday so I could relax and recharge my batteries. I told her Helen didn't like me going away, and that, of course, I didn't like being away from Helen either. Dr Hamilton wouldn't take no for an answer. She insisted on writing an immediate referral for the social care department, demanding they offer me emergency respite cover. Six days later, the council provided a live-in carer for two nights so I could get away, and the Carers First Centre set me up with cheap accommodation in a caravan in Perthshire.

If I had known then my wife would soon be taken from me, I would never have gone.

12

After finishing his cup of tea, Julian checked the cheap digital watch that, when at home, he relied on to keep him attuned to his wife's daily routine. When to feed her, when to let her nap, when to administer her medication.

Almost 1 p.m. He could please himself for the rest of the day and all of tomorrow too. The thought made him lightheaded; he didn't know what to do first. Catch up on some sleep? Indulge in a long shower? Luxuries he never had time for at home.

He stayed sitting at the table and continued gazing at the loch, immobilised by choice and freedom. At the end of his appointment with Dr Hamilton, she had encouraged him to relax during his time away. *Let yourself unwind, Julian. Enjoy being rather than doing.* Easier said than done. His mind and body were still on high alert, ready to respond to Helen's every noise and movement, despite the miles between them.

With a sigh, he retrieved his phone from his backpack and called Linda, the capable, middle-aged carer assigned to look after his wife. 'She's doing grand,' Linda assured him in a cheery voice. 'We're getting on like a house on fire.'

When he'd said goodbye to Helen that morning, she'd screamed as if the house *were* on fire. Thrown a violent tantrum and landed a furious punch on his chest. He'd considered cancelling the holiday, but Linda had insisted he go.

'She seems quite happy,' Linda said, 'no more lashing out. So far. That was a good right hook she got you with earlier.'

'It was nothing. Really.' Last year, Helen had given him a black eye that had lingered for weeks.

'She did tell me her legs were sore,' Linda said, 'so I gave her a massage, just like you showed me.'

'Great. You'll probably need to do another one at bedtime.' Helen's redundant legs caused her constant discomfort, her rigid muscles often in spasm. 'And if she can't sleep, just—'

'Give her one drop of the morphine. I know.'

'Yes. I don't like to use it too often but needs must.' After Helen's last hospital stay, he'd managed to get a prescription for Oromorph to help her sleep when the pain proved unbearable.

'It's all under control,' Linda said. 'You've got everything so organised, Julian. It's lovely to see how well you look after her.'

'And you've got everything you need in the flat?'

'I have, sweetheart. I shall treat the place like it's my own.'

Julian had cleaned his bedroom before Linda's arrival and changed the sheets on his narrow single bed. It felt odd to think of a stranger sleeping where he slept. Anxiety tugged at him as he thought of the metal cash tin hidden in his wardrobe. The tin containing the remainder of his and Helen's savings. Money the authorities didn't know he had kept from them. This money paid for the little extras that made his wife's life easier. Visits from a private physiotherapist. Vitamins and supplements. Repairs to the car that kept them connected to the outside world. He told himself Linda seemed like an honest woman. Not the type to go rummaging through his wardrobe and lifting up the pile of towels he'd hidden the cash tin under.

'She keeps asking for you,' Linda said.

'That's nice.' He wondered how long an absence it would take for Helen to forget him. The accident had left both her short- and long-term memories impaired. When she'd first regained consciousness after the crash, she appeared to recognise him and knew his name but showed no recollection of their history together. Had she asked after him because she missed him, or did she say his name out of habit? Or did she grasp, on some instinctive level, his duty to care for her and wanted to make sure he fulfilled it?

* * *

After ending his phone call to Linda with a promise to enjoy his time off, Julian decided to go for a walk. He put on the waterproof jacket and walking boots he'd bought from a charity shop three years ago but had never used and set off from the caravan, turning left onto the road and heading towards the arched stone bridge that linked the south side of the loch with the village of St Monzie. The dark clouds had travelled further up the loch, and a vigorous wind whipped the slate-grey water into waves.

His senses awakened. He inhaled the damp, earthy scent of decaying leaves. He heard the sharp, keen cries of a buzzard circling overhead and the mirth of ducks echoing across the loch. His arms swung beside him as he walked and he relished their freedom from wheelchair duty. It was good to move at his own pace. At times, his wife's limitations became his own, and he almost forgot he had an able body.

Guilt kicked in, and he felt lousy for having such thoughts. He recalled the praise Dr Hamilton had heaped on him during his appointment. Praise he feared he did not deserve. *You're a good man,*

Julian. I've never seen such a dedicated carer. He should be kinder to himself, he thought. Surely even a good man could feel overwhelmed by his responsibilities now and again?

With the bracing autumn air in his lungs and his arms swinging back and forth, he resolved to exercise more. Maybe he should start running again? The waistband of his jeans dug into his flesh as he walked, but he was sure it wouldn't take him long to shed his extra weight. The fitter he was, the more energy he would have to devote to Helen. Optimism bloomed within him as he envisaged this healthier, happier self. He would start today, now. He eyed the imposing hill that rose up behind the stone houses and cottages of St Monzie and decided to see how much of it he could climb.

When he reached the bridge, the clouds from the far end of the loch reached him, releasing vast sheets of rain that needled his face and seeped through his inadequate second-hand waterproof. He worried he might get soaked and catch a cold and then pass that cold to Helen, who might suffer another chest infection. The prospect of that happening made his bones ache with fatigue. He thought again of Dr Hamilton and how she had urged him to start looking after himself. *We don't want you reaching breaking point.*

At the time, he'd nodded in agreement, too scared to confess he might already be there.

* * *

Back at the caravan, he changed into dry clothes and sat at the table, intending to read. Exhaustion and poor concentration meant he'd only consumed trashy thrillers of late, but he'd brought his copy of Jack Kerouac's *On the Road* with him, determined to reread it. Rain streaked the windows and drummed on the roof of the caravan. He stared at the book's cover. He remembered his excitement when, a few months before the accident,

Helen had agreed to take a year's sabbatical from work so they could do some proper travelling together. Not their usual city break or camping trip to Brittany, but a long-haul adventure. She understood his urge to get away before committing to a degree course and to parenthood. All those years of fun he'd missed out on while looking after his dad. This would be his gap year, he'd joked.

He opened the book and began to read. He tried to concentrate, but the relentless pace of Kerouac's prose gave him a headache. He gave up after a few pages and listened to the rain instead. Another noise competed with it. A volley of long, pained bellows followed by a series of grunts and barks. The sounds seemed to surround the caravan on all sides. Rutting deer in the hills, he realised, their mating calls amplified by the water.

A restless energy filled him. A strange sense of anticipation. According to his watch, it was almost 3 p.m. Not long until sunset, thanks to the clocks going back the previous day. He decided to drive to the nearby village of Comrie and pick up a few supplies. Before leaving the flat that morning, he'd taken £150 from the cash tin. As a rule, he never used the savings for himself, but he had to leave £60 in cash in the caravan to pay for the accommodation and, with funds low in his current account, he didn't want to go away without some emergency money. After all, he'd told himself, he was only going away for Helen's sake, and he could always replace what he didn't use. Hardly as if he'd have much to spend it on in the middle of nowhere.

He locked up the caravan and set off. At the junction with the Comrie road, he glanced in the rear-view mirror, expecting to meet Helen's eyes. The car idled as he stared at the back seat. He'd folded it down to cover the gap her wheelchair slotted into. For a moment, it felt as though she didn't exist. He looked left and right along the road. If he turned left, the road would eventually lead to Glencoe and from there a man could carry on into all sorts of wilderness. A man could disappear if he wanted to.

He turned right and drove the eight miles to Comrie at a slow speed. The accident had left him a nervous driver. In the village, he parked on the main street. The low stone cottages and three-storey Victorian buildings offered an impressive array of shops and several cafés. A few people braved the weather – hurrying along the narrow pavements, umbrellas aloft.

A craving for coffee came over him. He dashed from the car into the nearby Shaky Toon café. Two elderly women occupied the table beside the steamed-up window, but the others were empty. Julian chose one at the back of the café, facing the door. A colourful poster on the wall informed him that Comrie, also known as the Shaky Toon, was situated on the Highland Boundary Fault and recorded more earth tremors than anywhere else in Great Britain.

'A cappuccino and a cup of hot milk, please,' he said to the young waitress when she came over. She scribbled his order on a notepad, her freckled brow creased with concentration. He couldn't see any other staff, and the girl gave the impression of a keen employee left in charge for the first time.

'Do you want the drinks right away or when the other person comes?' she said.

Realising his mistake, he cancelled the milk. 'It was for my wife, but she's... she's not here.'

The girl shrugged. 'Okay.'

As she walked away, he flashed the two elderly women in the window a rueful smile, but they paid him no attention. Women of all ages complimented him on his caring skills when he was out with Helen. Especially the older ones.

The waitress brought his coffee. Out of habit, he pulled it close, out of his absent wife's reach. He tried to relax but found it unsettling to have nothing to worry about. No brewing trouble to divert.

The door of the café swung open. A man bolted inside, water dripping from his green Parka jacket, from the rucksack on his back and from the tousled blonde hair that rested on his shoulders and framed a face Julian couldn't stop staring at. A disturbingly attractive face that made him dizzy. He gripped the edge of the table and wondered if the village had just experienced one of its famous tremors. If so, no one else seemed to have noticed it.

'That is some rain out there, right?' the man said to the waitress as he approached the counter.

American, noted Julian, although he couldn't place the accent accurately. Young too. Early twenties, maybe? Shorter than him and slender. Slim legs in tight black jeans. Neat feet in red Converse All Stars. The elderly women cast the stranger suspicious looks and raised eyebrows at one another.

The waitress mumbled something about the Scottish weather as a flush rose to her cheeks. This was the kind of man, thought Julian, who would have that effect on any girl, or woman. On anyone.

'Black Americano to go,' the man said, 'biggest size you got.'

While the waitress busied herself at the coffee machine, the stranger shrugged the rucksack from his shoulders with a weary sigh. He stretched his arms overhead and from side to side.

Julian watched, heart thumping against his ribs. A sudden lightness filled him. An almost unbearable sensation of freedom.

'Two pounds thirty, please.' The waitress placed the brown cardboard cup on the counter.

'Sure thing. No worries.' The man checked both pockets of his coat. 'Shit.' He unzipped it, revealing a baggy red and black striped jumper. He searched the pockets of his jeans. 'You gotta be kidding me.'

'Lost something?' the waitress asked.

'Just... gimme a second.' He bent down and unclipped the top of his rucksack. Julian watched his long fingers reach inside. A black T-shirt spilled from the top of the bag, followed by a book. A battered copy of *On the Road*. A jolt of adrenaline made Julian grip the table again.

The man abandoned his search and stood up. 'So, I got a lift here with this guy, and I think maybe I left my wallet in his car? Any chance of a coffee on the house?'

The waitress's cheeks flamed again. 'I don't think I'm supposed to do that.'

'Seriously? One coffee?' The man dragged his fingers through his hair. 'Lady, I haven't slept in three days. I'm like, totally soaked. I've had one of the worst days of my life and I really, really need a cup of coffee.'

His intensity made the waitress edge away.

'This isn't a homeless shelter,' said one of the elderly ladies, brushing cake crumbs from her fingers.

'Wow.' The man turned to face her. 'The milk of human kindness really overflows here, huh?'

Both women recoiled, mouths open with indignation.

'I'll get the coffee,' Julian said. All eyes turned to him, including those of the stranger. Bright blue eyes that sparked a molten heat low down in his belly. 'You can add it to my bill.'

The man's blue eyes glistened. 'That is... that is so kind, my friend. Truly. Like, that is the nicest thing anyone's done for me for a long time.'

Julian noted the dark hollows beneath the young man's eyes. Recognised his exhaustion. 'It's nothing.'

The man lifted his rucksack, swung it over his shoulder and grabbed the coffee. 'You, my friend, are a goddam saint,' he said to Julian, before striding across the café, yanking open the door and vanishing into the rain.

13

Julian sipped his coffee and waited for his fizzing nerves to settle. The elderly women departed, and the waitress announced she had to close up.

'Of course.' Julian put on his coat and went to the counter to pay.

'Thanks for helping me out,' the girl said as he handed over the money for both coffees. 'That guy was weird, eh?'

'I don't think he meant any harm.' He walked away without leaving a tip.

A dusky gloom had settled over the village. Julian glanced up and down the street. No sign of the stranger. He crossed the road to the Spar and browsed the aisles, selecting a jar of green pesto, a packet of spaghetti and a large bar of Dairy Milk. At the checkout, he noticed bottles of Glenturret single malt whisky for sale and had an urge to get drunk. Properly drunk. When had he last allowed himself to do that? At home he had to keep control of his faculties in case Helen needed him.

When the cheery man at the till told him the whisky cost £32, Julian hesitated. Could he really justify such an extravagance? He thought of the bottle of Bell's back at the caravan. Should he drink some of that instead? Deciding it wouldn't be right to use up the caravan owner's supplies, he decided to treat himself. The single malt would last him for ages. No harm in enjoying the occasional nip in the evenings at home.

He paid for his supplies from the wad of cash in his wallet, leaving himself with just over £100. Enough to pay for the caravan and for more supplies tomorrow. He headed back to the car, the bag containing the whisky bumping against his thigh. As he drove out of the village, he switched the radio on. 'Rebel Rebel' by David Bowie greeted him. He laughed and turned up the volume. He'd idolised Bowie in his youth. Put a Ziggy Stardust poster on his bedroom wall, but his dad had made him remove it. *I'm not having pictures of that queer in my house.*

Rain battered the windscreen. Julian turned his headlights on full against the encroaching darkness and kept his speed low on the winding road. As he approached a layby, he saw a slight figure in the gloom. A hooded figure with one arm outstretched and a thumb held up in the universal hitch-hiking sign.

Julian observed his left hand as it reached for the indicator. He noted his foot hitting the brake and his right hand guiding the Horizon into the layby. He wound down his window, and when the stranger's blue eyes met his, the molten sensation deep inside him returned.

'What d'ya know?' the man said.

'You'll catch your death in this weather.'

'Are you the only guy with a heart around here? I swear twenty cars have gone by.'

'Where are you going?'

'North, I guess. Some guy in the village said there was a bus heading this way later, but I figured I'd try to hitch a ride first.'

'I'm going as far as St Monzie. I'm sure there'll be a bus stop there.'

'Beats this rain, my friend.' The man put his rucksack in the boot before clambering into the passenger seat. 'I'm like, really wet, man. Sorry.'

'Don't worry about it.' A pungent scent rose from the man's hair and jacket. Weed, Julian suspected, although he hadn't encountered the stuff in years. The radio blurted out the opening bars of Spandau Ballet's 'True'. Julian switched the song off, not wanting the man to think he liked it. 'I'm Julian, by the way,' he said, hoping to put his passenger at ease, but unsure if he should offer his hand.

'Good to meet you, Julian.' The man kept his hands to himself. 'I'm Gabriel.'

'Like the angel?'

Gabriel gifted him a slow smile. 'Trust me, man. I'm no angel.'

The muscles in Julian's thighs slackened. He noticed Gabriel's nose was off-kilter. Bent to the right and the bridge slightly flattened. A natural asymmetry, he wondered, or the result of a fight?

He gripped the steering wheel, checked his mirrors and pulled out onto the road. Darkness had settled and his headlights bounced off a chevron on the first tight bend. Gabriel sank into his seat and, when Julian dared to glance across, he found his passenger had closed his eyes. Making the most of the comfort before hitting the road, he thought. Clocking Gabriel's pale lips and trembling shoulders, he turned up the heating and opened the vents in the dashboard. It didn't take long for the hot, noisy stream of air to circulate.

'You're a thoughtful guy, Julian.' Gabriel opened his eyes.

'You must be freezing.'

'Seriously, you shouting me that coffee back there and now this. Kinda restores my faith in mankind a little.'

'What made you lose it? The faith.'

'Let's just say I've had a run of shitty luck.'

'Sorry to hear that.'

'It is what it is.'

'Are you on holiday over here?'

'No. I'm British. Kind of.'

'Sorry. Your accent... I thought—'

'British mom, American dad. He was a pilot in the air force. She met him when he was stationed over here.'

'She went back to the States with him?'

'Yup. I was born in Ohio. Lived there for a while when I was a kid, but we moved around a lot. I lived in the States till I was nineteen.'

'My dad was in the army.'

'No way. Seriously?'

'Seriously.'

'Was he an asshole, too?'

Julian laughed. 'He had his moments.'

'What are the chances, huh? Two military brats.'

'Quite the coincidence.' Julian focused on the darkness ahead, resisting the urge to look at his passenger.

As soon as they entered St Monzie, Gabriel spotted a wooden bus shelter opposite the village shop. Julian pulled up next to it.

'What about bus fare?' he said. 'Do you have enough?'

'It's all good.' Gabriel gazed at the pounding rain. 'Guess I should check the timetable first?'

'I suppose so.'

Gabriel stepped out of the car and hurried over to the bus shelter. Julian rubbed a thumb along his lips. Please let there be a bus, he thought, there has to be a bus.

'No bus until tomorrow morning,' Gabriel said when he returned to the car. A confusing blend of terror and excitement swept through Julian.

'That's a nuisance,' he said.

Gabriel groaned. 'What does a guy have to do to get a break around here?'

'Listen. I don't know if it would help, but—'

'What?'

'I'm staying near here. You're welcome to crash for the night. Only if you want to. There's plenty of room, I could cook you something to eat.'

'Seriously, you sure you're not a saint?'

Julian smiled. 'It's not much of a place but you can get your clothes dry, get a good night's sleep and start again tomorrow.' His hands gripped the steering wheel. 'Only if you want to.'

When Gabriel nodded, glistening drops of rain fell from his tangled hair. 'I'd like that, Julian. Truly.'

14

When they entered the caravan, Julian switched on the overhead light and put the gas fire on high. Gabriel propped his rucksack against a table leg and shrugged off his sodden coat.

'Let me take that,' Julian said. He hung it on the hook on the back of the door, along with his own jacket.

Gabriel glanced around the caravan, taking in the dated décor.

'It's not my place,' Julian said. 'I'm just staying here.'

'Beats sleeping in a bus shelter, my friend.' Weariness crept through Gabriel's light-hearted tone. 'So, like, you're on holiday?'

'Sort of.'

'Where's home?'

'Edinburgh.'

'Beautiful city, my friend.'

'You've been there?'

'Sure. A few times. Whereabouts do you live?'

'You wouldn't know it. Shawfair Street is hardly a tourist mecca.' Julian noticed water dripping from the ends of Gabriel's hair. 'I'll get you a towel,' he said. In the bathroom, his pulse raced at his recklessness. What was he thinking of, inviting a stranger to stay?

What if something happened to him? Who would look after Helen then? He told himself to calm down. Gabriel didn't look the type to harm anyone. He was a young man down on his luck, and Julian wanted to help him. Nothing more.

'Here,' he said, holding out the towel as he stepped out of the bathroom. Gabriel had stripped down to a pair of navy boxer shorts, his wet clothes puddled on the floor around him. Julian stared at the younger man's smooth, toned torso and felt ashamed of his own saggy flesh.

'Thanks, man.' Gabriel took the towel. 'Mind if I take a shower? I'm kinda frozen.'

'Please. Yes. Go ahead.' Julian stepped aside as Gabriel sauntered into the bathroom. He cringed as he remembered his tatty washbag on the toilet cistern, his cheap lemon-scented body wash in the shower and his worn toothbrush by the sink, bristles splayed.

While Gabriel showered, Julian brought a wooden chair through from the bedroom and arranged his guest's wet clothes over it. Jumper over the back, jeans and T-shirt on the seat. He wrung out each of Gabriel's wet black socks and draped them on the wooden bar between the chair legs. Afterwards, he unpacked the supplies he'd bought in Comrie and left his backpack near the fire to dry. He pictured himself and Gabriel eating an early supper of pasta and pesto, washing it down with a modest nightcap and turning in for an early night. He would give his guest the bedroom and make himself comfortable on one of the long cushioned benches. He glanced at the bench nearest to him and saw his copy of *On the Road* lying there. He picked it up and placed it in the middle of the table.

'Man, I needed that,' Gabriel said when he emerged from the bathroom, towel tucked around his waist, boxer shorts scrunched in one hand. He stopped at the sight of his clothes spread out on the chair. 'Wow. That's... that is like above and beyond, man. I'm touched. Truly.' He smiled his slow, inviting trap of a smile, and Julian's breath stalled in his chest.

'It's nothing,' he said.

When Gabriel crouched to hang his boxer shorts next to the socks, he revealed for the first time the black angel wings tattooed across his back. Julian marvelled at the detail in the large feathered creations.

'Digging the wings?' Gabriel straightened up and strolled over to his rucksack.

Julian blushed. 'Very realistic,' he said, unsure how to critique a tattoo. He watched as Gabriel untied his half-empty bag and pulled out a pair of blue ripped jeans and a black T-shirt. 'You travel light.'

'This is all I got.' Gabriel straightened up. 'Everything I own is in this bag.'

'That must be liberating.'

'It's the only way to live, my friend.' Gabriel pulled the T-shirt over his head. 'I collect experiences, not possessions.' With no warning, Gabriel let his towel drop. Transfixed, Julian watched as the young man stepped into his jeans and tugged them over his bare buttocks. When Gabriel, fully dressed, turned to face him, heat crawled across Julian's chest.

Silence swelled between them, punctuated by the rain hitting the caravan roof. Julian waited for Gabriel to speak, but the young man's eyes were fixed on him with a curious, expectant look.

'How about a hot drink to warm you up?' Julian said. 'Tea? Or coffee? I think there's instant coffee here.'

'I'd rather take a shot of the good stuff.' Gabriel nodded towards the bottle of Glenturret sitting by the kitchen hob.

'Yes. Of course.' As Julian removed two glass tumblers from the kitchen's sole cupboard, he glanced at his watch. Not even half-five. A bit early to be drinking, but with the darkness outside it could be any time. He took off his watch and left it by the sink.

'Mind if I fix the lighting in here?' Gabriel switched on the two twin lamp sets attached to the caravan walls. Yellow light filtered through the pink tasselled shades. He turned off the overhead light, transforming the caravan into a dim place full of shadows. 'Perfect, right?'

'Perfect.' Julian christened the tumblers with whisky and brought them to the table. He and Gabriel sat opposite each other and raised their glasses.

'Cheers,' Julian said.

'Cheers, man.'

Their glasses met with a conspiratorial clink. Gabriel took a hefty gulp of whisky. 'That's better. Damn, that's good.'

Julian sipped his drink. The alcohol spread warm, comforting tendrils into his stomach.

'No way.' Gabriel reached for Julian's copy of *On the Road*. 'I'm reading this right now.'

'Really?'

'Like, for the twentieth time.'

'Same here. Roughly.'

'This is a day of strange coincidences, my friend.'

'Seems that way.'

They shared a smile, and this time, Julian knocked back a large gulp of the whisky.

'Glad I'm not hitching in that,' Gabriel said as the wind flung handfuls of rain against the large window. 'I really lucked out today, man. A Good Samaritan like you showing up and helping me out.'

'Anyone would have done the same.'

'Well, they didn't, my friend. You did. Not everyone is as decent as you.'

They clinked glasses again. Gabriel slid out from behind the table and fetched a silver tobacco tin from his coat pocket.

'Don't suppose you got any smokes?' he said when he sat down again.

'I don't smoke. Sorry.'

'Didn't think so. Any weed?' He laughed. 'Just kidding. You don't look the type.'

'Is that a backhanded compliment?'

'It's all good.' Gabriel produced a stubby joint from the tin along with a cheap plastic lighter. 'Guess we'll have to make this last.' Julian glanced at the hand-drawn 'No Smoking' sign on the kitchen cupboard door but decided to ignore it. He would air the place tomorrow, once Gabriel had gone.

After a deep inhale, Gabriel sank back against the faded pink cushions and let smoke trail from his nostrils. 'I gotta say, Julian, this is the safest I've felt for a long time. Here, in this place, with you. Truly.'

'Glad to hear it.' Julian forced himself to sit back and tried to look relaxed. When Gabriel offered him the joint, he hesitated before refusing. He'd only smoked dope a few times in his life, and it had always made him sick.

'Like, the shit I've been dealing with,' Gabriel said. 'I gotta confess it could get a man down.'

'What kind of shit?'

'I don't want you to think bad of me.'

'I won't.'

'You're not a judgemental guy, I see that. I feel I can trust you.'

'You can.'

'I got in with some bad people, that's all. Took some wrong turns.'

'What kind of turns?'

'I started selling this stuff a while back.' Gabriel brandished the joint. 'I worked in bars and nightclubs in London for a while, got into a drug scene, I guess. At first it was just small scale, but then I got in with some bigger league guys, you know?'

Julian nodded, even though he didn't.

'I'm talking a big operation,' Gabriel said. 'Harder drugs. I was doing good, making bank, but I was playing a ton of poker, you know? Bigger and bigger games and I was winning and then I wasn't and then I lost a lot. Like, a helluva lot, so I borrowed from people no man should ever borrow from and then I had to skim from my boss so I could pay them back. You get the picture? And trust me, my boss is a guy you don't wanna piss off. So, I had to hightail it out of there. These are people you gotta run from.'

'What will you do?' Julian said, intoxicated by the drama of it all.

Gabriel pinched the tip of the joint dead and placed it back in the tin. 'Who knows? Something always shows up, right? Way I see it, the universe has a path for me to walk, my own special pilgrimage. I just gotta wait for a sign to show me where to head next.'

Julian felt torn between worry for Gabriel's precarious situation and envy of his freedom. 'What about your family?' he said. 'Can't your parents help you out?'

'Both gone. Mom when I was nine years old. Ovarian cancer. They didn't even tell me. My dad sent me off to a summer camp and when I came back, she was gone.'

'That's awful.'

'She loved me, you know? We were super-close. Then she was gone and I was stuck with the old man.'

'You didn't get on with him?'

'I was rebellious, I guess. All kids get into trouble, right? I set a few fires, got in some fights, hated on my stepmom. No biggie. But he sent me to this military school in Columbus, real shithouse place. I stuck it till I was fifteen, then I ran away to San Francisco.'

'Did you reconcile with him?'

'He died in a helicopter crash when I was seventeen.'

'I'm sorry.'

'Don't be.' Gabriel raked his long fingers through his hair. 'He wasn't a good guy. Not to my mom, not to me. Not like you, Julian. Not kind like you. If he was alive now, the warped fuck wouldn't help me. He'd probably tell those guys where I was. Tell me to take my punishment like a man.'

Gabriel swigged the last of his whisky and explained that after his father's death, he'd used his British passport to come to England, hoping to get to know his maternal grandmother. 'Grandma was cool. A nice lady, but she died a few months after I arrived. My mom's brother wasn't interested in me. Kinda made me feel my mom was a bit of a black sheep, you know?'

'I am sorry.'

'It's all good. I'm used to being alone.'

'No one else then? No girlfriend to help you out?'

'No. There was someone but, you know, people let you down sometimes.'

'Sorry to hear that.' Julian pointed to Gabriel's empty glass. 'Another drink?'

'Always.'

Julian fetched the bottle from the kitchen, topped up their glasses and left the bottle sitting between them.

'So, what about you, my friend?' Gabriel said. 'What's your story?'

'Not sure I have one.'

Gabriel pointed to the gold band on Julian's ring finger. 'Well, you're not here with your wife. You taking some space? Getting a break away from your kids?'

'We don't have children.'

'Got marital woes?'

'Not quite.'

'She left you? You're the kind of nice guy a woman would leave.'

'No. Well, not exactly.'

'Don't you love her any more?'

'I care for her.'

'But you don't love her?'

'It's a long story.'

Gabriel smiled. 'I'm all ears, man. Hit me.'

15

Gabriel turned out to be a good listener. As they polished off the bottle of single malt, Julian poured out the story of his life, starting with a brief description of Helen's condition and then returning to his father's multiple sclerosis diagnosis when he was eight years old. He couldn't remember when he had last unburdened himself in this way. Something in Gabriel encouraged it. The younger man's eyes filled with sympathy when Julian described his curtailed childhood and the demands of his role as a young carer.

'I'm guessing a military man like that didn't dig being an invalid?' Gabriel said.

'No, not much.'

'Must have been a tough gig for you?'

'Little did I know it was a practice run for looking after my disabled wife.' Julian picked up the empty whisky bottle. 'Shit.'

'Got anything else to drink, buddy?'

Julian remembered the bottle of Bell's in the kitchen cupboard. 'Hang on.' He lurched out of his seat and fetched it. He would leave some money for it in the morning. No harm done. He sat down and poured them both another dram, amazed at how relaxed and lucid he felt. How in control of himself.

'What happened to her?' Gabriel rested a bare foot on the seat. 'How did she end up like that?'

Julian, who had never spoken in detail to anyone about the accident apart from the police, found himself telling Gabriel everything. He described the blue Volvo estate veering into their lane of the A9 and running them off the road just outside Pitlochry.

'The other driver wasn't to blame. There was black ice on the road. I escaped with a broken collarbone and whiplash, but Helen's side of the car took most of the impact.'

'But it wasn't your fault?'

'No.' Witnesses had confirmed Julian's lack of culpability. The Volvo had swerved without warning. 'But I was the driver. I felt responsible.'

'Not your bad, man. You gotta let it go.'

'Easily said.'

'You're a good guy, Julian.' Gabriel fiddled with the frayed denim covering his knee. 'It's in your eyes. You got kind eyes. Anyone ever tell you that?'

Julian averted his gaze. His father had often accused him of having his mother's eyes. A comparison meant as a warning, not a compliment. 'Being kind didn't stop me losing everything.'

'Why do the good guys get all the bad luck? It shouldn't be that way. Bet guys like you, looking after folk they love, save the government a ton of money, right?'

'Over two billion pounds a week. Unpaid carers are the reason this country—'

'And they expect you to live off shitty handouts? It's criminal, man.'

Julian gulped his whisky. 'At least I got one over on them.'

'Yeah?'

'The authorities do everything they can to avoid giving you any money. If you have a decent amount of savings, you don't qualify for a lot of the benefits. After the accident, I started taking out the little we had left and stashing it. I made sure they couldn't con Helen out of what she needed.'

'Gotta stick it to the man any way you can. How much you hide?'

'Nearly forty grand.'

'Way to go.'

'We've only got about £9,000 left and that won't last long. I want Helen to have any extras she needs, but they soon add up.'

'Nine thousand.' Gabriel nodded. 'That's still something.'

Julian rolled his shoulders back and forth as the relaxing effects of the whisky exposed the unbearable tension in his muscles.

'What's going on with the shoulders, buddy?' Gabriel said.

'Nothing. Just a bit stiff.'

'Let me fix that.' Gabriel edged along the seat towards him. 'I do a great massage.'

'No. There's no need.' Julian's right thigh trembled as Gabriel pressed against him.

'Come on.' Gabriel nudged him with a bony elbow. 'Really?'

Julian sensed the challenge in the young man's words. He turned to one side and sat cross-legged on the bench.

'That's better,' Gabriel said.

Julian tensed up as Gabriel knelt on the bench behind him. When the young man's hands rested on his shoulders, he jerked away.

'Jeez.' Gabriel pulled him back. 'How long has it been since anyone touched you?'

Julian thought of Helen's fist making contact with his chest that morning. 'A while.'

'You don't say.' Gabriel's fingers sank into him and kneaded his knotted shoulders. After a few minutes, Julian's flesh softened and submitted.

'You're good at this,' he said.

'I learned in San Francisco at this commune place I lived in. I worked as a sort of masseur for a while. Did pretty good with the older ladies.'

'I bet.' A faint pang of jealousy accompanied Julian's smile. 'I do quite a bit of massage myself, actually. For Helen. Helps her with the pain.'

'I bet you're good at it, too. Bet you got a real sensitive touch.'

Julian sighed as his muscles yielded further. He found himself telling Gabriel about the time, as a thirteen-year-old, he'd offered to massage his father's frozen shoulder muscles to help him sleep.

'He was lucky to have such a caring kid,' Gabriel said.

'He wouldn't let me do it. I think his exact words were, what's wrong with you, son? Are you a bloody poof?'

'Typical of a guy like that. My dad was the same.'

'I can imagine.'

'What do guys like that know?'

Julian twisted his head and looked into Gabriel's blue eyes. He felt what he hoped was an electric current of understanding pass between them.

'I gotta ask,' Gabriel said, delving deeper into Julian's flesh, 'what about your mom?'

'What about her?' Julian dropped his head again.

'You haven't mentioned her. Like, at all.'

Julian's stomach plummeted. Gabriel's hands slowed and traced gentle circles around his shoulder blades, as if aware of his discomfort.

'She left when I was eight,' he said, 'just after my dad got diagnosed.'

'Left?'

'Said she was going to Manchester to visit her mum, but she left the country and went to Australia.'

'Seriously?'

'Her sister had moved to Adelaide a few years before. I think the two of them made a plan to get her over there. My dad didn't have a clue.'

'Man, that is harsh.'

'They got divorced and she married some Aussie guy after a while.'

'You never saw her again?'

'She died when I was nineteen. She had a stroke.'

Gabriel's hands came to rest on his shoulders. The sudden stillness encouraged Julian to keep talking.

'I don't remember that much about her. Not really. Apart from her hair.' His mother had been a hairdresser and her hairstyle had changed as often as her moods. Long and blonde, happy and sad. Black and cropped, affectionate and cold. 'The last time I saw her was at the bus station in Folkestone when she got on the coach to Manchester. It pulled away and we waved to each other and then she was gone.' The previous day she'd had her hair cut into a bob and dyed red. A radical change that in hindsight looked to Julian like a warning. 'I always wondered what she thought about when the bus pulled away. What she was feeling.' Tears surged to his eyes. 'Sorry.'

'Don't apologise. You gotta get these feelings out. The cult of masculinity is toxic, man. It wounds us all.'

Julian gasped as Gabriel wrapped his arms around him. The young man smelled of the cheap citrus shower gel and a lighter, musky scent of his own. His blonde hair pressed against Julian's damp cheek.

'You don't have to do this,' Julian said.

Gabriel reached out and stuck his index finger into Julian's glass. 'I know.' He ran his whisky-soaked finger along Julian's bottom lip. Julian's arousal was immediate and obvious, but he didn't care. When Gabriel licked the whisky from his lip, Julian pulled him closer. The young man's lips were fleshy but chapped, his tongue delicate but insistent. Julian surrendered to the embrace and lost all awareness of time until a cramp in his left leg forced him to pull away. Gabriel laughed and suggested they move somewhere more comfortable.

In the musty bedroom, Julian switched on the bedside lamp with its pink, tasselled shade. Overcome with self-consciousness, he sat on the edge of the small double bed. Gabriel stood in front of him, peeled off his black T-shirt and threw it aside. Julian stared in wonder, not just at the young man's physique but also at the easy way he inhabited his body. How free he was with himself. He grabbed the waist of Gabriel's jeans and undid his top button.

'Stop.' Gabriel clamped a hand over his.

'Sorry. I thought—'

'Let someone take care of you for a change.' Gabriel sank to his knees and, with practised fingers, unbuckled Julian's belt and unzipped his jeans. Julian surrendered to the unfamiliar pleasure of being wanted and eased himself between the young man's eager lips.

'Don't stop,' he said, grabbing a fistful of Gabriel's hair. 'Please don't stop.'

16

Afterwards, they lay together, naked, Gabriel's head resting on Julian's chest. Wind rattled the caravan and amplified the bellows of the rutting deer.

'What the hell is that noise?' Gabriel said. He laughed when Julian explained. 'Do they go at it all night?'

'Sounds like it.'

'I like their style.'

Julian's turn to laugh. He realised how drunk he was. He wondered if guilt and shame would rush in when he sobered up. His fingers trailed across Gabriel's back, the black feathers sticky where he'd finished himself off.

When Gabriel caressed his stomach, his self-consciousness returned. In the heat of it, he hadn't noticed the difference in their ages and their bodies. 'Don't,' he said.

'Why not?'

'I'm a bit... I've put on a bit of weight lately.'

'I like you just as you are, big guy.'

'Big guy?'

'You're solid. I feel safe with you.'

'I'll take solid as a compliment.' Julian kissed the top of Gabriel's head. 'How old are you?'

'Twenty-four. You?'

'Forty-six. I must seem ancient to you.'

'You're not old, big guy. You're mature. Worldly. I like that.' Gabriel lifted his head. 'This wasn't your first rodeo, right?'

'My second.' Julian met Gabriel's curious gaze. 'I was your age, and Finn was a chef in the hotel I was working in. It didn't last long – he was only there for the summer.'

'Summer romance, huh?'

'I suppose so.' A happy summer, full of secrets. The thrill of returning home to his father each day with the smell of Finn all over him. The twisted pleasure in washing his father's defunct body with hands that had touched Finn everywhere. After Finn's departure, his father took a turn for the worse, and Julian had once again pushed this part of his sexuality deep down inside himself and locked it away.

'What about women?' Gabriel said. 'You like them too, right?'

'I think I've always been attracted to both.'

'Me too.'

Julian suspected Gabriel's tally of men and women would far outstrip his own. He had no desire to know.

'Another drink?' Gabriel sat up and flicked his hair back from his face.

'Sure.' Julian waited until Gabriel had strolled naked out of the bedroom before picking his T-shirt up from the floor and pulling it on.

Gabriel returned with a whisky bottle in one hand and his tobacco tin in the other. He climbed under the thin pink duvet beside Julian and handed him the bottle. 'Drink up.'

Julian removed the lid and raised the bottle to his lips but hesitated before drinking, reluctant to wash the taste of Gabriel out of his mouth. When he did take a sip, he realised whisky would forever remind him of this night. Of this man.

Gabriel reclined against a pillow, opened his tin and sparked up his joint. After a deep inhale, he offered it to Julian.

'Better not,' Julian said.

'Don't be such a pussy.' Gabriel inhaled and pressed his lips against Julian's. Julian opened his mouth and let the harsh, vegetal smoke infiltrate him.

'Good, right?' Gabriel said when they parted.

Julian nodded. When he exhaled, all remaining tension in his muscles dissolved. He couldn't remember when he'd last felt so relaxed. His body so light. So free. He passed the whisky to Gabriel.

'Thanks, big guy.'

'Look.' Julian pointed to the tiny window above the bed. The racing clouds had parted to reveal a sharp sliver of moon.

'Awesome.' Gabriel took a slug of whisky. 'This is crazy, right? You and me, meeting like we did.'

'I certainly didn't picture my day ending up like this.' Julian reached beneath the duvet and stroked Gabriel's hipbone. 'I'm glad it did.'

'That's life, right? Now and then the universe gives you just what you need.'

'I needed this. Very much.'

'I'm guessing you don't get it on with your wife these days?'

'No. Of course not.'

'What was the sex like before the accident?'

'Good. Better than good.' The best he'd ever known, and Helen had sworn she felt the same. A year after her return from the brain injuries unit, he'd wondered if intimate touch might awaken something in her. One night, after putting her to bed, he lifted up her pyjama top and stroked her breasts. He expected her to lash out, but she remained passive. He took her hand and pressed it between her legs, but she let it rest there, limp. He covered her breasts up, laid his head on her stomach and wept. He'd never touched her that way again.

'So, I gotta ask,' Gabriel said, handing Julian the bottle, 'what do you do for sex?'

'What do you mean?'

'Your wife's been out of action nearly ten years. What do you do?'

'I don't really do anything.'

'Seriously? Come on.'

'Seriously.' Julian swigged the whisky. 'Well, I haven't for a while.' He told Gabriel about his attempt to find satisfaction a few years after the accident. The advert he'd placed on a Casual Encounters website. *Man with disabled wife in need of occasional company.* The advert led to him meeting a woman called Maureen at her shabby flat in Dalkeith, but she'd treated him with a gentleness he couldn't bear. He wanted her to get on all fours so he could get the deed done without looking at her face, but she wouldn't oblige. He'd left feeling embarrassed, ashamed and unsatisfied. 'After that, I went once to a sex worker. I felt too awful afterwards to do it again.'

'You are truly in a prison of guilt, my friend.' Gabriel shook his head. 'Why don't you leave her?'

'What? She needs me. I can't just—'

'You got care homes up here, right? Put her in one of those.'

Julian sighed. 'It doesn't work like that.' He explained the authorities didn't consider her needy enough to take up one of the rare spaces reserved for adults under sixty-five. 'Not that I could leave her in one of those awful places.'

'It's not fair. None of it.'

'After the accident, one of the consultants told me she wouldn't live long. Two years, maybe three.'

'She must be tough.'

'What if my love's the only thing keeping her alive?'

'I don't think that's love.'

Julian stared at Gabriel. 'Don't tell me I don't love my wife.'

'If you love her, why are you letting her suffer like that?'

'I'm not.'

'Trapped in her body, no idea what's going on. What kind of existence is that?'

'You don't know what you're talking about. Yes, it's difficult, yes, she suffers, but there are moments of real wonder amongst it all. Some days, she even smiles at me.'

Julian's last, pitiful sentence caught him out. Tears, hot and unbidden, worked their way up his throat.

'Sorry, man.' Gabriel took the bottle from him and placed it on the bedside table. 'I was just saying.'

Julian waved the apology away, too choked to speak.

'Come on, big guy.' Gabriel opened his arms. 'Come here.' Julian curled into him and laid his head on the younger man's smooth chest.

'It's all good,' Gabriel said.

'It's not. It's really not.' He let out a volley of sobs. When they subsided, the first pulse of a headache stirred between his eyebrows.

'What would you do if you were free?' Gabriel said. 'If you didn't have Helen.'

Julian sniffed. 'But I do.'

'Okay. What if things were the other way around? What if you'd come off worse in the accident? Would you want Helen to waste her life looking after you?'

'That's not... how can I answer that?'

'Would you? I wouldn't put a burden like that on someone I loved.'

'You couldn't say unless it happened to you.'

'I'm saying it now, my friend. If it were me, I'd want the person I loved to do the decent thing and turn off the goddam lights.'

Julian's headache pulsed harder.

'Don't tell me you never thought about it?' Gabriel said.

'About what?'

'That she might have been better off dying in the crash.'

Julian remembered those first weeks after the accident. Helen in an induced coma, fighting for her life. A straight-talking consultant outlining the severity of her injuries to him. The question that had crept into his head. *Would it be better for her if she never woke up?*

'Maybe both of us should have died.' he said.

'I'm glad you didn't. Or you wouldn't be here with me now.' Gabriel pressed Julian's ear lobe between his thumb and forefinger. 'It must really suck, seeing someone you love suffer like that?'

'It does. Some days she's in terrible pain.'

'Haven't you ever wished for the pain to stop? Don't you want her to be at peace?'

'Yes. Of course. Sometimes.' A tingling sweat erupted on Julian's upper lip. His stomach lurched. He rolled away from Gabriel and sat up.

'What's wrong, big guy?'

Julian staggered to the bathroom and locked the door behind him. He lifted the toilet lid, bent over and vomited.

Haven't you ever wished for the pain to stop?

He heaved until he'd emptied his stomach.

'Julian?' Gabriel's voice, low and plaintive. 'Are you okay?'

'I'm fine. Go back to bed.'

The floor outside creaked as Gabriel moved away. Julian flushed the toilet, closed the lid and sat on it. His hands were shaking, his breathing shallow. The night's debauchery would do nothing for his blood pressure. He would pay for his careless behaviour. After a few minutes, he stood up and washed his hands and face in the tiny sink. He cleaned his teeth with his worn toothbrush but couldn't erase the taste of betrayal. Exhaustion swept through him and when he returned to the bedroom, he was relieved to find Gabriel had passed out. The young man lay on his stomach, his lean limbs taking up most of the bed. Julian claimed the edge of the mattress for himself and laid his throbbing head on one of the thin pillows. Before he switched off the bedside light, his eyes rested on Gabriel's black wings. The feathers hovered in front of his eyelids as he sank into unconsciousness.

* * *

He woke to find birch leaves plastered to the caravan window like yellow tears and an empty space in the bed beside him. His head pounded, and his throat was dry and raw. The air reeked of weed and whisky and, as he inhaled, the events of the previous night rushed back, prompting a stirring between his legs and a seedy surge of guilt.

'Gabriel?' he said, his voice a pathetic croak.

The caravan was silent. He hauled himself out of bed and stumbled into the living area. 'Gabriel?' He knocked on the bathroom door and, after a few seconds, pushed it open.

Empty.

Head pounding, he looked around the caravan. Gabriel's clothes had vanished, except for the black T-shirt, which lay crumpled on the chair. No Parka jacket hung on the caravan door. No sign of the rucksack.

Gabriel had gone.

Julian noticed his backpack lying on the table, surrounded by its contents. He hurried over, his stomach twisting when he spotted his wallet lying open.

He picked it up, expecting to find all his money gone, but, to his surprise, Gabriel had only taken £80, leaving him with two £10 notes. A scrap of paper stuck out from between them. On it, a message from Gabriel.

Sorry.

17

Two days after his return from the caravan, Julian woke at 6 a.m., heart racing, from a dream he could not remember. Helen's deep, irregular breathing filled his bedroom, seeping in through the baby monitor on his bedside table. Each night as he slept, his unconscious stayed attuned to the monitor. Even the sound of his wife's sheets rustling as her upper body tossed and turned could stir him. Last night, he'd woken just before midnight to the sound of her having a seizure. A mild one, thankfully, and she'd soon settled down again once he'd given her a drop of Oromorph.

Turning over, he found Gabriel's T-shirt on the pillow beside him. He must have fallen asleep with it there. He pressed his face against it and inhaled but found no trace of the young man's scent. If it wasn't for the shirt and Gabriel's note, which Julian had kept in his wallet, he could almost convince himself the encounter hadn't occurred.

After discovering Gabriel had fled, he'd considered returning home straight away, but his hangover prevented him. He'd spent his final day at the caravan in bed, feeble, self-pitying and full of shame. All that money gone, too. He'd have to take extra from his already stretched current account to pay for the caravan. What else had he expected from a character like Gabriel? He told himself to be grateful the troubled young man hadn't taken the lot. This courtesy, along with the apologetic note, he took as signs of respect and possibly affection. As rain had lashed the caravan, Julian wondered if any of the young man's colourful stories were true. He couldn't help hoping Gabriel wasn't in any danger. He'd even permitted himself a brief fantasy about Gabriel abandoning his journey north and returning to him.

Resting his cheek on the T-shirt, he summoned Gabriel's bright blue eyes and lazy, devastating smile. His smooth chest and taut brown nipples. The memory alone made Julian hard, but when he reached for himself, a loud groan erupted from the baby monitor and killed the moment.

He got up, put on his threadbare dressing gown and trailed through to his wife's bedroom. He found her still asleep, her long grey hair fanned out across her pillow. Whatever discomfort had made her groan wasn't strong enough to wake her. At some point during the night, she had cast the duvet off her upper body. Julian covered her up again and gave her a light kiss on her forehead.

The zippy whine of a speeding car lured him into the living room. He hurried across to the window and peeked through the curtains in time to see a boy racer tearing past, taking advantage of Shawfair Street's unreliable CCTV cameras. The street was located at the shabby end of Fountainbridge, an area that had so far resisted development and gentrification. Home to unkempt tenement blocks and low-grade takeaways and saturated with the reek of hops from the nearby brewery.

It's not such a bad place, he told himself as he picked up an empty mug from the windowsill. Some might find the street depressing, with its grey council bungalows and their old and sick occupants, but at least his neighbours understood his predicament.

Beverly, two doors down, would often sit with Helen if he had to nip out to get some shopping or pick up a prescription.

He carried the mug through to the galley kitchen and switched on the overhead light. The red linoleum floor made a sucking sound when he walked across it. Irritation surged through him. The floor was always sticky, no matter how much he washed it. As he rinsed the mug under the tap, he felt the draught coming in through the rotting back door. A gap had appeared between the door and the frame. A few weeks ago, he'd reported the damage to the council, but no one had come to repair it. He suspected months would pass before anyone did.

He filled the kettle and flicked it on. As he waited for it to boil, he stared out into the backyard. The glare from the kitchen window lit up the dark morning. He could see the green wheelie bin, the sagging washing line and the missing panel in the fence that led to the overgrown no-man's land between the fence and the nearby bypass.

He made himself a strong cup of tea and returned to his wife. Her overgrown eyebrows pulled together in a frown as he entered the room, but she didn't stir. He watched the deep grooves between her eyes contract and relax. Her pale, narrow face had aged way beyond her years, the severe lines on her forehead a testament to years of suffering.

One of her pillows lay on the floor, jettisoned over the safety rail during the night. Julian nudged it aside with his foot as he settled into the armchair beside the bed. The agency carers weren't due until 7.30 so he decided to leave Helen a while before waking her. Later, he hoped to take her to the music and movement group at the Carers First Centre in Stockbridge. When in the right mood, she enjoyed the experience.

As he sipped his tea, his gaze settled on the memory board he had put up on the wall opposite Helen's bed, in the hope she might connect with her past. A large cork board covered with photographs. Their wedding portrait at the centre – a black and white shot of them in the vintage 1960s outfits they'd worn for the registry office ceremony. Helen's skirt rested halfway up her thighs, showing off her slender legs. Next to this picture, another of them dressed up as Morticia and Gomez Addams for a Halloween party. Helen had always loved dressing up. She was the sociable, gregarious one, and she had made him more confident and outgoing. In return, he had given her stability. She'd told him he was her family. She'd told him he felt like home. His eyes travelled over images of them holidaying with friends in a cottage on Mull. Another snap showed his wife in work mode, surrounded by a group of formerly homeless teenagers she had helped with one of her charity's programmes. Hard to believe the woman in the bed beside him had once lived the life shown in the photographs.

What if things were the other way around? What if you'd come off worse in the accident?

Gabriel's questions pushed their way into his thoughts. He didn't want to answer them. He liked to think Helen would have cared for him, as he had for her, but how could he be sure? What about her desire to have children? Would she have considered motherhood more important than her duty to look after him? Even before the accident, he'd worried her longing to start a family could become an issue between them. In the months leading up to the crash, he'd started to wonder if he even wanted children. He liked the idea of him and his wife alone together, years of free and relaxed living ahead. No one else to look after or worry about. But Helen had it all sorted. A year of carefree travelling and then they would start trying. She would return to work after maternity leave, of course, and Julian would study part-time and do the bulk of the childcare. A perfect scenario, according to her, and her certainty had forced Julian to keep his doubts to himself.

I'd want the person I loved to do the decent thing and turn off the goddam lights.

Julian shook his head at Gabriel's naivety. What would someone so young and free understand about the complexities of his situation? He picked up the pillow from the floor and rested it on his lap. Then again, mercy killings did happen. If he had it in him, if he was that kind of person, he could extinguish his wife right now, this minute.

He smoothed the surface of the pillow. He was not that kind of person, and besides, he'd heard about such cases in the news. Two years ago, he'd followed the story of a man in his sixties from Glasgow who'd suffocated his wife to end the agony caused by her motor neurone disease. The man had escaped a prison sentence, thanks to a sympathetic judge and a note the wife had written in the early stages of her illness, in which she gave her husband permission to end her life when she could no longer enjoy it. Julian wished he'd pointed out to Gabriel that Helen wasn't sentient enough to make such a request. That even though he was his wife's Power of Attorney, he didn't have the power to make that kind of decision. He should have explained that even if he did find the law sympathetic after he'd committed such an act, he would forever be remembered as the man who'd killed his wife, rather than the man who'd devoted years of his life to caring for her.

* * *

Later that morning, Julian found himself wrapping Helen's squirming body in thick red ribbon.

'And unwind.' Shona, a fine-boned dancer with red hennaed hair, turned up the volume of the traditional jazz oozing from the sound deck at the back of the hall. Julian obeyed and smiled at

Helen as he unwound the ribbon. Happiness surged through him when she smiled back.

'Everyone move around the space,' Shona said. 'Let's go.'

Julian gave Helen the ribbon to hold as he gripped the handles of her wheelchair and set off across the shiny laminated floor. The Carers First Centre occupied a former church, and the church hall provided a perfect space for classes and events.

Shona's class was full, carers and care workers steering their charges as best they could, cracking up with laughter as they tried to avoid collisions. Julian's friend Kathy was there with her husband, Will, whose muscular dystrophy had claimed everything apart from his warm, broad smile.

'It's chaos today,' Kathy said as they met at the centre of the hall. They moved alongside each other, wheelchairs out in front. 'I'm getting a sweat on.' Kathy's garish, fashionable workout clothes failed to make her look younger than her sixty-eight years.

Julian bent forward. 'Good to see you, Will.'

'Helen, you look gorgeous today,' Kathy said, over the music.

'Doesn't she just?' said Julian. Earlier, Helen had allowed the women from the care agency to shower her, wash her hair and coax her into the thick black tights, denim skirt and purple jumper Julian had picked out for her. Afterwards, he'd plucked her eyebrows and made her green eyes stand out by applying a touch of lavender eyeshadow.

'You always dress her so nicely.' Kathy wiggled her hips to the music. 'She's very lucky to have you, Julian. Not many men could do what you do.'

Julian couldn't help a rush of pride. He remembered a rare scrap of approval his father had given him one day, after Julian had skilfully administered a syringe full of medication. *You're a good lad. You're nothing like your mother.*

'She's on cracking form today,' Kathy said. 'Haven't seen her like this for a long time.'

'Let's hope it lasts.' Julian knew from experience how fast his wife's moods could turn.

'By the way,' Kathy said, 'I've got a favour to ask you.' She told him about a disco she was organising for young carers at the centre in November and asked if he might help out. 'I need someone to do a few pick-ups. Maybe help out with the refreshments.'

'Happy to,' he said. 'If I can get a sitter for Helen.'

'Wonderful. I've asked a few others, but no one is as reliable as you, I'm afraid.'

'I'll do my best.'

'Thanks. I'll give you a call when we've fixed a date.'

They parted ways, and Julian and Helen continued circling the room. Autumn sun streamed through the hall's high windows, dappling the Halloween decorations pinned to the walls. Pumpkins, ghouls and witches.

Shona changed the music to 'Dancing Queen' by Abba and instructed everyone to form a circle. She then invited them to take a turn at the centre to show off their moves. Julian was the first in, spinning Helen round and round while everyone clapped. Helen beamed and rocked back and forth in her wheelchair. Then, unexpectedly, she held out the ribbon.

'Julian?' she said.

He peered into her eyes and found uncertainty there, as if she feared he might reject her offer.

'Thank you, my love,' he said. He took one end of the ribbon, she kept hold of the other and they engaged in a teasing tug of war. Everyone cheered, and Helen laughed in response. Julian felt a rush of affection for his wife. He remembered how, before the accident, they would often sway cheek-to-cheek to Frank Sinatra in their living room or strut around the kitchen to 1970s disco. Good times he'd forgotten about. He wondered if Gabriel had somehow reawakened these memories? As if their encounter had invigorated him and, in a strange way, brought him closer to his wife. Her wide smile and animated face gave him a glimpse of the old Helen, the woman he'd loved, and, for a moment, he almost believed she might come back to him.

Shona turned up the music. Helen's rocking motion grew more frenzied. Her head tilted to one side; her eyes rolled in their sockets.

'Helen?' He dropped the ribbon and rushed over to her. 'Everyone stay back,' he said, 'she's having a fit.' He knelt beside the wheelchair and placed his hands on her twitching thighs. 'I'm here, my love. I'm here.'

18

HARD TIMES

Memories of Helen are never far from my mind. Last week, while attending a black-tie charity ball at the Savoy, I heard the band play a cover version of Abba's 'Dancing Queen', and suddenly all I could think about was Helen and I dancing together to that very song at the final music and movement group she attended.

That was the last time we ever enjoyed an outing together. In the weeks leading up to her death, Helen struggled with her health more than usual. The epileptic seizures she experienced on occasion became more frequent and, due to the pain in her legs, she could only sit in her wheelchair a few hours a day. The rest of the time she remained in bed.

I felt powerless. Once again, I could not prevent my wife from suffering.

Unable to leave her unattended, I was trapped indoors. Only when our dear neighbour, Beverly, agreed to sit with Helen could I go out to get food and other essentials. As the sky outside took on the muted greys of November, I stopped getting dressed in the mornings, unable to see the point, and I rarely showered. I even forgot to take my blood pressure medication. All that mattered was looking after Helen. Putting her welfare first. I spent any free time I had lying on the sofa, staring at the TV. I watched numerous episodes of *Dreams in the Sun*, the programme where couples venture abroad to find their ideal holiday home. I couldn't help picturing myself and Helen living such a life. Long, lazy days by the pool. Boozy lunches in the square of some picturesque village or market town. Heaven.

Back in reality, life sometimes had a hellish quality. I found it very frustrating that no one could tell me what this latest dip in my wife's wellbeing might indicate. Was this the start of a serious decline? Was I worrying for no reason? After an especially difficult night, during which Helen had experienced a severe seizure, a doctor came for a home visit. A kind, brisk woman, she told me Helen was in relatively good shape and that I didn't need to worry about losing her anytime soon. She did add that my wife might plateau at her current state of health with no improvement. Many of you might think that a depressing possibility, but I didn't care. All that mattered was having Helen with me.

During this period, my wife slept poorly, despite her increased medication. One night, as I sat in the armchair beside her bed, waiting for her to settle, I felt as though the outside world didn't exist. As if she and I were the last survivors of a zombie apocalypse.

Hours passed, but I did not move from the chair. I couldn't stop thinking about what might have been if the accident had never happened. The memories Helen and I could have made together. The life that never came to pass. If only we had set out on our journey five minutes earlier that morning, or five minutes later.

The next day, my good friend Kathy called to see if I was still interested in helping out with the Young Carers disco at the Carers First Centre. When she told me the event would take place on

Wednesday 24 November, I had to say no. Beverly wouldn't be able to sit with Helen on a Wednesday night and, even if she could, I wasn't sure I should leave Helen in her current condition.

I did not know then that 24 November was a date I would never be able to forget.

19

Wednesday 17 November, a week before his wife's death, Julian woke at 5.30 a.m. after a difficult night. Helen had roused him just after 1 a.m. with long, pitiful moans from the baby alarm. It had taken a second drop of Oromorph to get her back to sleep.

He rolled over and listened for the sound of her breathing. Nothing. He reached for the baby monitor in the dark and held it close to his ear. Agonising silence followed by a cough and a sharp inhale.

He sighed. Beneath the duvet cover, Gabriel's T-shirt nestled between his thighs. When he got up, he pulled it on over his head, the creased fabric stretching to accommodate his chest. He covered it with his dressing gown and set off to check on his wife.

He found her still asleep. In the dim glow cast by the nightlight on her bedside table, he gazed down at her. He watched the tiny convulsions of her body as she slept, the contorted expressions that flashed across her thin face at regular intervals. No respite from pain, even when unconscious. What kind of life was that? Could he really, in all good conscience, describe her as alive? He thought of how all the stars in the sky, even the brightest ones, had exploded and burned out years ago, their light taking so long to reach the earth they appeared to be living but were in fact already dead.

In the hallway, on his way to the bathroom, he spotted a white envelope, luminous on the doormat. Too early for the postman, he thought. He picked it up and found his name scrawled on the front, in wild loopy handwriting he recognised at once. He ripped open the envelope and read the note inside.

> *Hey big guy,*
>
> *I got your money for you. Sorry to borrow like that. Didn't know what to do so I kept moving, but now I'm in Edinburgh! I'd like to pay you back, and I'd really like to see you. Meet me today, 3 p.m. at the Hermitage of Braid. You'll know that place, right? I'll wait in the car park. If you don't come, I'll understand, but I sure hope you do.*
>
> *G.*

Julian unlocked the front door and ran out into the darkness in his pyjamas. No sign of Gabriel. He peered at the nearby streetlight, as if expecting to see the young man slouching against it, cigarette tip glowing.

Back indoors, he made himself a strong tea and, standing in the draughty kitchen, he read the note again while he drank it. Anxiety competed with excitement. Gabriel knew where he lived. Gabriel wanted to see him again.

He recalled mentioning Shawfair Street but was certain he'd given no further details. Gabriel must have staked the street out. Maybe, thought Julian, Gabriel had seen him emerging from the flat when he'd taken Helen out onto the front path in her wheelchair for a breath of fresh air yesterday.

The idea of someone watching him, of someone *seeing* him, both disturbed and thrilled him. He told himself Gabriel had acted with discretion and sensitivity. The young man could have approached him in the street or rung his doorbell, putting Julian in an awkward position. He could have put the money in the envelope with the note and left without them ever meeting again.

If you don't come, I'll understand, but I sure hope you do.

Julian pressed the note to his chest and smiled.

* * *

When the agency carers rang the doorbell two hours later, he had already showered and dressed. He opened the door and was relieved to recognise one of the two women standing there. Most days brought unfamiliar carers to the house, and he often had to guide them through everything and be on hand to supervise.

'Hello, Wendy,' he said. 'Long time no see.'

'Hello, Mr Julian.' Wendy, a wiry Filipina well past retirement age, was capable, efficient and good at dealing with Helen. She introduced the younger, weary-looking woman as Carol.

'Can I leave you ladies to it?' Julian asked. 'I need to go and see my neighbour.'

When he reached Beverly's bungalow, he found the living room light on and could see her sitting upright in her armchair, watching breakfast television. Beverly, now in her early sixties, had fractured her lower spine in a fall on an icy pavement over twenty years ago, an accident that had left her unable to work and in constant pain.

He rang the doorbell and waited. It always took Beverly a while to get out of her chair and shuffle along the hallway with her stick. He noticed fresh graffiti on the door of one of the garages opposite. Typical. Earlier in the year, he'd complained to the council about vandalism in the area, but no action had been taken to improve CCTV coverage of the street and catch the culprits.

Beverly answered the door in a purple crushed-velvet tracksuit.

'Hello, sweetheart,' she said.

He asked if she would sit with Helen for a couple of hours that afternoon. 'I've got a few errands to do.'

'Aye, I'll sit with her.'

'You're an absolute star.'

'Mind it's Wednesday, though.'

Every Wednesday, Beverly's niece picked her up at 6.30 p.m. and took her for a curry and an hour at the nearby Gala Bingo. The highlight of Beverly's week, and she'd already wound her bleached hair around rollers in preparation.

'Don't worry,' Julian said. 'I'll be back.'

'Hang on.' Beverly pointed at his left shoulder. 'You've got a guardian angel.'

'What?'

'Look there.'

Julian glanced at his shoulder and spotted a white feather.

'Means you've got an angel watching over you,' Beverly said.

'Is that so?' He plucked the feather off with trembling fingers. 'Lucky me.'

20

Julian couldn't remember the last time he'd visited the Hermitage of Braid. Before the accident, he and Helen would often come to the area between the Braid Hills and Blackford Hill for a walk.

He pulled into the car park just before 3 p.m. and found Gabriel waiting, the hood of his Parka raised despite the absence of rain, a cigarette dangling from his lips. When Julian stepped out of the car, Gabriel flicked the cigarette away and walked towards him, arms outstretched. Before he could refuse, Julian found himself embroiled in a tight hug.

'Damn, it's good to see you,' Gabriel said into his chest.

When they pulled apart, Julian scanned Gabriel's face and found it pale and drawn. Thinner than he'd remembered it. 'When did you last eat?' he said.

Gabriel's slow smile turned his concern to lust, that molten sensation flaring up at the base of his spine.

'Always the good guy.' Gabriel glanced around the car park. 'Let's walk.'

Side by side, they walked in silence, past the Hermitage of Braid, the large gothic house from which the park derived its name. The Braid Burn flowed beside them, swollen with the recent rain. The few remaining leaves of the oak trees shivered overhead in the bitter breeze. A golden retriever ambled past in the dull November light, followed by an old man inching along with a stick.

When a choice of paths presented itself, Gabriel picked the one on the left, a secluded route that would take them high above the river and into the trees. Julian's gut contracted, a signal of either fear or excitement. He wasn't sure which.

After nearly ten minutes of walking, they reached a clearing shielded by oak trees on one side and gorse bushes on the other. Gabriel sank onto the wooden bench at the clearing's centre.

Julian glanced along the path that led onwards to Blackford Hill. He reminded himself they could be disturbed at any moment.

'Come on, big guy.' Gabriel patted the empty space beside him. 'Take a load off.'

When Julian sat down, Gabriel removed the hood of his coat and rested his blonde head on Julian's shoulder. 'I've thought about you a lot, my friend.' He laid a hand on Julian's thigh. Julian hesitated before placing his own on top of it.

'Where are you staying?' he said.

'A hostel. Real dive of a place.'

'You look like you've been sleeping rough.'

'Might as well be.' Gabriel slid his fingers between Julian's. 'Sorry for taking off like that.'

'It's okay.'

'I'm not used to people being good to me.'

'I've been worried about you.'

'I gotta keep moving, you know? These guys that are after me got contacts everywhere. I'm taking a risk even being in a big city.'

Julian swallowed. 'Then why did you come?'

Gabriel slid his hand free and sat up. From the back of his jeans, he produced a slim fold of cash. 'I got hold of some money and I wanted to pay you back.'

Julian thought it best not to ask where the money had come from. 'Keep it,' he said, 'you need it more than I do.'

'That is beyond kind.' Gabriel pocketed the money without hesitation. 'Truly.'

A grey squirrel darted across the ground in front of them. It paused at the base of the oak tree opposite and regarded them with shrewd black eyes before darting up the trunk.

'You wanna know why I really came back?' Gabriel stared at him with his wild blue eyes. 'Way things are, I think I'm gonna have to leave the country.'

'Really?'

'Yup. But I couldn't go without seeing you.'

Julian's heart thudded as Gabriel leaned in and kissed him. When the touch of their tongues made him moan, Gabriel's hand reached between his thighs.

A dog barked in the distance. Julian pulled away. 'Sorry,' he said.

'It's cool. Really. I just wanted to see you.'

Julian smiled. 'That's why you stalked me?'

'I'm a good detective, that's all. Remembered your street name, hung around there for a while till I saw you. No harm in that, right?'

Wasn't there? Julian didn't know. Couldn't think straight.

'I saw you with Helen,' Gabriel said. 'Made me kinda sad.'

'For who?'

'Both of you. Can't be much of a life.'

'It's the life I have.'

'It isn't fair.'

Julian succumbed to the self-pity blooming within him. 'Tell me about it.'

'Things could change. If you want them to.'

'What do you mean?'

'What if someone were to help Helen out?'

'Help her? How?'

'Release her from her earthly suffering.'

'And who exactly is going to do that?'

Gabriel glanced in both directions. 'Me.'

Julian stared at him. 'Stop messing about.'

'Hey, I'm 100 per cent serious.'

Nervous laughter rose and died in Julian's throat.

'She's not the same person she was before the accident,' Gabriel said. 'You told me so yourself. You said you were lucky if she gave you a smile.'

'That's not... no. I said when she does smile, it's a wonderful moment that makes everything worthwhile.'

'No, you meant it was rare. The woman's miserable, right? How could she not be?'

'That's not her fault.'

'It's not yours either.'

'You're talking about... you know what I mean. It's a crime.'

'Sure, that's how the law would see it, but we'd know different. What do we care if right now, at this point in history, helping a woman like Helen isn't right in the eyes of the law?' Gabriel's thigh pressed against Julian's. 'I mean, plenty of things are lawful now that were illegal once upon a time, right?'

Julian felt a release in his solar plexus. A door opening deep within him.

'You're a good guy, Julian. One in a million. What about you? What about your life?'

The door slammed shut. 'What about Helen's?'

'You're not getting any younger, big guy. What if it takes years for her to die? What then? You think the government's going to look after you? Think you'll get a thank you for all your hard work?'

The future that might await him had often crossed Julian's mind. As soon as Helen died, his benefits would stop. He might be in his fifties or his sixties with no career to fall back on. No private wealth to top up his state pension. No life insurance policy to cash in.

'I could always be a care worker,' he said, with a half-smile.

'This isn't funny. This is your life.' Gabriel caressed Julian's shoulder. 'I wanna help you, man. I wouldn't take this risk for just anyone.'

Julian shrugged him off. 'I don't want you to take it at all.' He looked both ways along the path but couldn't see anyone approaching.

'Hear me out,' Gabriel said and proceeded to outline his plan. All he needed, he said, was for Julian to be out of the house for a couple of hours. Out of the house doing something that would provide a good alibi. He promised he would make sure Julian was beyond suspicion. 'I'll make it look like a break-in gone wrong. That sorta thing happens, right?'

'Sometimes. That doesn't mean—'

'And she won't suffer. I'll make sure of it.'

'You've really thought this through.'

'This is your show. You're the boss. I won't do anything unless you give me the word.'

'Gabriel. Please, I—'

'It has to be soon, though. I can't wait around forever.'

'This is crazy. If you get caught, I'd be an accessory to murder.'

'Most victims know their murderers, right? There's usually some connection between them. Me, I don't know Helen. Never met her. Without a motive, cases like this are impossible to solve.'

'You've met me.'

'Have I? No cameras here, my friend. Doubt there were any by the side of that loch.'

'What about the café?'

'The police would only try to link us if they catch me. Which they won't.'

'They might.'

'I've been doing illegal shit for years and never been caught. Not by the law, anyway.'

'Not yet.'

'Especially if I disappear afterwards.' Gabriel slid from the bench and knelt in front of Julian. 'If I leave the country right after, we got nothing to worry about.'

In the dimming light, Gabriel's blonde hair had an unholy glow. Julian longed to lose his fingers in it.

'I mean, I gotta have some cash to get away.' Gabriel looked up at him with pleading eyes. 'But you can help me with that, right?'

Julian remembered boasting about his hidden money to Gabriel. A pitiful amount in the grand scheme, but, he supposed, to someone in Gabriel's position, it offered a viable way out. A fresh start. Disappointment, dark and hollow, overwhelmed him. If only Gabriel hadn't mentioned money. He berated himself for his naivety. Did he really think that after their one brief encounter, Gabriel would care enough about him to take such a risk for free? How ridiculous. He considered taking £9,000 for himself and running away, leaving Helen to the mercy of the social care system, her final years spent in a council care home. He soon dismissed the idea. He didn't have enough money to hide away forever, and no doubt the authorities would track him down. Maybe even charge him with abandonment and neglect. Guilt coursed through him at the thought of Helen, alone in a dismal care facility, reliant on the kindness of strangers. She'd never survive without him. Her death would be a lonely, lingering one. He could never subject her to such a cruel ending.

'So,' Gabriel said, 'how about it?'

Julian sighed. 'If you're really in that much danger, I could just give you some money. Five hundred, a thousand maybe. Enough to get you a flight somewhere safe.'

Gabriel shook his head. 'I need more than that to start over.'

It occurred to Julian that if Gabriel wanted to, he could break in and take the money. He didn't need to offer his help. Surely that made the offer genuine?

'I wanna turn my life around, Julian. I'm a victim of circumstance, just like you. If we do it my way, we both get to be free. Don't you want that?'

Julian pictured the black wings on Gabriel's back unfurling and carrying him away. His arms rested on Gabriel's shoulders, as if trying to ground him.

'And hey,' Gabriel said, 'one day you can come find me, or I'll come find you.'

A deep sadness welled up in Julian. As if someone like Gabriel would ever choose to be with him.

'And we'll both be the people we really are,' Gabriel said. 'Right?'

'You really think it's that simple?'

'Sure.' Gabriel smiled. 'Come on, big guy, what d'ya say?'

21

CHOICE AND CONSEQUENCE

It is only fitting that in the final chapter of this memoir I confess that my decision to leave my wife unattended haunts me still. The truth is, I only did so because I wanted to help some people in need, a desire Helen would have understood. That's the kind of woman she was. Always keen to help others.

Ever since my good friend, Kathy, had asked me to assist with the Young Carers disco, I'd felt bad about having to refuse. I couldn't help feeling sorry for those kids. I knew only too well how hard life was for them – the burden of responsibility, the social isolation, the missed opportunities. With less than a week to go until the disco, I rang Kathy and volunteered to help out. She was delighted as she needed someone to serve refreshments and also to pick up several young carers from the Sighthill housing estate. Without my help, they wouldn't have been able to attend.

Many of you may find it impossible to comprehend the choice I made by leaving Helen alone that night. At the time, I told myself a couple of hours away wouldn't matter. Due to Helen's recent poor health, I hadn't ventured out socially for weeks. I'm sure many of you can understand how lonely and depleted that had left me. I needed to connect with humanity again. I expected to return home recharged and refreshed, more ready than ever to look after my wife. I believed my short absence would prove beneficial to us both.

When I left home that night, Helen had just fallen asleep, thanks to her pain medication. I can only hope she had no idea what was happening to her. Mercifully, the police found no signs of a struggle.

As I said at the press conference after the murder, numerous individuals and institutions were complicit in Helen's death. Media coverage pointed out that the neglected CCTV cameras in our street were partly responsible for the lack of evidence. Helen's killer had gained entry to our flat through the back door. A door I had reported broken to the council weeks before the murder, but they had failed to respond. And what of the volunteer sitter service that Carers First used to offer before the government cut the funding for it? Had that still been in place, Helen might be alive today.

As a victim of a terrible crime, it was distressing to even think the police might consider me a suspect. In the first few weeks of the investigation, my neighbour, Beverly, had to go to the station more than once to confirm what she had seen on the night of the murder. I'd invited her to pop in before her niece picked her up to go for dinner. I gave her a box of Milk Tray to thank her for a recent spate of neighbourly favours, and we had a nice chat. Helen was smiley and responsive when Beverly popped into her bedroom to say hello, even though she was already drowsy. Beverly left us just before 6.30 p.m. Five minutes later, Helen was fast asleep and I left the house, my journey to Sighthill to pick up my allotted young carers captured on numerous functioning CCTV cameras. Beverly confirmed to the police that our flat was in good order when she saw it. Nothing out of place. I suppose they needed to confirm I didn't ransack my flat myself. As there was only a five-minute delay between me arriving home at around 9.15 p.m. and my call to the emergency services, they were able to rule out my involvement in the crime.

While I was relieved to no longer be under suspicion, I still had to grapple with my unresolved questions about Helen's death. I may be finishing this memoir here, but what happened to my wife is, for me, a story that will never end. One question above all torments me to this day.

Will the person responsible for her death get away with murder?

AFTER

22

At 6.30 p.m. on the day after the trip to the beach at Cala de Deià, Julian was down on the pool terrace, scrubbing a sun-baked trail of pigeon shit from the surface of the wrought-iron table. In half an hour, Gabriel, if punctual, would arrive and make his way to this very table to drink the cocktails Olivia had insisted they enjoy poolside.

His stomach dipped. He concentrated on cleaning the table, his body both jittery with nerves and heavy with fatigue. Last night, unable to sleep, he'd lain still beside his wife, listening to the lush din of the mountain frogs that found their voice in the darkness. The distant toll of the church bell in Deià marked every hour of his wakefulness. Hours spent wishing Olivia had never invited Gabriel for dinner. Why did she always have to be so polite? If only Gabriel had a phone, he'd thought. He could have called him and suggested they meet alone at a bar in Deià or Sóller instead. Dark possibilities tortured him until dawn. What if Gabriel had grown tired of protecting their secret and wanted to confess? Unlikely, he told himself. What if Gabriel suspected him of the same desire? He would have to reassure the young man. Show him he had nothing to fear.

He tackled the disintegrating white muck with increased vigour. Was Gabriel in some kind of trouble, he wondered? Had he come in search of money?

I always hoped I'd see you again.

As if, he thought. As if someone as young and good-looking and free as Gabriel would want to see him again. He wouldn't. Would he?

After Helen's death, he'd had to cut Gabriel out of his mind. Gabriel had urged him to fully believe the story they'd concocted for the police. Only then would it work. Only then could they protect each other. Julian had found this selective amnesia easier than he'd expected. It was easy to believe Gabriel wasn't real because none of what had happened felt real to him. Their encounter at the caravan, the plan they had made together. All of it had an imaginary, hallucinatory quality. Until he'd returned home to find Helen dead.

'Hello, darling.'

Julian, intent on his task, had failed to notice the slap of his wife's sandals as she approached.

'I think you can stop cleaning now,' Olivia said, a large tray of glasses and plates balanced on her hip. 'The stain's gone.'

'Just making sure.' He stepped away from the table so she could deposit the tray.

'Don't worry,' she said, unloading the plates and glasses. 'Everything will be perfect.'

'I'm not worried.'

'It's nice for you to have a friend over for a change.'

Olivia found it sad that his former life, laden with so much responsibility, had prevented him from making lasting friendships.

'I'm not sure I'd call him a friend,' Julian said. 'I hardly know him.'

'Well, he seemed very pleased to bump into you.'

How had Gabriel known where to find him, Julian wondered? He'd tweeted once about his Mallorcan holiday before leaving London. Had that led Gabriel to him? For Gabriel to have followed them to the beach, he must have been watching them from outside the villa. What if this surveillance had started even earlier, in London?

'Does he smoke?' Olivia asked. 'He looks the sort.'

Julian thought of Gabriel's mouth hovering close to his, exhaling a coil of pungent smoke into him. 'I'm not sure.'

'I'll leave this here just in case.' She placed a small glass ashtray on the table. 'It's going to be a beautiful evening.'

'Yes.' The sea, azure and still. Pink wisps of cloud dotting the sky.

'It'll cool down later. Always does up here in the mountains.'

Julian hoped so. Sweat already sullied the back of his tropical print shirt. He thought about changing into something else but worried Olivia might find such fuss over his appearance odd.

'That outfit looks good on you,' his wife said. He'd matched the shirt with his beige chinos. 'Those deck shoes I got you really do go with anything.'

When he complimented her appearance, she waved the praise away. It touched him, the effort she'd made on his behalf, her navy kaftan accessorised with the sparkly silver Birkenstocks she reserved for evening wear and a pair of square diamond earrings that glittered when she moved her head. Sweet, solid Olivia. He decided he was glad she'd invited Gabriel to the villa. Gabriel would see how happy he was in his new life. Gabriel would understand how much good had come from what they had done together.

Olivia glanced at the vintage Cartier watch that had once

belonged to her mother. 'Let's go and have a quick check on the food.'

Fear gripped Julian at the thought of Gabriel telling Olivia something he shouldn't. He pushed the thought away. Stirring up the past wouldn't benefit either of them. They were both custodians of a secret neither could afford to reveal.

In the kitchen, Olivia plated up the tapas she'd prepared beforehand – stuffed peppers, wedges of mushroom tortilla, blue cheese and walnut croquettes. Julian singed slithers of orange skin for the cocktails and made sure they had plenty of ice. The two of them moved around each other with synchronised ease. They were a good team, thought Julian. He didn't want anything to change that.

'I'll heat up the patatas bravas and sauté the asparagus when we're ready for it,' she said. 'It's a shame we don't know if he's a vegetarian or not. I could have done my garlic prawns.'

'This'll be fine.'

'He should have let us pick him up. I wonder where he's staying.'

Before they'd parted ways at the beach, Gabriel had refused Olivia's offer of a lift to the villa, claiming his friend Kai would drop him off. Julian had glanced around the beach, looking for the skinny man Gabriel had waved at earlier. The man was nowhere to be seen, and Julian had wondered if Gabriel even knew him.

'Didn't he say something about going to Ibiza?' Olivia wiped her hands on a dishtowel. 'What sort of work does he do?'

'I don't know. I keep telling you I hardly know the guy.' The words rattled out of him, snappish, defensive. He didn't even know Gabriel's surname, but he could recall with ease the whisky-infused taste of the younger man's lips.

Olivia frowned. 'What's wrong?'

'Nothing.' He explained he'd met Gabriel while on a respite break from Helen. 'Thinking about it makes me feel bad,' he said.

'Not long after that she was dead, and I'd spent part of those final weeks away from her.'

'Darling, there's no need for you to feel guilty.'

'It's still hard sometimes.'

'It always will be.'

'That kind of loss... it's hard to explain to anyone who hasn't experienced it.'

Olivia held out her arms. 'Please forgive me.'

'There's nothing to forgive.'

They came together in a clammy hug. When Julian had proposed to Olivia, she'd asked him never to lie. Made him promise they would share everything with each other. Julian had agreed. Everything he felt he could share with her, he had done.

The entryphone's shrill buzzer sounded from deep within the villa.

'That must be him,' Olivia said. 'He's early.'

Julian tightened his grip on her. 'I love you, Olivia Pearson.'

'Soppy fool.' She smiled up at him. 'Go and let him in.'

23

After Julian had pressed the button on the entryphone that opened the tall metal gates at the villa's entrance, he stepped out into the courtyard, heart hammering against his chest.

Gabriel sauntered through the parting gates, a tanned figure in blue jeans and a white T-shirt. His black flip-flops scuffed up the dust as he walked. His hair hung loose; his mirrored glasses glowed rose-gold in the sun. He carried a navy rucksack over one shoulder and a white carrier bag swung at his side.

'Buena noches, mis amigos,' he said.

'Buena noches to you,' said Olivia, hurrying out into the courtyard. 'Welcome.'

Gabriel greeted them with a tight hug and kisses to both cheeks. 'Don't worry, my friend,' he said when he caught Julian staring at his rucksack. 'I'm not moving in, I'm just between abodes. My buddy Kai and I are gonna crash in Deià tonight.'

Despite doubting Kai's existence, Julian still felt an uninvited stab of jealousy.

'Wow.' Gabriel gazed up at the front façade of the villa. 'Would you look at this place?'

The mellowing light highlighted the pink hue of the villa's stone and accentuated the deep red of the bougainvillea that framed the heavy wooden door and covered the nearby outbuilding. When Gabriel declared the place awesome, Julian couldn't disagree.

'Thank you, Gabriel,' Olivia said. 'We like it.'

'And you, check you out.' Gabriel patted the shoulder of Julian's shirt. 'You are all about the colour tonight.'

Julian, unsure if this was a compliment or not, wished he had chosen a more sedate top. Gabriel's hand lingered on his shoulder, and Julian sensed the eyes behind the glasses inspecting him.

'Come on in,' Olivia said, 'we've got cocktails ready.'

'Awesome.' Gabriel offered the carrier bag to Olivia. 'Little something for my hosts.'

'Thank you.' Olivia reached into the bag and pulled out a bottle of brown liquor. 'Spanish whisky. How novel.'

'I know this guy here likes his whisky,' Gabriel said, with a nod in Julian's direction.

A tremor travelled up Julian's spine.

'We'll try some after dinner,' Olivia said. 'Julian, why don't you take Gabriel's bag?'

'Thanks, my friend.' Gabriel passed Julian his rucksack. 'You're a gent.'

'My pleasure.' When Julian hoisted the bag onto his shoulder, the strap cut into his flesh. 'Welcome to our home.'

* * *

Once he'd deposited the rucksack in the hallway, Julian rushed upstairs to his bathroom, sat down on the toilet and emptied himself. Afterwards, while washing his hands, he looked his reflection in the eye and told it to pull itself together.

He came downstairs to find the kitchen empty. He hurried out onto the terrace and along to the rocky steps that led to the pool. Near the bottom of the steps, he peeked through the gap in the bougainvillea and froze at the sight of Olivia and Gabriel deep in conversation at the wrought-iron table. When he walked out onto the terrace, his wife looked up at him. He thought he saw shock flit across her face, but, as he got closer, she smiled at him in the soft evening light.

'Gabriel and I were just chatting about America,' she said.

'Your lady's seen more of my country than I have,' said Gabriel.

'I travelled all over the States in my early twenties.' Olivia sighed. 'Loved it.'

'What a place you've got here, my friend,' Gabriel said as Julian took a seat at the table. 'What a view.' He speared an oily black olive with one of the silver toothpicks Olivia had laid out. 'I gotta say, this island is one of the most stunning places I've travelled to.'

'Seen much of it, have you?' Julian said.

'Mostly Palma and a little up the west coast.'

Had he, Julian wondered? Or had he been close by all this time? Watching them. Gabriel's guileless expression gave nothing away. Julian hoped his own could match it.

'Let's get into these Negronis.' Olivia poured each of them a crystal tumbler of deep carmine liquid from a glass jug and added a twist of orange peel as garnish. 'To friendship,' she said, raising her glass.

'I'll drink to that,' Gabriel said, as the three of them clinked glasses.

Julian sipped his cocktail. Strong and bitter. Strong enough to settle his nerves, he hoped.

'Damn, Olivia.' Gabriel's ice clinked in his glass. 'You sure know how to mix a drink.'

Olivia laughed. 'Far too much practice in my youth, I'm afraid.'

'What else is youth for, right?' Gabriel removed his sunglasses and tossed them on the table. 'You're a lucky man, my friend. Got yourself a good woman there, that's for sure.'

Julian's guts knotted as he met Gabriel's eyes. 'Can't disagree with that.' He turned his head and focused on Olivia's adoring gaze.

'This is too much.' Gabriel swigged his drink. 'Sitting here with you after all this time. Can you believe it?'

'Isn't life funny?' Olivia said. 'The way it brings people together.'

'Sure is. Look at how I met your husband.' Gabriel gave Olivia an edited version of that first encounter. Julian picking him up on the rain-drenched road. Julian warming him up with whisky and giving him a bed for the night. 'What if someone else had picked me up on that road?' Gabriel said. 'I wouldn't be here with you good people now.'

Julian shifted in his seat. If he hadn't stopped to pick up Gabriel, Helen might still be alive and he would not be sitting here now. Unsure what to feel about this fact, he pressed his leg against Olivia's. His wife's warm, solid flesh acted like ballast. Grounded him.

'Bet he never mentioned it, right?' Gabriel said. 'He's too modest.'

'He is.' Olivia patted Julian's thigh. 'I'm always telling him that.'

'I know he said it was nothing,' Gabriel said, 'but I've never forgotten it.'

Julian's glass shook in his hand. 'I didn't mean it was nothing.'

'Would you like some cheese?' Olivia offered Gabriel the cheese platter.

'Why not?' Gabriel picked up the cheese knife and cut a wide hunk of Manchego. 'You guys shouldn't have gone to all this trouble. I'm touched. Truly.' Ignoring the side plates and napkins Olivia had arranged on the table, he bit into the cheese. 'Whoa. This is immense.'

'Everything's vegetarian tonight,' Olivia said. 'We weren't sure if—'

'Oh, I eat meat.' Gabriel smiled. 'We're top of the food chain for a reason. It's nature, man. We're just animals, right? Survival of the fittest.'

'It's still quite warm, isn't it?' Julian undid the top button of his shirt. 'Meant to be even hotter tomorrow.'

'Did you keep in touch with each other after that night?' Olivia asked.

'No,' said Julian, irritated by her persistence.

'I skipped the country not long after.' Gabriel sliced more cheese. 'Went to India for a while.'

'I adore India.' Olivia reached for the cocktail jug and topped up Gabriel's glass. 'Which part were you in?'

'The North, mostly. Himachal Pradesh.'

'The Himalayas are glorious. What were you doing there?'

'Working on a farming project with some local people.'

'For an NGO?' Olivia asked.

'More of a private enterprise,' Gabriel said.

'What did you grow?' Julian asked.

'Indigenous crops.' A smirk played about Gabriel's lips.

Did he mean weed, Julian wondered? So much for a fresh start.

'We made good money, but honestly, for me, it was a chance to retreat from the world, you know? Get right with the universe.'

Gabriel looked like he had achieved that goal, thought Julian. He didn't look like a man troubled by conscience.

Gabriel pulled out a packet of Marlboro Lights and a plastic lighter. 'Do you mind?' he asked Olivia.

'Not at all.' She pushed the glass ashtray across to him and gave Julian an 'I told you so' look. 'I love going abroad,' she said, 'but we've given up long-haul travel for environmental reasons. Haven't we, Julian?'

Julian nodded and sipped his Negroni. Olivia, who had already travelled the world, wanted to make amends for the carbon footprint of her youth. He'd hoped they might enjoy global adventures together, but she refused to take any flight longer than eight hours.

'Nothing beats the freedom of travel,' Gabriel said.

'I wouldn't know,' said Julian, prickly with resentment. He was about to add that his longest foreign trip was his three-week honeymoon in Provence with Helen, but Olivia and Gabriel started a conversation about Indian beaches he could contribute nothing to. A discussion that lasted until the cocktail jug was empty and the fading light had woken the solar lamps around the edge of the pool. The three of them moved up to the top terrace where Olivia had set the table with blue ceramic plates and antique silver cutlery. She sat Julian at one end of the table, Gabriel at the other and, after bringing out the platters of vegetarian tapas, she sat herself in the middle. Julian had little appetite but kept his glass topped up with dry Mallorcan white wine.

'Darling?' Olivia handed him the dish of peppers. Their singed skins glistened with olive oil and bulged with the rice and vegetables stuffed inside. He took one. How was he supposed to chew and swallow like a normal person enjoying a normal meal? How could he, with Gabriel sitting opposite him? Gabriel exchanging small talk with his wife. Not even the setting could comfort him – the spread of the sea ahead and the mountains behind blushing pink in the fading daylight. The mingling scents of rosemary and lavender from the terracotta pots at the edge of the terrace.

Gabriel bit the head off a stalk of asparagus. 'This meal. Wow.'

Julian picked at his food while Gabriel and Olivia polished off most of the tapas and swapped stories of San Francisco and the Californian coast. Olivia opened another bottle of wine. The air cooled around them as light drained from the sky.

'Gracias,' Gabriel said, pushing away his plate. 'Y esta comida es deliciosa.'

'Where did you learn Spanish?' Olivia asked.

'I only got a few phrases. I'm no expert.'

'Your accent is perfect,' Olivia said. 'Isn't it, Julian?'

Julian shrugged. 'I suppose.'

'I'm good at faking stuff,' Gabriel said. 'I picked up some basics when I was in Ibiza.'

'Yes, tell me about Ibiza,' Olivia said. 'What are you planning to do there?'

'So, I've done a season before.' Gabriel licked olive oil from his fingers. 'I drive DJs around, make sure they got everything they need. Gets pretty crazy.' He shook his head as if recalling memories too outlandish to share.

'And after the season ends?' Olivia said.

'Who knows, right? Let's see what the universe has in store for me.'

'Still living out of your rucksack?' Julian said.

'Sure am, my friend. It's all about freedom for me.'

'As it should be at your age,' said Olivia.

'Freedom's important at any age, right?' Gabriel's wide blue eyes settled on Julian, making him reach for the wine.

Olivia released her throaty laugh. 'This is why I adore the young. So much optimism. I don't suppose you've even hit thirty yet, Gabriel?'

'Not quite. Little way to go.'

'What about your love life?' Olivia asked. 'Anyone special just now?'

'Don't embarrass him.' Julian, keen to hear the answer, topped up his wine.

'No one special,' Gabriel said. 'Hasn't been for a while.'

Julian had an image of the younger man dropping his towel in the caravan and exposing himself without shame. 'Sorry,' he said, as he splashed wine onto the table.

'What about your family?' Olivia said. 'Will you go back to the States to see them?'

Gabriel shook his head and gave Olivia a brief summary of his parents' deaths.

'Oh dear,' Olivia said. 'That's awful.'

Gabriel shrugged. 'It is what it is.'

'Mine are gone too,' she said. 'You never stop missing them.'

'Orphans, all three of us,' added Julian.

They gazed at the view in silence. The sky had divided into layers – pearly blue, grey and dusky pink on top. Pretty but not striking, thought Julian. Not yet. Soon, without warning, deep pinks and burnt oranges would fill the sky.

'I read your book,' Gabriel said.

'Really?' Julian gulped his wine.

'Your memoir.' The emphasis Gabriel laid on the second syllable of 'memoir' gave it a mocking tone. 'I read it a ton of times.'

'Olivia encouraged me to write it,' Julian said.

Olivia nodded. 'I felt Helen deserved to have a voice, and a friend of mine runs a little publishing company so we were able to get it done quickly.' She smiled at Julian. 'It was nice for us to do something for Helen together.'

'I mean, it's hardly a bestseller,' Julian said. 'We've sold some online, and it's popular in the caring community. Any proceeds go straight to Helen's charity, of course.'

'You did a great job, both of you. Truly. It's so moving.'

'He really brings her to life,' Olivia said.

'Totally. It's like in death she's got this voice she never had in life, right? I mean, it's tragic, sure, but if she hadn't died like that, no one would have heard of her.'

Olivia frowned. 'I'm sure she'd rather no one had heard of her.'

'I think what Gabriel means,' said Julian, 'is that Helen didn't die in vain.'

'That's right,' Gabriel said.

'Her charity's already doing great things.' Julian's feet tapped against the tiles. 'And I've found my purpose, I suppose. My calling.'

'Someone's gotta give a damn about this stuff, right?' Gabriel fixed him with his innocent, deceptive eyes. 'You're a better man than I am, that's for sure.'

A familiar molten heat oozed from the base of Julian's spine. He tried to ignore it. Prayed for it not to spread.

'Poor Helen,' Olivia said. 'I'm still so appalled that someone could do that to a defenceless human being.'

'At least she's free from pain now,' Gabriel said. 'That's how I like to think of it.'

'I think about that night a lot,' Julian said quietly. 'I really hope she didn't suffer.'

'She wouldn't have known it was happening.' Gabriel leaned forward. 'I'm sure of it.'

Julian felt a long-held inner tension dissolve. 'Thank you.' He thought he saw relief flash across Gabriel's face. It occurred to him Gabriel might have come in search of closure. To make sure Julian knew he had acted with mercy, as promised. Perhaps some vital exchange had just occurred, leaving them free to move on with their lives.

'Would you look at that?' Gabriel pointed at the crimson gash that had appeared in the sky. 'Time is marching on.' He turned to Olivia. 'Is there a phone I can use? I should call Kai and see about my lift.'

'Of course. Use the landline in the hall. It's an old-fashioned, dial thing, I'm afraid.' As soon as Gabriel disappeared into the villa, Olivia leaned back in her chair.

'My goodness,' she said, 'he's quite a character.'

She gave a contented yawn and stretched her arms overhead. A hostess pleased an evening had gone well but also relieved it would soon be over. She picked up the plates nearest to her and stacked them. Julian wanted to picture them in the kitchen together, enjoying a final glass of red wine as he washed and she dried, but he couldn't quite believe the evening would end so simply. That closure had finally occurred.

When Gabriel returned and told them Kai had taken off to Palma with some girl and wouldn't be coming to pick him up, Julian was not surprised. Gabriel insisted he would get a taxi and find a room in Deià for the night, but Olivia, snapping back into hostess mode, insisted he would do no such thing.

'He'll stay here tonight,' she said. 'Won't he, Julian?'

Julian, unable to refuse or resist, nodded. 'Ma casa es ta casa.'

'You mean mi casa es tu casa, right?' said Gabriel.

Julian sighed. 'If you say so.'

24

As soon as Julian woke, he turned over to check on Olivia. She was still asleep, her breath whistling in her nostrils. He rolled onto his back and stared up at the fan's slow, creaky rotation. He hadn't expected to sleep but must have drifted off just before the dawn that now filtered through the shutters. He rubbed his eyes, still unable to believe that right now, in the room directly below him, lay Gabriel.

He slipped out of bed and pulled on a T-shirt and shorts. With one eye on his wife, he twisted the large metal key in the bedroom door. He'd locked it after she'd fallen asleep, uncertain whether he intended to keep Gabriel out or himself in.

He crept out of the bedroom and down the wooden staircase. The door to the guest room was shut. He hovered outside it, ears straining, but heard nothing. What if Gabriel had changed his mind about staying and left during the night? This possibility brought him both relief and alarm.

The door handle squeaked as he pressed on it. He paused, pulse skittish, until the silence encouraged him to ease the door open.

Gabriel lay naked on his back, the white sheet draped over his hips protecting his modesty. One arm hung over the side of the double bed, the other, bent at the elbow, rested on the pillow. Sun streamed through the open shutters, bathing his bare feet.

Julian watched the rise and fall of the younger man's chest. Last night, after dinner, he'd hoped they might have a chance to talk alone. After a dessert of almond cake and ice cream, Olivia had produced Gabriel's bottle of whisky and suggested the 'boys' have a nightcap together. But Gabriel, yawning, had refused and allowed Olivia to show him to the guest room.

Julian edged inside and approached the bed. On the bedside table lay a black wallet, bulging with cash and a worn copy of *On the Road*. It looked to Julian like the same one Gabriel had carried with him when they first met.

Gabriel coughed and rolled over to face the wall. Julian stared at his black wings for some time before backing away and softly closing the door.

* * *

By 9.30 a.m., after Olivia had gone for her walk and Julian had completed his morning swim, they sat together on the top terrace, sipping their first coffee of the morning and picking at leftover almond cake for breakfast. The day was already warm, and the latest forecast had predicted several weeks of higher-than-average temperatures for the time of year.

'Should we wake him?' Julian said, the balls of his bare feet tapping against the warm terracotta tiles.

'No.' Olivia raked a hand through her hair. 'Let him rest.'

Julian had the image of Gabriel taking root in the bed. Long shoots curling round the mattress springs, making a prisoner of him.

Olivia let out a contented sigh. 'This is the life. Isn't it, darling?'

He nodded but couldn't quell his rising unease. Gabriel had no cause to make trouble, he reasoned. They had both fulfilled their part of the deal. Neither had let the other down.

To distract himself, he picked up the copy of *The Mallorcan Daily Record* Olivia had bought in Deià the previous day. A story on the second page caught his attention. *Police Reopen Investigation into German Teenager's Suicide.*

'I remember that happening at the time,' Olivia said, 'nearly twenty years ago now. Poor kid fell off a hotel balcony, but his family have always believed it was murder. They've been trying for years to get the case reopened.'

Julian's unease flared in his chest. 'Maybe they just don't want to face the truth?'

'Doesn't matter, really. The police here aren't known for their competence and if there's anything to be hidden, I'm sure they'll hide it.'

Julian dropped the paper on the table. He had no desire to read about the reopening of a cold case. Especially not now, with Gabriel in his guest room.

'What shall we do today?' Olivia said. She made several suggestions – the beach, the art gallery in Sóller, lunch in Valldemossa. 'We can decide once we know what your young friend's plans are.'

'I'm not sure he's the type to make plans.'

'He does seem a bit directionless.'

'He doesn't need plans. He's a free agent. He can do what he likes.'

'He strikes me as needing guidance.'

Julian filled his mouth with almond cake and did not reply.

'Once we know where he's going, we'll decide.' Olivia sipped her coffee. 'If he's meeting his friend in Palma, we could drop him off in

Sóller and he can get the train.' She laid a hand on Julian's thigh. 'It would be nice to be home in time for a long siesta.'

Julian swallowed his cake and forced a smile. During the night, unable to sleep, he'd woken Olivia and made love to her with a fervour that had surprised them both. Her coy smile suggested to him she was hoping for a repeat performance. When she leaned towards him, he planted a tender kiss on her upturned lips.

'Jeez, you guys. Get a room.' Gabriel appeared, his board shorts and T-shirt creased and his hair sleep-tangled. 'Just messing,' he said, claiming the seat at the top of the table. 'Love's a beautiful thing, right?' He accepted the coffee Olivia poured for him but refused the offer of almond cake. 'Never been a fan of breakfast.'

'Did you sleep well?' Olivia asked.

'Like a dead man. Didn't hear a thing.'

Julian's neck flushed as he recalled Olivia's guttural cry of plea-sure in the night. 'Do you need to ring your friend again?' he asked Gabriel.

'No point. If Kai's with a really hot girl, he's not gonna surface any time soon.'

'Well, wherever you're headed, we're happy to give you a lift,' Olivia said.

'What beautiful humans you are.' Gabriel drained the last of his coffee. 'I gotta know, do you have any pictures of your wedding day here? I'd love to see some.'

'We wouldn't bore you with them,' Julian said.

'I've got on some on my iPad.' Olivia picked up the coffee pot. 'I'll fetch it and top this up at the same time.'

She bustled away, accompanied by the purposeful slap of her sandals. Gabriel took a packet of Marlboro Lights and his lighter from his pocket.

'You can't smoke at breakfast,' Julian said. 'Olivia wouldn't like it.'

'Whatever.' Gabriel smiled. 'I'm cool with delayed gratification.'

Julian's legs trembled. He glanced through the terrace doors. No sign of his wife. She must be upstairs, looking for her iPad. 'How did you know I'd be in Mallorca?'

'I overheard Olivia telling one of her friends. They were in this café near your house and—'

'Our house in London?'

'Sure. Where else? Nice place, by the way.'

'How long have you been watching us?'

'First thing I did when I got back in the country was find you.' Gabriel frowned. 'What else would I do?'

Julian could not recall any sense of being followed. No shiver down the spine. No nudge of intuition.

'I figured it would be better if we met here,' Gabriel said. 'Make it look coincidental.'

'Here we are, boys.' Olivia and her slappy sandals burst onto the terrace. She topped up their coffee cups before settling down and scrolling through the photos on her iPad. 'Got them.' She moved her chair closer to Gabriel and talked him through the pictures of the intimate, low-key ceremony. Julian smiled and nodded along but couldn't stop thinking about Gabriel rushing to find him on his return from India. *What else would I do?* As if Julian really had been the first and only thing on his mind.

'I gotta say, you both look damn happy.' Gabriel peered at the iPad. 'It's a beautiful thing when the right people meet each other at the right time.'

'It is,' Olivia said, her eyes shining.

'That's the real deal, right there,' said Gabriel. 'Two good people celebrating their love and promising to look after each other. Doesn't get any better than that.'

'Well put,' Olivia said.

'Talking of celebrations,' Gabriel said. 'I bet this guy here had a killer bachelor party, right? What was that like, my friend?'

'A stag night?' Julian said. 'I didn't have one.'

'I had a lunch thing with my closest girls,' Olivia said, 'but he—'

'It wasn't that kind of wedding,' Julian said.

'Oh. Okay.' Gabriel tapped the side of his cup. 'That's kinda sad.'

'Not at all,' Julian said. 'I didn't want one.'

'Hey, Olivia, how about I take hubby here to Palma tonight for a proper bachelor party?'

'That's not necessary,' Julian said.

'I disagree, my friend.'

'I'm not sure my good wife would approve.' Julian threw Olivia a pleading look.

'Come on. Don't insult her. You're not that kind of woman, right, Olivia?'

She laughed her husky laugh. 'No, I'm not.'

'Come on, big guy. It's my shout, all the way.'

'Really,' Julian said, 'there's no need.'

'Not often you get an offer like that, darling,' Olivia said.

'He deserves it, right? Always doing stuff for others.'

Olivia caressed Julian's neck. 'It might do him good to let his hair down.'

'That's what I'm saying.' Gabriel rubbed his hands together. 'How about it, buddy?'

25

'Here's the man,' Gabriel said when Julian returned to their table. 'Drinks are up.'

Julian hoisted himself onto his high bar stool. In the five minutes it had taken him to visit the bathroom, the margaritas Gabriel had insisted on ordering had arrived. Gabriel lifted one of the thin-stemmed glasses and placed it on Julian's side of the table.

'The taxi driver was right about this place,' Gabriel said. 'Pretty good, huh?'

Julian nodded. The rooftop bar at Hostal Cuba had a spectacular outlook – Palma Cathedral, still impressive in the distance and, on Julian's left, the bay of Palma and the marina. Behind him lay the sloping terracotta roofs of the Santa Catalina district – once home to Palma's fishermen. But Julian found himself too tense to enjoy the setting. Too tense to appreciate the beautiful, mostly young people occupying the tables around him.

'Only the best for you, my friend. Tonight's on me, don't forget. My shout.' Gabriel raised his glass. 'Cheers.'

'Cheers.' Julian clinked his glass and took a long sip of the sour margarita. The strong tequila undercurrent tasted almost chemical.

White crystals of salt from the rim of the glass stuck to his lips. He licked them off and swallowed them.

'That's a killer margarita,' Gabriel said.

'I wouldn't know, I've never had one before.'

'Jeez. Good job you got me in charge of this bachelor party.'

Julian flinched as, beneath the table, Gabriel's espadrille brushed against his deck shoe. 'This isn't my stag night,' he said tucking his feet out of reach.

'Come on, man, go with it. Get a drink in you.'

'Don't rush me.' The taxi ride to Palma – forty minutes on the twisting mountain road – had left him with a throbbing behind his eyes that was only just wearing off. The dance music pulsing out from the bar's hidden speakers didn't help. Gabriel appeared to like it, his fingers drumming along on the table.

Julian braved another sip of his cocktail. He was hungry and shouldn't be drinking on an empty stomach. Gabriel swallowed most of his drink in seconds and waved to a nearby waiter. As he did so, his black linen shirt rode up, exposing the strip of tanned midriff between the shirt and his tight black jeans.

'Duo, por favor,' he said, gesturing to his glass.

Almost 8 p.m. and the heat of the day had only just begun to recede. A breeze came in off the water, cooling the sweat beneath Julian's tropical print shirt. He doubted the temperature would drop below twenty degrees all night. His beige chinos already clung to his thighs.

'A toast.' Gabriel raised his almost empty glass. 'To you, my friend.'

Before Julian could raise his glass off the table, Gabriel knocked his own against it with an extravagant clink.

'You really got it going on with this new life of yours, huh?' Gabriel said, with no trace of resentment. 'Didn't I tell you everything would work out?'

started his second margarita. When he saw Julian approach, a vast smile spread across his face.

'You're back,' he said.

Julian hopped onto his seat, finding the manoeuvre much easier than before. 'These margaritas are quite magical,' he said, lifting his glass. 'Cheers.'

A long sip. That bitter, chemical undercurrent again. Dazzling flashes on the surface of the sea captured his attention. As he marvelled at them, a calm confidence overwhelmed him. Gabriel had kept his word. He'd stayed away until it was safe, and now they could put a fitting end to unfinished business.

Gabriel lit another cigarette. Julian watched as smoke snaked from its tip.

'This music isn't so bad,' he said, legs jigging beneath the table. Gabriel threw back his head and laughed. 'What?'

'Nothing, my friend. It's all good.'

Another swig of margarita. Julian licked salt crystals from his lips. He and Gabriel smiled at each other and sat in silence for a while. The kind of easy silence, thought Julian, that could only exist between two people with no secrets from one another.

The volume of the music increased, and Julian swayed along to it. Heat flushed through his body. He undid the second button of his shirt. A violent thirst gripped him. He drank the rest of his margarita but that did nothing to soothe his throat.

'I'm very thirsty,' he said, 'maybe we should get some water?'

'You're looking a little hot there, buddy.'

'I am. Very hot. Is it me?'

'It's just the Molly kicking in.'

Music vibrated through Julian's body. 'What?'

'The ecstasy. The E.' Gabriel's pupils loomed black and large. A surge of adrenaline made Julian gasp.

'Gabriel,' he said, 'did you spike my drink?'

26

After Gabriel had confessed to spiking his drinks with MDMA powder – *just a little, big guy, just to get you in the mood* – Julian knew he should leave the bar and take a taxi home, but he didn't. He knew he should be furious, but when he opened his mouth only laughter came out. He had a sense of his edges dissolving, of spreading outwards, of some hidden inner self bleeding into the warm night air.

'You okay, buddy?' Gabriel said.

'I'm not quite myself.'

'But in a good way, right?'

After that, time collapsed. They drank water and several more 'special' margaritas and chatted with two earthy girls from Lancashire at the next table. Girls with long drinks and short dresses. Girls who giggled at everything Gabriel said and took every opportunity to touch his arm or lean against him. Julian admired the casual way Gabriel flicked his hair back from his face and the polite but aloof attitude that made both girls work to keep his attention. Hard to blame them, Julian thought, as the golden evening light formed an aura around Gabriel's head. When the less attractive girl turned away from Gabriel and began flirting with him, Julian felt blessed with a little of that aura and flirted back. Harmless fun. Gabriel rewarded him with a conspiratorial wink.

Sunset. Julian strolled with Gabriel beside the oily green water of the marina, away from Santa Catalina and the old town, towards the end of the bay that housed the towering cruise ships and, according to Gabriel, the most entertaining nightlife.

'Sure you're okay?' Gabriel said.

Julian nodded. He was more than okay.

'You and me against the world, big guy,' Gabriel said. 'You and me.'

Julian stared into Gabriel's dilated pupils. 'I don't even know your surname. How crazy is that?'

'King. Gabriel King.'

'Nice to meet you, Gabriel King.'

They walked on. As they approached the far end of the bay, they passed a hen party of Spanish women dressed in police uniforms, all of them waving handcuffs.

'Guilty as charged,' Gabriel said as the women walked past.

They saw gangs of drunk British men on the prowl, and when they met a stag party all dressed in tropical print shirts, instant friendships formed, and Julian and Gabriel tagged along with the men to a nearby Irish pub where a football match dominated several large screens and Gabriel and Julian joined in with football chants and drank bottles of Spanish lager and Julian felt so bonded to these strangers, these men he would normally look down on, and time collapsed and they were on the street and in a long queue that glided forwards and sent them past two wide bouncers and in through a black door and Julian realised he was in a strip club.

'First time?' Gabriel said. Julian nodded and inhaled air rank with sweat and perfume. They sat at round tables and ordered beer, and Julian couldn't stop staring at the women with so little on, all close enough to touch and holding onto poles, and he took a moment to admire their fitness levels because it couldn't be easy to move in such an athletic fashion all night. Conscious of staring too hard, he joined in a conversation about England's chances in the next World Cup. Every man involved in the debate wore a glazed expression and kept glancing over at the dancing women while pretending not to. Except for Gabriel. Gabriel looked and clapped and whistled. Julian wondered how it would feel to care so little about what other people thought.

A woman in a sequinned thong spun herself around a pole and sank into the splits. With a stab of shame, Julian remembered Olivia's donations to Women Against Sex Slavery. He thought of sex with Olivia in the early days. How, when he couldn't manage an erection, she'd taken his limp length in her mouth and coaxed it to life. She believed his body had remained loyal to Helen and couldn't accept his newfound happiness. It's just guilt, she'd told him.

'Let's ditch these jerks,' Gabriel said. They left the strip club, and after a meandering walk through carnivalesque streets they joined another queue, this time in front of a tall building bathed in red light and vibrating with a muffled boom.

'Time to get your groove on, buddy.'

When they reached the nightclub door, Gabriel paid the entrance fee and dragged Julian inside and onto the heaving dance floor. A tight pack of people wearing scant clothing, a DJ up on a podium like some kind of God. The bass shaking everyone and everything.

'I don't know how to dance to this music,' Julian said, but Gabriel closed his eyes and surrendered to it, and as Julian mimicked Gabriel's writhing hips, another layer of self dissolved, and he wondered how many skins he had and how far he could unpeel himself, and all that mattered was the beat and he closed his eyes too.

He opened them to find Gabriel's face close to his.

'How do you feel?' Gabriel said in his ear.

At that moment, everyone around them put their hands in the air and, with a great rush of joy, Julian did too.

'Free,' he said.

Time collapsed. Julian danced until sweat dripped from his face. Until he had danced the past out of himself. Until Gabriel took his hand and led him through the crowd. At one point they lost each other, but Julian didn't panic. An invisible tether connected them. He could feel it, strong as rope, and he followed it to the edge of the dance floor where he found Gabriel waiting.

Gabriel guided him down some stairs, along a corridor and into an outside courtyard, and how warm the air was, so warm, and the music in the courtyard had a slower pulse and a dark heart but Julian couldn't stop dancing.

'Feeling good, buddy?' Gabriel said.

'Amazing. I feel amazing.'

'Wait here. Gonna get us a little something.'

Gabriel headed to the nearby bar, where Julian saw him talking to a young guy with spiky black hair. The two of them disappeared into a dark corner, but Julian, still sensing the invisible tether, didn't worry. When Gabriel reappeared, he flashed Julian five hand-rolled joints that he tucked into his cigarette pack.

'Let's shoot,' he said.

They left the club and swaggered along the promenade, past huddles of bedraggled revellers. The sky boasted crimson glimpses of dawn. They passed two parked police cars, lights flashing. On the promenade, a cluster of cops had three burly men face down on the concrete. Julian and Gabriel sailed past the ruckus as if invisible and, once out of range, they shared a secret smile.

They walked and walked, past the marina and over the road to the ancient city walls. The sky grew lighter, until only a few stubborn stars remained, refusing to leave the party.

Before long, they found themselves on the Passeig des Born with its shuttered-up designer clothes stores. They climbed a set of steep steps and found themselves alone with the gothic masterpiece of a cathedral at their backs, the bay of Palma in front of them and daylight coming in fast.

'What a night,' Julian said.

'Epic, my friend.'

They sat on the low wall overlooking the bay. Gabriel lit one of the joints, inhaled and passed it to Julian. When Julian took his first drag, the pungent smoke scalded the back of his throat. Unlike last time, he knew he wouldn't throw up. He'd accessed some new level of being. Transformed himself. He wondered if he was one of those people with the right constitution for hedonism. Imagine not knowing that all his life.

'Weed helps with the comedown,' Gabriel said. 'Takes the edge off.'

Julian handed the joint back. He didn't want to come down. He wanted this feeling of freedom to last forever.

Gabriel smoked while they watched motor launches zip across the bay to luxury motor yachts.

'Check those beasts out,' Gabriel said. 'How about we get us one of those?'

Julian laughed. 'Why not? Where would we go?'

Gabriel shot him a sideways glance. 'Anywhere you like.'

The muscles in Julian's back softened and released. A pleasant sensation.

'They have like a ton of those boats off Ibiza. This one time I got invited to a party on one and Kate Moss was there and some movie star guy but I didn't know who he was.'

'Sounds fun.' Julian realised Gabriel's forthcoming job in Ibiza might, like Kai, be a fiction. He also realised he was enjoying the illusion of Gabriel far too much to care.

'It's always crazy there. I'm looking forward to it.' Gabriel crushed the joint out on the wall. 'Maybe I'll take the ferry over from here. More fun than flying, right?'

'What happens after Ibiza? What will you do then?'

Gabriel shrugged. 'Portugal, maybe. Got a few buddies out in the sticks there, living off the land. Doing the whole self-sufficient thing.'

Julian sensed Gabriel's black wings unfolding beneath his shirt, ready to carry him away on another adventure. He glanced down at the wall, where one of Gabriel's slender, tanned hands rested, and covered it with his own. 'Stay,' he said.

Gabriel turned his hand over so their palms touched. 'Stay?'

'For a week or two. We can hang out. You could put Ibiza off, couldn't you?'

A flock of black birds erupted from the buttresses of the cathedral and circled overhead.

Gabriel's slow smile materialised. 'I guess.'

27

'Careful, darling,' Olivia said, 'you need to watch your footing here.'

Julian, too late to heed the warning, stumbled over a rock. As he straightened up, he knocked his head on the gnarly branch of an olive tree. 'Shit.'

'Are you okay?' Olivia, ahead of him on the path, stopped and turned.

'Fine.' He mustered a smile. 'Lead on.'

It was just gone 7.30 a.m. and Julian, who had spent the previous day and most of the night sleeping off his adventure in Palma, had offered to accompany Olivia on her morning walk. An offer prompted by guilt. An offer he now regretted as the unsympathetic sun gazed down on him. He sensed the day's heat lying in wait and cursed himself for forgetting his Panama.

'The view's great once we get through the trees,' Olivia said. They were descending through the scrubby terraces below the villa. Carob trees appeared either side of them, dangling their dark, curling pods. Optimistic birdsong filled the air. Julian, still fragile, found it irritating. He felt bruised all over, as if he had fallen from a great height. A grimy dread crawled through him. Was this the comedown Gabriel had warned him of?

He hadn't seen his guest to ask him. Yesterday morning, after they'd returned from Palma in a taxi, Gabriel had passed out in the spare room and still hadn't surfaced. Olivia had been the one to suggest Gabriel should stay the night so he could recover. No chance of him going anywhere in that state, she'd said.

Olivia strode on ahead, a buoyant figure in shorts, T-shirt and sturdy hiking boots, a small backpack bouncing between her shoulder blades. Julian ambled behind, his sockless feet slipping around inside his trainers. The path veered to the right and narrowed. Tall shrubs hemmed him in on one side, smooth grey boulders on the other. His pulse thumped at his temples. He wished he'd taken painkillers before setting off.

The path dipped and rose. Flashes of cobalt blue appeared through the greenery. A few minutes later, the shrubs dwindled away, leaving a wider, exposed length of path along the cliff.

'Glorious, isn't it?' Olivia said, approaching the edge.

Julian nodded, out of breath. He joined his wife and stared out at the sea. The vastness of it left him disorientated. He glanced down. Far below, spumy water lashed against jagged black rocks.

'So dramatic.' Olivia took her phone from the pocket of her shorts and insisted Julian get a snap of them with the view in the background. He stood with one arm around his wife and forced a smile as he took the picture.

'Lovely,' Olivia said, when she inspected the results.

Julian peered over the edge of the cliff. The sucky heave of the sea made him nauseous. 'Can I have a drink?'

With an indulgent smile, Olivia slid her rucksack off her back and opened it. 'Someone's still a little worse for wear,' she said, handing over a flask.

'Maybe a little.' He opened the flask and took a slug of icy water.

'So peaceful here,' Olivia said.

Julian glanced at the wall of pine trees that rose up behind them. To his right, in the distance, he could see the coastal trail that connected Deià to Sóller. The unkempt path they stood on served as an access route to the trail from the villas on their part of the hillside.

'It's like having our own private viewpoint here,' Olivia said. 'You hardly ever see anyone walking this way.'

'I hope you bring your phone when you're walking alone.'

'Of course I do.'

'Just to be on the safe side.'

'No need to fuss.'

Julian wiped his mouth and handed the flask back. Another glance at the water below made the back of his knees tingle. He took a step backwards.

Olivia laughed. 'I've got some boiled sweets in my bag if you want one.'

He refused the offer but felt a strong tug of tenderness towards her. Yesterday, after closing the guest room door on Gabriel, he'd staggered upstairs and passed out fully clothed on the bed. Sometime in the afternoon, he'd woken to find Olivia had left a glass of sparkling water and a packet of ibuprofen on the bedside table.

'Did you overdo the "indigenous crops" on your night out?' she said, putting the words 'indigenous crops' into air quotation marks.

'Sorry?'

'I wasn't born yesterday.' She slipped the rucksack straps over her shoulder. 'I've got a pretty good idea what your young friend was up to in India.'

Julian shook his head. 'No, I really think he was doing some kind of community farming project.'

'Darling, you're so naive sometimes. Smoking dope is what most travellers do when they're over there. When I went to India back in the day, I smoked my share. Not that it agreed with me. Made me paranoid.'

The screech of a bird in the pine trees made Julian spin round. He peered into the patches of dappled shade beneath the branches but saw only a carpet of dry brown needles and a cluster of large grey rocks.

'Himachal Pradesh is a lawless area,' Olivia said. 'I looked it up online yesterday.'

'What for?' He didn't like the thought of Olivia researching anything to do with Gabriel.

'Apparently the mountains are full of travellers living illegally,' she said. 'People on the run from God knows what.'

Julian swallowed. 'And people like Gabriel. Free spirits on a misguided search for enlightenment.'

Olivia laughed. 'Yes, those too. India's full of them.'

They set off again, in the direction of the coastal trail. A dark foreboding settled over Julian. He had yet to broach the subject of Gabriel remaining as their guest and, as his headache flourished in the heat, he wasn't sure he wanted to. What was the point of Gabriel staying on? What could possibly come of it? He almost wished he might return to the villa and find Gabriel gone. Out of his life for good.

'Wait for me,' he said. Olivia stopped and when Julian caught her up, he pulled her towards him for a kiss. A kiss that made him think of Gabriel taking his hand as they sat by the cathedral and pulling him to his feet. Gabriel leading him through silent, winding streets, past shuttered windows and solid wooden doors. Gabriel pushing him against an ochre wall and surrendering his lips and tongue.

An echo of euphoria ran through him.

'About Gabriel,' he said when he and Olivia parted.

'What?'

'I'm not convinced he should go to Ibiza. Not yet, anyway.'

Olivia glanced up at him. 'Why not?'

'He's a good kid, but he is a bit lost. I doubt a party season in Ibiza will help him find his way.'

'And you will?'

'He's in need of guidance. You said so yourself.'

'You can't stop yourself, can you?'

He recalled biting Gabriel's lower lip. The trickle of blood he'd licked and sucked.

'Always helping people.' Olivia smiled. 'You're meant to be on holiday.'

'Helping people is what you and I do.' Julian kissed her again. 'Just for a week or two. He'll be gone before my birthday. Maybe I can help him work out what to do with his life.'

'Project Gabriel.'

'That's the one.'

'What's his surname, by the way? Do you even know it?'

'Of course. It's King.'

'Gabriel King.' She turned her eyes seaward. 'He does seem to look up to you.'

Gabriel taking his hand again and leading him into the back-yard of a restaurant. Recycling bins, rickety wooden chairs and cigarette butts on the ground. Gabriel down on his knees, looking up at him with eyes full of mischief.

'Yes,' Julian said. 'He does.'

28

For the next few days, when in Olivia's company, Julian and Gabriel played the roles of host and guest, mentor and mentee, unlikely friends. Roles they maintained when she accompanied them on excursions to the beach at Cala de Deià and to the nearby hillside village of Valldemossa. Excursions made in the cramped Fiat 500, Olivia in the driving seat with Julian beside her and Gabriel folded into the back.

In Valldemossa, they joined the throng of day trippers meandering the ancient cobbled streets. They visited the Carthusian monastery, a sprawling building with a plain façade of golden stone. Inside, they walked around the whitewashed cells where Frédéric Chopin had spent the winter of 1838 with his lover, the French writer, George Sands.

'To think he actually worked on the Preludes here,' Olivia said, as they stood around Chopin's Pleyel piano.

'Kinda romantic, huh?' Gabriel said. 'This writer chick ditching her husband to come hang out here with Chopin for the winter.'

Julian clasped his hands behind his back and said nothing. Every day that passed brought Gabriel's departure closer. Gabriel appeared resigned to the fact he would have to leave but had made Julian promise they would make the most of every moment together.

'I'm not sure she found it that romantic,' Olivia said. 'The weather was awful, the locals disapproved of them and Chopin got ill. She'd have been better off staying in Paris.'

Gabriel shrugged. 'People do crazy shit for love, though, right?'

During these outings, Julian found himself on edge, restless, trapped in a state of permanent arousal. A state he only found relief from when Olivia was out of the way. In the mornings, when she went for her walk, he would put on his swimming shorts and head downstairs to the guest room, where he would rouse Gabriel from sleep by stroking his wings and seeking out his pliant lips and his hot, stale morning breath. The first time, they didn't make it out of bed; the second time, they trailed down to the pool and relieved each other in the deep end.

At night, after dinner, Olivia would go to bed and leave them to drink whisky on the terrace. I'll leave you boys to chat, she would say, and at that moment Julian would feel an intense rush of love and gratitude towards her. She thought she was giving him space to give Gabriel a pep talk, but instead the two of them would take the whisky down to the pool and escape into the olive grove to devour one another. Afterwards, they would swim beneath the stars, the frog chorus croaking at full volume. Once clean, Julian would creep into bed, chlorine masking his betrayal.

* * *

On the morning of the fifth day, just before eleven o'clock, Olivia drove them all into Deià to get food supplies and to have a coffee. They deposited the Fiat in the car park opposite the five-star La Residencia hotel. The winding mountain road left little room for pavement on either side, forcing them to walk down towards the centre of the village in single file. Gabriel took the lead with his usual slouching gait, eyes shielded by his mirrored glasses, his legs on display in a pair of denim shorts. Olivia followed behind him, her solid figure allowing Julian only the occasional glimpse of his lover's toned calves. He gazed at the villas clinging to the hillside instead. The lopsided jumble of terracotta roofs made Deià look like an expensive shanty town.

Olivia swivelled her head, one hand on top of her straw hat. 'Did you email Mike?'

'What?' he said.

'Mike. You said last night you would email him about the funding application.'

During the night, unable to sleep, he'd given in and typed *Gabriel King* into the search engine on his phone. To his relief, he'd found no trace of the young man sleeping in the guest room. In the online world, Gabriel did not exist. As he was wondering whether deleting Gabriel from his search history could appear more suspicious than leaving him there, Olivia woke up and asked him what was wrong. Unable to tell her the truth, he'd claimed to be anxious about the outcome of a recent funding application he and Mike had made to the Wellstood Foundation. An application that, if successful, would double the current income stream of the Helen Griggs Awards. Olivia had held him close and declared him adorable for caring so much.

'I'll do it later,' he said. Mike had emailed him yesterday about some minor administration matters, but he hadn't bothered to reply. Could he not have a few days off? Tetchy and sweaty, he wished himself back at the villa, asleep by the pool. The deck shoes he'd worn to please Olivia were once more nipping at his heels.

A constant stream of vehicles passed by. Tourists in cars and coaches. White vans stuck behind them with impatient drivers.

When the local bus to Palma hurtled past, Julian jumped away from the kerb of the narrow pavement. His arm reached out to shield his wife, but she had already stepped out of danger.

It was just after 11 a.m. and the village was gearing up for another busy day. Groups of enthusiastic hikers in shorts and dusty boots strode past them in both directions. Backpackers occupied the benches outside the post office, drinking takeaway coffees and smoking. The pavement widened out. Well-dressed couples strolled arm in arm, pausing to peer into the shady interiors of shops selling traditional crafts and cotton clothing.

They passed an estate agent's. It was closed, but two young women in denim shorts were examining the property adverts on the noticeboard outside.

'Wow,' one of them said, 'I'd kill to live here.'

'Who wouldn't, right?' Gabriel stopped beside the girls and peered at the noticeboard.

Julian flinched as Olivia linked her arm in his. 'Let's go to Sandrino's for coffee.'

'I'll catch you guys up,' Gabriel said.

After pointing out Sandrino's to Gabriel, Olivia steered Julian along the pavement. He couldn't resist a backward glance. Gabriel placed a cigarette between his lips and one of the girls brought a lighter to it. Whatever Gabriel said next made them both laugh.

'Look at those girls,' he said, 'their tongues are practically hanging out.'

Olivia laughed. 'I suppose your guest is quite good-looking.'

'Yes. I suppose he is.'

'In an obvious way.'

Julian had no problem with Gabriel's obvious beauty. Nor with the imperfect, crooked nose that only enhanced it.

'Olivia?' A voice from behind them. 'Olivia Pearson?'

Julian turned to see a tall, slender woman in a yellow sundress.

On top of her long bleached hair sat a straw hat even wider than Olivia's. An older man stood beside her, short and wiry with a shock of white hair and a matching moustache.

'Libby bloody Ashworth,' Olivia said. 'I don't believe it.' The two women kissed each other on the cheek, crushing the brims of their hats together.

'Simon, darling,' Olivia said. Simon stepped in for an embrace. Afterwards, Olivia introduced Julian and a round of handshakes followed.

'Libby and I spent many summer holidays together in Deià in our youth,' Olivia explained. 'Her parents had a lovely villa down by the beach.'

'They sold it fifteen years ago,' Libby said. 'I've never forgiven them.'

'Neither have I,' said Simon, in the booming, authoritative voice Julian associated with all the males he'd met in Olivia's social circle.

'How are the twins?' Olivia asked. 'They must be at uni now.'

'They are.' Libby beamed. 'Both my girls doing PPE at Oxford. Can you believe it?'

'Amazing,' Olivia said. 'Where are you staying? How long are you here for?'

With one eye on Gabriel and the fawning girls, Julian listened as Libby wittered on about their holiday apartment in Palma.

'We only come a few weeks every year,' she said. 'Now we don't have the children to entertain, I can shop and sunbathe and my husband can indulge his passion for yachts.'

'Are you a sailing man, Julian?' Simon asked.

'No. Afraid not.' Julian noted Simon had on deck shoes identical to his, as well as a pair of beige chinos. Julian wished he'd worn different clothes. He felt he was following the dress code of a club he could never belong to.

Olivia invited Libby and Simon to join them for coffee but, to

Julian's relief, they refused. Libby explained they were on their way to pick up a yacht in Port de Pollença.

'He's leaving me all alone while he takes to the high seas for a week,' she said.

'You love having a break from me,' Simon said. Libby laughed a tinkling, coquettish laugh that made Julian cringe.

'Olivia, you'll come to Palma and visit me, won't you?' she said. 'We can have lunch. Do a bit of shopping.'

'That would be lovely.' Olivia slipped an arm around Julian's waist. 'If I can tear myself away from this one.'

'It's wonderful to see you so happy,' Libby said. 'We heard about you and Lars on the grapevine. I thought about getting in touch, but you know how it is.'

'It's fine, really,' Olivia said.

'First William leaving you and then Lars.' Libby shook her head. 'You didn't deserve that.'

'It was all a long time ago.' Olivia sighed. 'Anyway, by the end, Lars had become more of a project than a husband.'

'You and your projects,' Libby said, 'you never could resist a lame duck.' She looked at Julian and her cheeks flushed.

'We read all about you in the paper, Julian,' Simon said. 'Lovely story.'

'He doesn't mean... not your other wife,' Libby said.

'God, no.' Simon shook his head. 'That was awful. Tragic.'

Julian's chest tightened. He glanced up the street. The girls had gone and Gabriel stood with one foot resting on the wall, cigarette hanging from his lips.

'He means meeting Olivia was a happy ending,' Libby said.

'It is.' Julian planted a kiss on the top of Olivia's head. 'We couldn't be happier.'

The following morning, before breakfast, Olivia suggested Julian might like to take Gabriel for a bike ride.

'We have bikes?' he asked.

'Two. In the outbuilding. They haven't been used for a while.'

Julian followed his wife to the villa's front courtyard and into the airless outbuilding. Amidst the jumble of boxes and old furniture, they found two old-fashioned bikes with wicker baskets attached to the front. Patches of rust dotted both frames. One bike had a rear wheel missing and the other, although in better shape, had handlebars that wobbled too much for Julian's liking.

'Shame,' Olivia said, 'would have been fun to get out on these.'

'Never mind,' he said, relieved. He didn't think the bikes looked fit to negotiate the busy roads, and he didn't fancy the exertion of cycling up the steep access road. 'Actually, I thought I might take Gabriel to Palma for the day. Do some sightseeing.'

'You go ahead, darling.' She brushed dust from her hands. 'The cleaner's arriving soon. I want to show her around and get her started.'

'Sure you don't mind?'

'Not at all. Although I'm not convinced you'll get Gabriel out of bed. He did go a little heavy on the red wine last night.'

'Maybe a little.' When Julian had slipped into the guest room earlier, he'd found the air infused with stale alcohol. Gabriel, fast asleep, had shaken off his touch and refused to stir.

The cleaner arrived after breakfast, a middle-aged Spanish woman with a gleaming bun of black hair at the nape of her neck. Olivia left Julian on the top terrace and proceeded to give her a tour of the villa.

Gabriel appeared in his black shorts, bare-chested, eyes bleary with sleep. He sat at the head of the table and poured himself a coffee.

'Sure thing, big guy,' he said when Julian proposed the trip to Palma. 'Let me drink this and take a shower and I'm all yours.'

He stroked his chest as he sipped his coffee. Julian's skin tingled in the same spot, as if Gabriel were touching him there.

This time they took the bus into Palma. There was a bus stop a few metres from the junction of the villa's access road and the main route to the capital. The journey took forty-five minutes. They departed the bus on the Avenue de Jaume III just after 11.30 and wandered beneath the street's covered arcade, past clothing and jewellery stores. When they turned onto the Passeig des Born, Gabriel declared himself thirsty and persuaded Julian to take a seat outside a nearby bar.

'I suppose a sparkling water wouldn't go amiss,' Julian said.

When an elderly waiter appeared, Gabriel ordered for them in Spanish. Minutes later, the waiter returned with two Aperol spritzes.

'Come on,' Gabriel said, when Julian declared it too early to drink. 'Live a little.'

The first drink didn't last long so they ordered another and sipped it beneath the shade of the plane trees towering overhead.

They talked about the people entering and leaving the expensive clothes stores. Where they might have come from, where they might be going. Julian didn't know if he felt lightheaded because of the alcohol or because of Gabriel's leg resting against his beneath the table.

'If we want to see the cathedral, we should probably get going,' Julian said, after draining the last of his drink. 'It does tend to get busy.'

'I guess.' Gabriel's blue eyes had a lazy, inviting look about them.

'Where are your glasses?' Julian realised he hadn't seen Gabriel in them all morning.

'Forgot them, man.'

'Let's get you a new pair.' Julian slipped forty euros under the base of his glass. 'Come on.'

'Can't hurt to look, I guess.'

They wandered over to the shop opposite the bar. The window display contained silver mannequins dressed in fashionable jeans and T-shirts. A young Spanish man with a shaved head presided over the interior. He wore the same style of loose blue jeans as Gabriel. In response to Julian's request for sunglasses, he produced several pairs of mirrored aviator shades from a glass cabinet.

'These Armani ones are the best,' he said, handing them to Gabriel. 'Only 300 euros.'

Gabriel tried them on. 'What d'ya think, big guy?'

'They do look good.'

'Thing is,' Gabriel said, '300 euros is way out of my league.' He steered Julian to the other side of the shop. 'I gotta be honest, big guy. I'm all outta cash.'

'Let me treat you.'

'No way. I couldn't.'

'I want to.'

'Really? Thanks, man.' Gabriel looked so touched it made Julian want to hug him.

'Let's do you too,' Gabriel said. 'You could do with some new pants.'

'Oh.' Julian looked down at the beige chinos he'd matched with his white linen shirt, his deck shoes and his Panama. A respectable, climate-appropriate outfit, he'd thought.

'Dude, you're gonna be fifty, not seventy.' Gabriel gathered up several pairs of blue jeans and two pairs of tapered linen trousers and hustled him into a changing cubicle at the back of the shop. Self-conscious but excited, Julian tried each pair on, transforming in the mirror to a younger, hipper self.

'I don't look like an old man trying to be young?' he said, as he admired himself in a pair of stylish blue jeans.

'Are you kidding me?' Gabriel locked the cubicle door. 'Come here.'

They emerged ten minutes later, Julian wearing the loose blue jeans and a satisfied smile. The assistant gave no sign of suspecting the pleasures they'd just enjoyed. He agreed to cut the labels off the jeans so Julian could wear them out of the shop.

'We need a few more things,' Gabriel said when the assistant started adding up the bill. He picked out a pair of black leather espadrilles in Julian's size. 'The deck shoes have to go, man,' he said.

'Seriously.' Julian slipped his feet into the espadrilles and agreed immediately.

'I'll keep these on as well,' he said. He also allowed Gabriel to add a pair of black flip-flops to the purchases, as well as a straw pork-pie hat and several T-shirts. Gabriel encouraged him to leave the deck shoes at the store, but Julian, unwilling to upset Olivia, asked the shop assistant to put them in one of the bags.

An expansive lightness swelled within him as he handed over

his debit card to settle the bill. As if he made such extravagant transactions all the time.

Laden with bags, they stepped out of the cool, air-conditioned shop into the sun's fierce embrace. When Gabriel suggested lunch, Julian took him to the old town where they discovered a beautiful courtyard restaurant. An elegant, discreet venue with pink bougainvillea trailing down the walls and no prices on the menu.

'This place won't be cheap,' Gabriel said.

Julian hesitated. The bill from the store would make a big dent in what was left of this month's wages. He remembered the credit card he kept hidden in the back of his wallet. 'Who cares?' he said, the expansive lightness filling him once again. 'Let's treat ourselves.'

Gabriel smiled. 'No one's ever been good to me like you, big guy.'

Julian admired his revamped reflection in Gabriel's glasses. 'Champagne to start?'

30

Julian regained consciousness with a gasp, like a man coming back from the dead. It took him a moment to register he was back at the villa, lying on his bed. The window shutters were closed, but the white light at their edges told him early morning had passed. He sat up, head spinning. According to his travel clock, it was almost noon.

'Christ.'

He still had on his white shirt and the new jeans he'd purchased the previous day. A red line marked the vamp of his absent espadrilles. He dragged himself out of bed, changed into shorts and a T-shirt and made his way downstairs on wobbly legs.

'Olivia?'

No sign of his wife in the kitchen. Breakfast plates and glasses sat in the sink. The top terrace was empty so he made his way across the grass, flinching beneath the sun's hot, accusatory glare.

'Olivia?'

On the rocky steps, he saw her through the gap in the bougainvillea. She was lying on a sunbed beneath the shade of an umbrella, holding a paperback, a blue sarong draped over her swimming costume. The sunbed beside her was empty, but when he stepped out onto the pool terrace, he saw Gabriel lying face down on the bed next to it, warming his wings.

'You're alive.' Olivia lowered her book as he approached. When Gabriel turned his head and gave him a wave, sunlight glinted off his new Armani glasses.

'Sorry.' Julian claimed the empty middle sunbed, grateful for the umbrella's protection. 'I didn't realise I'd had so much to drink.'

Olivia removed her reading glasses. 'Poor little mouse.' Julian thought he detected an edge of sarcasm to her voice.

'I'm fine,' he said, without conviction.

'You passed out in the taxi coming back from Palma. Gabriel and I had to carry you upstairs and put you to bed.'

'Sorry.' He groped around in his mind for some recollection of his arrival home. The last memory he could dredge up was of him and Gabriel drinking Negronis at a beachside bar at sunset.

'It's my bad.' Gabriel rolled onto his side, exposing his taut, tanned stomach. 'Truly, Olivia. The drinks were my idea.'

With a subtle sideways glance, Julian saw the trail of fine blonde hairs that started at Gabriel's navel and disappeared beneath the waistband of his swimming trunks. A trail he had followed many times with his tongue. Sweat had matted the hairs together. Julian could almost taste their saltiness.

'My husband doesn't need me to punish him,' Olivia said. 'The hangover will do that.'

Julian frowned. In place of his usual black shorts, Gabriel wore a pair of navy ones with luminous yellow stripes down each leg. Had they bought them yesterday? He wound back through the day to the three-hour lunch – *yes, a second bottle of champagne. Why not? Pinot Noir for the meat course. Absolutely.* He remembered now how they'd staggered through the old town afterwards, hemmed in by the tall, colourful buildings, and he remembered Gabriel dragging him into a shop playing thumping dance music.

What else had they bought? How many other shops had they visited?

He groaned and massaged his forehead.

'You need a cold one of these, my friend.' Gabriel picked up a bottle of San Miguel from the ground and took a swig.

'No. Christ.' Julian lay back and closed his eyes. 'I'll be fine. Just need a minute to regroup.'

To his relief, the others stopped talking. The pounding in his forehead subsided. A pigeon in one of the nearby trees cooed in a slow, luxurious fashion. When he let his heavy arms dangle over the side of the sunbed, Olivia grasped his left hand and squeezed it. Seconds later, Gabriel's thumb traced a circle on the inside of his right palm. A smile spread across Julian's face as he returned both gestures of affection.

Gabriel withdrew his hand. 'How about a dip, buddy? It'll make you feel better.'

'Can't face moving yet.' Julian opened his eyes in time to see Gabriel stand up and roll his shoulders, the black wings rippling along with his muscles.

'Bombs away.' Gabriel tossed his glasses onto the sunbed and took a run up to the pool. He hit the water with a smack, dislodging a plume of spray.

'Remember being his age?' Olivia said. 'We could drink like that and get up the next day and do it all over again.'

'Not really. When I was his age, I never had the chance to behave badly.'

'Poor darling.' Olivia squeezed his hand again. 'I forget sometimes.'

'I really am sorry about last night. Maybe I'm trying to relive a youth I never had.'

'No one would blame you for that.' She released his hand. 'I can't believe how many shopping bags you came back with. Quite the spree.'

'I needed a few bits and pieces. Not often I treat myself, is it?'

'True. I assume you treated Gabriel to the sunglasses too?'

Julian bristled. Surely he could do what he wanted with his own money? 'The glasses were on sale. I felt bad buying stuff for myself when he needed things too.'

'I don't want anyone taking advantage of you. That's all.'

I gotta be honest, big guy. I'm all outta cash.

'For goodness' sake. He isn't taking advantage.' Julian pushed away the memory of Gabriel's confession in the clothes store. 'He's got a bit of money, but I'd rather he saved it. I know what it's like to have to watch the pennies.'

'I'm not talking about money. I'm talking about your good nature.'

Her warm, concerned tone banished his irritation. She was only looking out for him, as any loving wife would.

'Well, thanks to my good nature and yours,' he said, 'we've made a breakthrough.'

'Really?'

'He's talking about going back to studying. In the States, probably.'

Over lunch in Palma, he and Gabriel had agreed on this story. Julian hoped Olivia would feel happier if she knew her hospitality had produced results.

'Well done you,' she said. 'A win for Project Gabriel.'

Gabriel launched into a splashy front crawl, churning up the pool's cool green water.

'I hope so,' Julian said. 'He's a bright kid. Be a shame if he didn't make something of himself.'

'Yes. It would, I suppose.'

He cleared his throat. 'Would it be possible for him to stay a bit longer? I know we said two weeks, but if we let him stay another few days, he'll be here for my birthday.'

Olivia fiddled with the edge of her sarong. 'Is that what you want?'

He shrugged. 'Just thought it might make it more of an event.'

'It's your birthday. I only want you to be happy.'

Julian examined his reflection in Olivia's glasses. He saw the same man she did – upright, caring, respectable. He remembered how much he'd wanted to be that man.

'Thanks, my love,' he said.

'As long as I get you back to myself after that.'

'You will.' He meant it. His birthday would be the cut-off point. His affair with Gabriel a lusty blip in the otherwise honourable progress of his life.

'How about something to eat?' Olivia swung her freckled legs over the side of the sunbed. 'You'll feel better.'

Julian's stomach gave a rebellious leap. 'I doubt it.'

'A bit of bread and cheese won't hurt.' She stood up and, after wrapping her sarong around her waist, strode over to the steps and disappeared.

Julian lowered the back of his sunbed and lay on his front. With drooping eyes, he watched a line of large black ants moving back and forth across the paving slabs. His eyes closed, and he hovered in a pleasant limbo – neither awake nor asleep. Aware of water splashing in the pool behind him and the low drone of nearby insects. Unaware how much time had passed. A few minutes? Half an hour?

Gabriel's wet hand slipping beneath his T-shirt roused him.

'Don't be naughty,' he said.

'Let me put some suntan lotion on you.'

'I'm not in the sun.'

'Do as you're told.' Gabriel leaned close to his ear. 'I just wanna touch you.'

Julian pulled his T-shirt over his head and cast it aside. The lid of a suntan lotion bottle popped, and seconds later, Gabriel's hands roamed across his back, exerting a soothing, suggestive pressure. When the hands delved inside his shorts and caressed his buttocks, Julian felt a stir between his legs. A low moan escaped him as Gabriel's lips brushed his cheek. As he turned his head to meet the kiss, he spotted his wife's Birkenstocks on the ground next to her sunbed.

'Stop it,' he said. 'Olivia might see us.'

'Relax, big guy.'

'I'm serious.' Julian rolled onto his side, forcing Gabriel to pull back his hands. 'We can't afford to be careless.' He sat up and glanced towards the villa.

'I get it.' Gabriel's mouth settled into a sulky pout as he threw himself onto his sunbed.

'Don't be like that.'

'Forget it.' Gabriel lay on his front, concealing the bulge between his legs.

Julian sighed. A few minutes later, Olivia appeared on the terrace, carrying a tray. He resolved to be more cautious. She could easily have crept up on them. How was he supposed to know where she was without the warning slap of her sandals?

'Here we are, boys,' she said, placing the tray with its platter of bread, cheese and olives on the end of Julian's sunbed. 'Help yourselves.' She pushed her feet into her Birkenstocks.

'You're not staying?' Julian sat up and edged towards the tray, his legs daring to leave the umbrella's shade.

'I'm afraid I've got a few phone calls to make.' Olivia smiled. 'Be careful in this heat, darling. You could easily get burned.'

31

When Julian woke at 6 a.m. the next day, he found the bed beside him empty and a note on his wife's pillow.

Couldn't sleep. Gone for an early walk.

After cleaning his teeth and washing his armpits, Julian sauntered down to Gabriel's room. Inside, the air was thick and warm and laced with sweat. Julian slipped beneath the sheet and pulled Gabriel's wings towards him.

'Hey, big guy,' Gabriel murmured.

'We need to talk.' Julian nuzzled Gabriel's shoulder.

'Sounds ominous.'

Julian explained the deal he'd struck with Olivia.

'She wants me out of here after your birthday?' Gabriel said.

'That's what she told me.' Julian's pulse thudded in his ears. 'She has been very accommodating.'

'But this is fun, right?' Gabriel pulled away and sat up. 'Aren't we having fun?'

'That's not the point.'

'It's okay for you. With your fancy new life, your money.'

'What about the money I gave you? What about your fresh start?'

'You think a guy can start over with a few lousy grand?'

'Surely you could have found something more productive to do than growing drugs in the Himalayas?'

'Hey, I was good at that shit.'

'Where's all the money you made?'

'What, like I was gonna carry it home in a suitcase? Come on. Six months in Goa used up most of it. By the time I'd bought fake visa stamps for my passport and a fake driving licence, it was gone.'

'I thought you wanted to change your life?'

Gabriel reached behind him for a pillow. 'I had to hide away after what I did for you.' He pummelled the pillow into shape and slid it behind his head. 'Let's not forget that, my friend.'

Body trembling, Julian sat on the edge of the bed. The secret they shared hung between them in the room's sweaty fug. Unable to find the words to banish it, he got up and walked away.

* * *

'Are you okay?' Julian asked Olivia when she returned from her walk. The dark, puffy crescents beneath her eyes concerned him.

'Couldn't sleep for the heat,' she said. 'I'll take a sleeping pill tonight.'

'Since when did you take sleeping pills?'

'I always bring some on holiday in case the heat gets to me.'

She insisted on accompanying him for his morning dip. He wanted to swim fast and hard and cleanse himself of the argument with Gabriel, but she wanted to talk as they accumulated laps together. She outlined the busy morning of admin duties she had planned – a call with her accountant to discuss the complex process of vesting one of her trusts and she had a funding application to read through from Women Against Sex Slavery.

They paused for breath at the deep end, Julian standing. Olivia, whose feet did not touch the bottom, hung on to the side of the pool.

'Have you emailed Mike?' she said. 'You mustn't get behind with things.'

'I'll do it later.' He dived below the rippling surface to escape further questioning.

As he traipsed downstairs after his shower, he saw Olivia at the front door, buzzing the villa's gates open. He got to the door in time to see Gabriel steering one of the bikes from the outbuilding through them.

'Where's he going?' Julian asked.

'He wanted to go off on a little adventure, so I let him take the good bike.'

'I wouldn't call it good. It's hardly fit for purpose.'

'He seemed to think it was fine. I've given him the code for the gates and a spare key.' She turned to go inside. 'Make sure you get the key back when he leaves.'

As Julian watched the gates close, a forlorn longing gripped him. A premonition of how it might feel to say goodbye to his lover. On his way down the hall, he stuck his head into the guest room, reassured by the sight of Gabriel's rucksack propped against the wardrobe.

After breakfast, Olivia set up her laptop on the table and claimed the top terrace for herself. Julian retreated to the upstairs living room with his computer and spent an hour reading and replying to various emails, including one from *Caring World* magazine, asking if he would do a guest slot as an agony aunt. He accepted the offer, although he had no desire to deal with the problems of strangers right now. A new email from Mike explained their application to the Wellstood Foundation had progressed to the next round, requiring them to provide a more detailed breakdown of how they would use the potential funding. Julian sighed and set about estimating the costs of more hours for Mike and for the free-lance social media expert they'd discussed hiring. The task annoyed him. The thought that his earnings relied upon him performing good deed after good deed. At 10 a.m., he called Mike.

'Hiya, mate,' Mike said. Julian pictured him at the kitchen table of his Camden flat, cappuccino in hand, his bushy black beard groomed to perfection. He was delighted to hear of Julian's plans to give him more hours. They also discussed how much of the potential grant they would allocate to a number of carer support services across the country.

'This money would be a total game-changer, mate,' Mike said.

'It would,' said Julian, although his mind had already wandered to Gabriel. He couldn't shake the notion Gabriel might ride the rusty old bike to the nearest police station and announce he had something to confess. No, he told himself. Gabriel wouldn't say anything to the police. He wouldn't incriminate himself like that. Would he? These thoughts made Julian feel like a fragile object Gabriel could drop at any moment.

He ventured downstairs to make a coffee. When he went outside to ask Olivia if she wanted a cup, he found her pacing around the dry grass, her phone to her ear.

'Yes, I can do a bank transfer,' she said. 'No, no, I'd rather we just got started. Yes, tomorrow would be good. I'm happy to pay extra to speed things up.' She turned her head and saw him. Julian pointed to the empty cup beside her laptop, and she gave a thumbs up. 'By email will be fine.'

When he returned with two fresh cups of coffee, he found her seated at the table.

'That was Liberto from Casa Feliz,' she said. 'You wouldn't think sorting out a regular cleaner would be so hard.' She took the coffee from him. 'Thank you, darling.'

He sat at the head of the table. Hot, dry air licked at his skin. He found himself longing for rain.

'I found this on the bedroom floor.' Olivia pulled a crumpled slip of paper from her kaftan pocket and pushed it across the table. 'I wasn't prying. It was just lying there.'

Julian smoothed out the paper. His skin prickled as he recognised it as a till receipt from the restaurant in Palma where he and Gabriel had eaten lunch.

'Yes, it was a pricey meal,' he said. 'If that's what you're getting at.'

'It's a credit card receipt. Since when did you have a credit card?'

'The bank offered me one. I didn't ask for it.'

'Bloody things are a con,' she said. 'You know what I think about them.'

'It's hardly a big deal.'

Her long, deep sigh of disappointment irked him. Did he have to earn her love too, good deed by good deed? Could he not make a mistake now and again?

'If you need extra money,' she said, 'you only need to ask.'

'I'm fine.' He did need extra money, but he had no intention of asking. His extravagant purchases had used up most of his wages, and, after checking his online banking, he'd discovered he'd taken out 300 euros from a cashpoint in Palma to give to Gabriel. An act of generosity that had taken him into overdraft.

'I won't use the credit card again,' he said. 'We were just having fun and I was... I was showing off. I wanted to spoil him. He sees me as a sort of father figure, I suppose.'

Olivia stared at him. 'And what is he to you?'

Julian sensed a crackle in the hot, dry air between them. 'What do you mean?'

'Do you regret marrying me?'

'No.'

'Is Gabriel like a son to you? Is that what you want? If you met someone younger, you could still have a child.'

'Is that what all this is about?' Julian masked his relief with a show of concern. 'Don't be silly. You know I don't want children.' He moved next to his wife and put his arms around her. 'Trust me. I don't see Gabriel like a son at all.'

* * *

Olivia slept in the afternoon. When Julian woke her just after five, she appeared refreshed and cheerful, their earlier disagreement forgotten. Gabriel returned soon after but went straight to his room and locked the door.

Julian made a salade niçoise for dinner and the three of them ate on the terrace, the mountains behind them bathed in a rosy glow.

'Go anywhere exciting on the bike?' Julian asked.

'Just enjoyed a real long ride,' Gabriel said. After that, he resisted Julian's attempts at small talk.

Olivia, chatty after a few glasses of Chablis, appeared oblivious to the awkward atmosphere. She quizzed Gabriel about his nascent study plans and Gabriel made a point of answering her with courtesy and enthusiasm.

'I'm thinking maybe social work,' he said, 'something like that. I've been around, seen a few things. I figure I could help people.'

'That's very commendable,' Olivia said.

'And I got my ticket all sorted out for Ibiza.' Gabriel pushed away his half-eaten salad. 'Figured I'd take the ferry, soon as we get the big birthday done.'

Julian's stomach knotted. After the way Gabriel had behaved all day, he should surely find this announcement a relief. He should, but he didn't.

'Only four days until you're fifty, darling,' Olivia said. 'The countdown is on.'

Julian placed his cutlery on his plate, unable to continue eating. 'Can't wait,' he said without enthusiasm. 'Have you booked Sa Vinya?'

'Everything's organised,' Olivia said. 'You just leave it all to me.'

When his wife said she wanted an early night, Julian, afflicted by an uncomfortable blend of anxiety and guilt, accompanied her. He waited in bed for her to finish in the bathroom. She emerged naked, her full, heavy breasts and springy mass of pubic hair on display. He looked away, but when she clambered into bed beside him, he reached for her, his body fidgety with unspent desire. 'Come here, you,' he said, but she told him she'd just taken a sleeping pill. After kissing his forehead, she turned off her bedside light and left him lying in the dark.

32

'I'm going into Palma,' Olivia announced over breakfast the next day. 'Libby's invited me to an exhibition at some new gallery and then we're going for lunch.'

'Oh. Okay.' Julian smeared apricot jam on his toast. 'That'll be fun.'

'You don't mind?'

'Of course not.' He wondered what he would do all day. Earlier, while Olivia was out for her walk, he'd gone to the guest room and found the door locked. How long did Gabriel intend to ignore him for?

'Are you okay, darling?' Olivia asked. 'You look tired.'

'Didn't get the best sleep.' He'd dreamt about his mother. Her first nocturnal visit for many years. In the dream, he'd watched her climbing aboard the bus that would take her away from him forever. He wondered if she'd had any idea of the effect her departure would have on him. That he would soon become a carer to his father and then, years later, to his wife, all the while trying to prove he was nothing like his mother.

When Olivia drove away from the villa just after ten, Julian took a novel down to the pool. Before settling down to read, he attempted to tidy up the rockery. The dislodged stones were heavier than they looked, and he was sweating by the time he'd shoved them at random into the collapsed rockery wall. A patch-up job, but it would do.

He collapsed onto one of the sunbeds and picked up his book. He decided to check on Gabriel in an hour but, thirty minutes later, Gabriel appeared with a towel around his waist.

'Morning,' Julian said.

Gabriel dropped his cigarettes onto the sunbed beside Julian and let his towel fall to the floor. He was naked.

'Am I forgiven, then?' Julian said.

Gabriel smiled. 'We'll see.'

When Julian reached for him, Gabriel turned away and dived into the pool.

'Tease,' Julian said, when Gabriel surfaced. He lay back and admired the ease of his lover's strokes, relieved at this apparent change of mood.

Ten minutes later, Gabriel hauled himself out of the pool. After moving his cigarettes aside, he flung himself onto the sunbed next to Julian's and turned onto his side. Water rolled from his wings and trickled down his spine to the dip between his buttocks. When he reached out his hand, Julian took it and let Gabriel pull him onto the sunbed.

'Sorry,' Julian said. The tension of the previous day dissolved as Gabriel guided him inside him.

Afterwards, they covered each other with suntan lotion, massaging it in with strokes that alternated between feather-light and pleasurably painful.

'Any chance of a beer, big guy?' Gabriel said.

Julian kissed him hungrily. 'You're very demanding.'

'In the best way, right?'

Julian slapped his buttocks. 'Back in a minute.' He sauntered barefoot and naked across the hot flagstones, a jaunty whistle escaping him as he bounced up the rocky steps and onto the dry grass. It occurred to him this was how his life would be, if he and Gabriel were together. Just the two of them.

In the cool, dim kitchen, he took two bottles of San Miguel from the fridge and a bottle opener from a nearby drawer. Turning around, he noticed for the first time a large black sports bag sitting by the door that led to the hallway. A pink feather duster poked out of one end. From the hallway came a high voice singing in Spanish and seconds later, a slender woman in a blue housecoat burst into the kitchen, her arms full of bed linen. She froze at the sight of Julian's naked body.

'Christ.' He grabbed the tea towel hanging next to the sink and held it in front of his crotch. 'I do apologise.'

The woman laughed. 'Is okay.'

Julian recalled Olivia on the phone yesterday, discussing booking a cleaner. 'You're from the agency?'

'Sí. Yes.' She was younger than the previous woman. Glossy red nails, arched eyebrows. 'The agency give me the key and also number for gates.'

'My wife didn't tell me you were coming.' Why had Olivia booked a cleaner so soon after the other one? The villa was hardly dirty. He edged away from the sink, staying front-on to the bemused woman. 'I'll go back to the pool,' he said. 'Leave you to get on.'

'Okay.' She turned her head away. 'No looking.'

'Thank you.'

Back at the pool, he found Gabriel sprawled on a sunbed, clothed only in his Armani sunglasses. 'Cover yourself up,' he snapped, throwing a towel over him.

'What's with the mood, my friend?'

Julian dropped the beers and bottle opener on his sunbed. As he pulled on his shorts, he told Gabriel about the cleaning woman's unexpected entrance.

Gabriel laughed. 'Sounds like she got a load of you.'

'It's not funny.' He prised open a beer and took a sip.

'You're right.' Gabriel sat up, the towel only just covering what it needed to. He helped himself to a beer. 'This situation of ours is in no way amusing.'

They drank in silence. Sitting on the edge of the sunbed, Julian watched a line of ants hurrying across the flagstones. Their busyness angered him. All that diligence, all that hard labour and for what?

'These are not the lives we're meant to be living, man.' Gabriel reached for his pack of Marlboro Lights.

'Speak for yourself.'

Gabriel lit a cigarette. 'We gotta be together, big guy. You know it.'

'Don't make me tell you to grow up.'

'We started a journey together, and to protect each other we've had to live these other lives for a while. We did what we had to do.' Smoke leaked from Gabriel's mouth. 'It was like a rollercoaster and we had to ride it. Me getting away, you with the police. Now we can get off the ride.'

'It's that easy?'

'Look at everything you did for me. This life you built, all the charity stuff, your memoir... all to keep me safe, right?'

For Helen, Julian thought. He'd done it all for Helen. Hadn't he?

'The only thing we gotta sort out is Olivia.'

The hairs on the back of Julian's neck lifted.

'I know it won't be easy,' Gabriel said, 'but we—'

'What are you talking about?'

'You gotta leave her, man.'

'Oh.'

'You gotta get a divorce.'

'Why would I get a divorce?'

'What's the point of marrying a rich chick if you don't divorce her?' Gabriel flicked his ash on the ground. 'Cut her loose, get your paycheck, and let's you and me start over.'

Julian pictured the pre-nuptial agreement on Arnold's desk. The black line on which he had signed his name. 'I love Olivia.' He wiped sweat from his forehead with an already sticky palm.

'Marrying a rich chick was a smart move, my friend. Did you plan that or was the universe just looking out for us?'

'I can't divorce my wife.'

'Not overnight, no, but we'll figure something out, right?'

'Gabriel. Please. I—'

'Just think about it, big guy.' Gabriel rested a hand on his knee. 'That's all I ask.'

33

On the evening of his fiftieth birthday, Julian laid out his recent purchases on the bed and deliberated over what to wear. He picked up the navy linen trousers Gabriel had chosen for him and slipped them over his boxer shorts.

Olivia emerged from the shower, her bare skin exuding an unfamiliar musky smell. Julian assumed it came from the expensive shower gel she'd bought in Palma the previous day. She'd surprised him by returning home laden with shopping bags. Libby had forced her to spoil herself, she'd said. Julian had admired all her purchases, her uncharacteristic lavishness diminishing his guilt. She'd joked about the two of them being corrupted, and he'd responded with nervous laughter.

'The water went cold,' she said. 'Is Gabriel still in the shower?'

'Probably.' Gabriel did enjoy long showers. Julian had enjoyed one with him that morning. Gabriel's birthday gift to him. 'Maybe you should ask that Liberto guy to send a plumber out to look at the boiler.'

'Maybe. I'll think about it.'

For Christ's sake, he thought. Why didn't she get the whole water system replaced? She could afford it.

'Are they the right length?' Olivia pointed to his tapered trousers.

'It's the style, apparently.' Julian looked away as she opened a round tub of scented body cream and applied it to her freckled skin. In the shower that morning, Gabriel had asked him again to leave her. *You and me, big guy, we're a done deal.* Julian had promised him they would talk tomorrow, once he'd got his birthday out of the way. Whatever happened, thought Julian, Gabriel would have to leave the day after tomorrow, just as they'd promised Olivia. He slipped on a black linen shirt, aware of the liquid thump of his heartbeat in his ears. Surely his blood pressure must have rocketed over the past few days?

He turned around to find his wife in a lacy jade-green bra that forced her breasts into sumptuous cleavage. As she picked up a pair of matching knickers, he noticed she had trimmed her pubic hair, a grooming task she usually neglected. Her exposed labia, long and dark brown, unsettled him.

'Wow,' he said. 'That's... you look nice.'

She flashed a shy smile as she stepped into the knickers. 'Thought I'd make an effort for your big day.'

Her uncertainty in her own appeal both moved him and introduced an unwelcome pressure. He gave her the kiss he sensed she was waiting for.

'I love you,' she said.

'You too.' He did love her, didn't he? If he could just get Gabriel away for a while, he would have time to think. Time to work out what he really wanted.

She pulled away and put on a new wraparound dress in the same shade of green as her underwear.

'That colour suits you,' Julian said. He slipped on his black espadrilles and appraised himself in the wardrobe mirror, uncertain now if the outfit was too young for him. Did he look ridiculous?

'Not sure about the shoes.' Olivia pushed past him and peered into the bottom of the wardrobe. 'Here we go.' From beneath his relegated Panama hat, she produced the brown suede loafers she'd bought him for Christmas. 'Try these.'

'Not sure they'll match.'

'Try them, darling. For me.' He gave in and put them on. 'Perfect,' she said.

'I suppose,' he said, unconvinced. 'What time did you book Sa Vinya for?'

'We're not going there.'

'Why? I thought you said—'

'I've prepared a little surprise.' Olivia dabbed Chanel No. 5 onto her wrists. 'We're going to the Residencia hotel.'

'Oh. Was the restaurant fully booked?'

'You're fifty, Julian. We're doing this in style. Cocktails and tapas and I've invited Libby and Simon.'

'What? Why?'

'To make it more of a party. Isn't that what you wanted?'

'I don't know them.'

'It'll be fun. Trust me.'

* * *

An hour later, Julian found himself sitting at a glass-topped table on the terrace of La Residencia, nearing the end of his second vodka martini. Olivia sat to his right, Libby and Simon on his left. Gabriel sat opposite him, exuding the air of an off-duty rock star in his tight black jeans, white linen shirt and mirrored sunglasses. He had attracted attention from the moment they'd arrived. Two long-limbed teenage girls sitting at a nearby table with their parents kept staring at him and whispering to one another. Women seated with their husbands had stolen more than one admiring glance. Even the pianist playing the white Steinbach at the end of the terrace kept looking up to admire Gabriel's profile.

'I'd forgotten how divine this place was,' Olivia said.

'The main building was originally a monastery, you know?' Simon said in his booming voice. He gestured to the main complex behind them – two manor houses in traditional golden stone with terracotta-tiled roofs. 'A Cistercian order.'

Julian glanced again at Simon's navy loafers, identical to his own in all but colour. He sighed and swirled his remaining martini around his glass before swallowing it.

'Simon's a bit of a history buff,' said Libby.

'Cistercian monks like totally believed in the value of manual labour.' Gabriel lit a cigarette. 'They found enlightenment by working with their hands.'

'Gosh. How fascinating.' One of the straps of Libby's lacy white sundress had fallen over her shoulder, and she made no attempt to replace it. Julian found her middle-aged attempt at bohemian waif very unattractive.

'I had a similar experience in India,' Gabriel said. 'Working on the farm every day gave me an incredible sense of peace.'

'Yes, I imagine working with indigenous crops would do that.' Olivia reached into her handbag for her phone. She checked the screen, tapped out a text and put the phone away.

'Anyway,' Simon said, 'the monks brought irrigation here. Hence the gardens.'

They all admired the bright green lawns below the terrace, and the lemon trees and poplars lining La Residencia's driveway. Every detail added to the hotel's rustic elegance.

'Talking of irrigation,' Julian said, 'I think we need another martini.'

'Better not argue with the birthday boy,' Olivia said.

Julian signalled one of the efficient, apron-clad waiters over and ordered another round of martinis and a selection of tapas. He did so in a polite but authoritative voice. The waiter, attentive and deferential, made him feel he belonged in the refined surroundings.

'What's your room like, Libby?' Olivia asked.

'Wonderful,' Libby said. 'I haven't stayed here in an absolute age.'

Julian zoned out of their conversation and stared at Gabriel. Smoke trailed from the younger man's nostrils. Julian smiled and thought he detected a flicker of a smile in return. If he kept his eyes straight ahead, Julian could almost pretend the others weren't there. That he and Gabriel were enjoying these drinks alone.

'Isn't she, Julian?' Simon said.

Julian frowned. 'What?'

'Generous. Your wife. Treating us to a room here.'

'Yes. She is.' Julian rubbed Olivia's thigh, reminded that she had made all of this possible. Without her, he would not be sitting in this five-star hotel drinking excellent martinis as the dwindling sun cast a rose-gold haze over the nearby olive groves, the sloping hills and the distant sea.

'Look.' Olivia nudged him and nodded towards the hotel entrance. An elegant, elderly woman pushed a wheelchair out onto the terrace. In it sat a man Julian assumed to be her husband. A bald, skeletal man beset by jerks and twitches. 'Poor woman,' Olivia said. 'Maybe he's got Parkinson's?'

Julian nodded, his nerves jangling. Only when the woman and her husband turned the corner of the terrace and disappeared from view did he relax.

The fresh drinks arrived, accompanied by platters of tapas. They clinked glasses and ate skewers of garlic prawns and rare, tender beef. The terrace filled up with people, every table taken apart from the one behind Julian with a reserved sign on it.

'So, young Gabriel,' Simon said, wiping his chin with a napkin, 'Olivia tells us you're off on your travels again soon.'

'Yessir. Back home to the US of A. Eventually.'

'Oh, to be your age,' said Libby. 'All that freedom. All that choice.'

'Freedom isn't only for the young,' said Gabriel.

'Only a man still in his youth would say that.' Simon wiped his fingers. 'Where did you and Julian meet?'

'In Scotland,' Julian said, on Gabriel's behalf. 'Some years ago.'

'And you just bumped into each other again?' Libby said.

Olivia reached for her drink. 'Quite the coincidence, isn't it?'

'This guy was a true friend to me then, and as for now, what can I say? And Olivia, you have been like, the most awesome hostess.' Gabriel raised his glass to her. 'I'm super grateful. Truly.'

'Not at all.' Olivia lifted her glass. 'Been lovely to have a guest at the old place.'

'I remember Villa Soledad always being full of people,' Libby said. 'Olivia's parents were fabulous hosts.'

'Daddy did love a party,' Olivia said.

'We children would play in the pool until all hours while the adults were drinking and dancing away.'

Simon glugged his martini. 'Olivia, my wife tells me that when you were teenagers here—' He broke off, distracted by a young woman walking towards them. The clingy fabric of her black, strapless dress showed off a slim, boyish figure, at odds with her full breasts.

'Stop staring.' Libby gave Simon a playful slap on the arm. 'My husband is not the most subtle of men.'

A long swathe of black hair lay over the woman's bony shoulder. As she passed their table, Julian saw a shaved patch on the other side of her head. He also noticed the tattoo on her lean, tanned arm. A long twist of red roses interspersed with thorny black stems.

'Don't worry, wife,' Simon said, when the girl sat at the reserved table behind them, 'she looks a bit too racy for me.'

At the other end of the table, Gabriel removed his glasses. His cool blue eyes remained impassive, but Julian could see his interest in the girl.

'Time for your present, darling.' From her handbag, Olivia produced a small square box wrapped in silver paper.

'Thank you.' Beneath the wrapping, Julian found a black box with scuffed corners. He lifted the hinged lid to reveal a chunky watch with a thick strap of stainless-steel links. Roman numerals decorated the black face.

Simon gave an appreciative whistle. Libby clapped her hands like an excited child.

'That is sweet, my friend,' said Gabriel, giving the watch a cursory glance before looking again at the woman at the next table.

'It's a Rolex Sea Dweller. It belonged to my father.' Olivia lifted the watch from the box. 'Put it on, darling.'

Julian slipped his left hand through the strap. He snapped the clasp shut and found the watch a perfect fit.

'I had a link taken out,' Olivia said.

He held up his wrist. The watch sat heavy on him. The weight of quality, of luxury. What a gift to give him.

'A classic vintage piece,' Simon said. 'Worth a lot of money these days.'

'I love it,' Julian said. Did he? Would he ever get used to the weight of it?

'He was so much fun, your father,' said Libby.

'He was.' Olivia smiled. 'Not an easy man to have as a father, but fun, certainly.'

'Now, the watch is all well and good, Olivia,' said Simon, 'but is it enough to satisfy a man's midlife crisis? Shouldn't you have got him a sports car instead?'

'Stop teasing,' Libby said. 'Just because you bought a Porsche when you were fifty, like the cliché you are.'

Simon chuckled. 'Had to stop driving it a few years ago. Played havoc with my sciatica.'

'Julian isn't like that,' Libby said. 'Are you?'

'I don't really like driving,' Julian said. Libby and Simon showed no sign of remembering the car accident that had paralysed his wife and left him a nervous driver, but Olivia slipped a hand into his, her fingers stroking the pristine watch face.

'Excuse me, folks. Nature calls.' Gabriel rose from the table and headed into the hotel. Olivia ordered another round of drinks. Talk turned to Simon's recent sailing trip – the beauty of the Balearic Islands, his despair at the 'great unwashed' soiling it.

'Someone's found a friend,' Olivia said.

Julian turned to see Gabriel bending over the young woman's table, bringing his lighter to the cigarette she held clamped between her scarlet lips. What an obvious chat-up move, Julian thought. She could easily have used the box of hotel matches on her table. Gabriel didn't appear to mind. When she gestured to the seat opposite her, he claimed it.

'What about his drink?' Julian said. 'Should I take it over?'

'Leave them to it,' Olivia said. 'Let the young folk enjoy themselves.'

Julian turned his back on Gabriel. He tried to listen in to the conversation on the next table, but Gabriel was too far away and, as his fellow drinkers shed any remaining sobriety, the volume level at his own table increased. Now and then he twisted in his seat and caught a glimpse of Gabriel sipping from a drink the girl must have ordered for him.

'I've got an idea,' he said, after finishing his cocktail. 'Let's go back to the villa.'

'Really?' Olivia said.

'Ooh, yes.' Libby splayed a hand across her tanned chest. 'I'd love to see it again.'

'We've got champagne there and plenty of wine.' Julian rubbed his hands together. 'Let's recreate the old days, get a bit of a party going.'

'That would be fun,' Olivia said.

Simon suggested they get a driver from the hotel to take them there. 'He can come and pick us up later and bring us back.'

'Perfect.' Julian jumped to his feet. 'I'll let Gabriel know it's time to leave.' He hurried over to the next table and tapped Gabriel on the shoulder. 'Sorry to interrupt,' he said, 'but we're about to go.'

'Oh, okay.' Gabriel pointed to his companion. 'Julian, this is Nina. Nina, Julian.'

'Hi, Julian,' Nina said, her English clipped with an accent he couldn't quite place.

'You go on ahead, big guy,' Gabriel said. 'I'm gonna stay here and keep Nina company for a while.'

Julian's stomach dipped. 'But how will you get back?'

'Don't worry about me, my friend.' Gabriel smiled. 'I'm all good.'

* * *

Julian lay on the cream sofa in the living room. According to the heavy, alien Rolex on his left wrist, it was just after 4 a.m. He picked up his glass of water from the floor and gulped it back. A headache fizzed behind his eyes. He'd had far too much to drink, but not as much as Olivia.

At some point during last night's party on the pool terrace, Julian had stopped counting his wife's drinks. She'd topped up everyone's glasses with champagne at regular intervals. Julian had sipped from his slowly, too distracted by thoughts of Gabriel to let himself go. He'd endured hours of dull conversation about sailing and politics with Simon and several displays of uncoordinated dancing from Libby and Olivia, who'd screamed like teenagers when Julian had played a selection of eighties hits on his laptop for them. He'd cringed as Olivia gyrated to Duran Duran's 'Hungry Like the Wolf', her cleavage on the verge of escape from her dress. Their guests left sometime after 1 a.m. As Julian had helped Olivia upstairs, she'd told him in slurred words that she wanted him, but, to his relief, she'd passed out as soon as he'd deposited her on the bed.

He succumbed to fitful dozing until the first breaths of another hot, still day stole through the shutters of the living room window. Before long, he heard the scrape of the front door opening and the slam as it shut. He hauled himself off the sofa. Time to tell Gabriel he'd had some time to think and had decided they should go their separate ways. After all, it made sense that Gabriel would want to sleep with a younger, more attractive person. Nothing surprising about that. They would have to accept their incompatibility in a mature fashion.

After tiptoeing from the living room to the bedroom to check Olivia was still asleep, he crept downstairs. He found the door to the guest room ajar and Gabriel inside, casting off his crumpled shirt.

'Hey, big guy,' Gabriel said.

Julian closed the door. When he spotted an angry red bite mark on Gabriel's chest, just above the left nipple, all hope of mature behaviour deserted him. 'Enjoy yourself?' he said.

'I guess.' Gabriel yawned. 'What did Olivia think? Bet she was pleased to see me getting some action?'

When they'd arrived back at the villa last night, Julian had expressed concern over Gabriel getting picked up by a stranger. Olivia had told him not to be silly. *Don't you want the boy to have a bit of fun?*

'Is that why you did it?' Julian said.

'You jealous, big guy?'

Julian gazed at the bite mark. 'I'll leave her,' he said. 'I'll leave Olivia.'

Gabriel stretched himself out on the bed, his hipbones protruding from the waistband of his jeans. 'You really wanna be free?'

Julian felt a familiar sensation. A door deep inside clicking open. 'Yes.'

'You'd better mean it.'

Julian hesitated. 'What about tomorrow? You're supposed to be going.'

'Relax, man.' Gabriel folded his hands behind his head. 'Leave Olivia to me.'

34

The following morning, Julian stirred to find his wife sprawled beside him, a pillow over her head.

'Olivia?' Fear snaked through him. 'Olivia?'

'What?' she said, her voice thick with sleep.

'Nothing. I... why have you got a pillow over your head?'

'You were snoring. All night.'

She rolled away from him, one hand clamping the pillow in place. He slid out of bed and padded downstairs. In the guest room, he found Gabriel's packed rucksack lying on the unmade bed but no sign of Gabriel. In the kitchen, he found a note propped against the kettle.

Taken the bike into the village to get us some pastries. G.

Julian poured himself a glass of orange juice and took it outside, the terrace tiles already warm beneath his feet. He sat at the table, eyes dazzled by the azure brilliance of sea and sky. Gabriel was supposed to be taking the bus to Palma in the early afternoon and, from there, the evening ferry to Ibiza. Yesterday, all three of them had survived their hangovers and sleep deprivation by napping in the shade by the pool. When Julian did manage to get Gabriel alone for a few minutes after dinner, the younger man had promised him they would talk the next day.

He sat and waited, hopeful Gabriel would return before Olivia awoke. They needed some kind of plan. If Gabriel did go to Ibiza, that would give him time to decide how to tell Olivia he was leaving her. It was a scene he couldn't even imagine. Sitting on the terrace, caressed by the warm air and gazing at the sensational view, he wondered why he would even want to leave. Once again, he thought of the pre-nuptial agreement. Even without it, would Olivia be obliged to give him money after such a short marriage?

'Morning, darling.' Olivia appeared behind him. When she bent down to peck his cheek, he caught a waft of minty toothpaste. 'How lovely,' she said when he explained Gabriel had gone to fetch them breakfast.

She made them a pot of coffee and checked her emails on her phone as they drank it. Julian pretended to be interested in the list of raffle prizes she read out for a Women Against Sex Slavery dinner in September.

'What time is it?' he asked. 'Gabriel should be back by now.'

Olivia glanced at his wrist. 'Why haven't you got your new watch on?'

'I don't want to damage it. Thought I'd save it for best.' He'd put it back in its scuffed box and left it on his bedside table.

'Don't be silly. I'd like you to wear it.'

'What if it gets damaged?' He'd already done some online research into the watch's value. The model he now owned, known as a Great White, was very collectable. He'd seen a number of them priced at £40,000 in online auctions.

'It's fully insured,' Olivia said.

'Fine. I'll wear it.'

Olivia checked her phone. 'It's nearly 9.30.'

'It can't be taking him this long to buy pastries.'

'Maybe he bumped into Nina in Deià?'

'She's gone. Remember?'

Last night, over a dinner of spaghetti and pesto, Olivia had quizzed Gabriel about his conquest. Where was she from? What did she do? Gabriel had provided some basic information. Nina was the twenty-five-year-old daughter of a German father and a Spanish mother, and she'd grown up in Berlin. She'd been in Mallorca almost a year, working in bars and nightclubs in Palma, and now she was about to go off travelling. She wanted to be a novelist and had come for another trip to Deià because her favourite erotic writer, Anaïs Nin, had stayed there. According to Gabriel, she'd decided to treat herself to a night at La Residencia before heading across to the east coast the next day.

'Oh yes,' Olivia said to Julian. 'Gabriel said she was going to Pollença, didn't he?'

'Can't say I recall.'

'Although he didn't seem too sure about her plans.'

'Why should he be? It was only a one-night stand.'

Another half-hour passed. Upon hearing the faint buzz of the entryphone, Julian leapt from his chair and dashed through the villa to the front door. When he opened the gates, a small white van with the La Residencia logo on the side drove into the courtyard. The smiling driver leapt out and presented Julian with an extravagant bouquet of flowers.

'Thank you,' he said. The card tucked inside contained a gushing thank you message for Olivia from Libby and Simon.

The gates closed as the van pulled out onto the access road. Julian shut the front door with his foot, the pungent lilies tickling his face.

As he headed down the hallway, the phone rang. He hurried back and picked up the chunky white receiver.

'Hello,' he said. A male voice with a Birmingham accent asked to speak to Julian Griggs. 'That's me. I'm Julian Griggs.'

'You're Gabriel's mate?'

'Yes. Why, what's happened?'

'There's been a bit of an accident.'

35

Three days later, Julian sat at the table on the top terrace, his laptop in front of him. He stared at the open document on the screen. His contact from *Caring World* magazine had sent on five letters for the agony aunt slot he'd agreed to fill, and he had a week to get the replies written. The first came from a woman caring for her dementia-stricken mother. The only day care centre that could cope with the mother's challenging behaviour had recently closed down. The last line of the letter made Julian's pulse flutter.

I'm at the end of my tether. What should I do?

He looked to the end of the table where Olivia sat, fingers pecking at her iPad. Her lips were pressed together in a thin line, a clear reminder she was still annoyed with him.

He looked back at the letter and started writing his reply:

Take a deep breath. It is vital to examine your situation rationally, so that fatigue and frustration don't force you to do anything rash.

A rhythmical tapping drifted through from the kitchen. Tap, pause, tap. Julian and Olivia turned their heads towards it.

'Hey, guys.' Gabriel hoisted himself through the doors, supported by a pair of metal crutches. 'Another amazing day, right? Will this sunshine ever end?'

'Morning,' Olivia said, in clipped tones. 'Sleep well?'

'I was like, totally out of it.' Gabriel hauled himself to the head of the table, his bandaged left foot hovering off the ground. He flung himself into a chair. 'Those painkillers the hospital gave me are the real deal.'

'How's the ankle?' Julian said.

'Like, super tender.' Gabriel attempted to pull the chair beside him closer but couldn't reach it. With a sigh, Julian got up and brought the chair near enough for Gabriel to rest his injured foot on. 'Thanks, man.'

'You might as well get Gabriel some coffee while you're up,' Olivia said.

'That'd be awesome,' Gabriel said. 'I guess I should eat something too, right? Soak up the drugs. Just bread or something.'

Julian closed the lid of his laptop and stepped from the heat of late morning into the cool, dark interior of the villa. In the kitchen, he put a pot of coffee on the hob and cut several slices of the baguette Olivia had picked up from Deià earlier. A tremor ran through his hands as he wielded the bread knife. Only three days into his guest's extended stay and his nerves were already fraying. His limbs were heavy, his mind sluggish. He craved time alone with Gabriel. He craved the sense of lightness and possibility only Gabriel could provide.

The accident had involved Gabriel on the bike and a middle-aged couple from Birmingham in a Ford Fiesta. The Fiesta had pulled out from the car park in Deià just as Gabriel rode past. No one's fault, according to Gabriel. The bike's handlebars had wobbled and he'd lost control of it. After the collision, the Birmingham couple, Rob and June, had insisted on taking him to the A & E department of the Sones Pases University Hospital in Palma, where a doctor had diagnosed a bad sprain to the left ankle. After Rob and June had dropped Gabriel back at the villa, Julian had helped him into the guest room and onto the bed and fetched extra pillows to keep the injured ankle raised.

'Did you do it on purpose?' he'd asked.

'What do you think?'

'You cycled out in front of a car?'

Gabriel had smiled. 'That's how much I wanna be around you, big guy.'

Julian finished preparing the breakfast and carried it out to Gabriel on a tray. He topped up his wife's cup with fresh coffee and kissed the top of her head. She ignored the gesture, too busy staring at her phone.

'Thanks, man.' Gabriel sipped his coffee. 'I gotta say, I really appreciate you guys letting me stay on until this thing heals up. Truly.'

'It's the least we could do,' Olivia said with a curt smile.

'Absolutely,' Julian said. It hadn't taken him long to guilt Olivia into letting Gabriel stay. After all, he'd pointed out, she should never have encouraged him to use the bike in the first place. Not when it was in such bad condition. What if the accident had been more serious? She'd agreed but had made it clear Julian would have to look after Gabriel; she had no intention of waiting on him.

'You'll have to entertain yourself today, I'm afraid,' Olivia told Gabriel. 'Julian and I have work to get on with.'

'And we might take a drive out somewhere later,' Julian said, keen to keep Olivia happy. 'If you fancy that, my love?'

She nodded, her eyes flicking between phone and iPad.

'All good with me.' Gabriel tore an oval of baguette in two. 'You guys do what you gotta do. You won't even know I'm here.'

Julian stared at the grazed skin on Gabriel's left arm. A raw, red ladder descending from his T-shirt sleeve. Gabriel's reckless antics had given him a fright. Reminded him how far his lover would go to get what he wanted. Yet, as his eyes lingered on the scar, he had an urge to lick it. He hadn't touched Gabriel for days, not properly. What was he going to do? Could he really leave Olivia?

A crescendo of pealing bells interrupted his thoughts. Olivia picked up her phone.

'Yes, hello, Liberto.' She pushed back her chair and stood up. 'Thanks for returning my call.'

'Ask him about a plumber,' Julian said, but she had already turned away from him.

Julian and Gabriel sat in silence until the slap of Olivia's sandals had faded away.

'See,' Gabriel said, 'told you to leave her to me.'

'I feel bad for taking advantage. She's a decent woman.'

'Buys us more time though, right? We can get a plan together.'

'I can't just walk out on her.'

'Chill out, big guy. No one's saying you gotta do that.'

'I thought—'

'Maybe we don't need to rush this. It might take a little while.'

Julian sagged with relief. 'Exactly. That's what I mean. We've only been married just over a year. I doubt—'

'So, for me, it's obvious. I should come to London.'

'Really?' Could that work, Julian wondered? If Gabriel could find a job and a place to live, they could see each other in secret for a while. A few years even, until his marriage had lasted a respectable length of time.

'I come to London and you rent me a place to stay for a while.

Give me a little money to live off, just until we can figure this thing out.'

'Gabriel. I—'

'It's not like I need much. I live a simple life, right?'

Julian picked up Olivia's purposeful approach and held a finger to his lips.

'All good?' he said when she returned to the terrace.

'Yes.' She resumed her seat and picked up her iPad.

Tension gathered in Julian's forehead. What Gabriel had suggested was a dream. A dream he could not afford. He opened his laptop and tried to concentrate on the dilemma of the poor woman in the letter. *I'm at the end of my tether. What should I do?*

'Hey, big guy,' Gabriel said, 'any chance you can get my cigarettes from my room?'

'Yes. In a minute. I need to—'

'I'd kinda like to lie by the pool. Will you give me a piggy-back down there?'

'Let me finish this first.'

'Whatever, man. No rush.'

Julian sighed and attacked the keyboard with jittery fingers.

It is crucial during this stressful time that you do not make any decisions you will come to regret.

* * *

Mid-afternoon. Julian sat alone on the top terrace, swigging a cold beer, wide awake despite the soporific heat. Olivia had retired upstairs for a siesta and on the pool terrace, out of sight, lay Gabriel. Julian had carried him down the rocky steps earlier, irritated and aroused as Gabriel had nibbled his earlobe. Once settled on the sunbed, Gabriel had grabbed Julian's hand and slipped it inside his shorts. Julian had resisted and warned Gabriel they had to be cautious. There would be no point having a plan if Olivia found out about them.

'Besides,' he'd said, unable to resist a dig, 'it might not be safe, considering you've been sleeping around.'

'No worries there,' Gabriel had assured him, 'Nina was all about the safe sex.'

Julian thought back over Gabriel's offer to come to London. The younger man's nerve annoyed him. The assumption he would support him. He would have to take some of the blame for that, he realised. He'd flashed his lifestyle around in order to impress, and what else could he expect from someone like Gabriel? Someone with Gabriel's background.

He drained the rest of his beer. At some point, he knew, he would have to disappoint his lover. He couldn't afford to keep him, no matter how much he might want to. Imagine the life he could lead if he had greater resources of his own. He fantasised about an amicable divorce in which Olivia gave him the villa. What long, lazy days he would spend here with Gabriel. Sleeping, eating, fucking.

The fantasy unnerved him. He reached for his laptop and opened it. He'd answered all but one of the letters, filling his replies with assurances that caring for someone was a valuable and meaningful occupation, even if society failed to recognise it as such. *Find small moments of joy in every day and let these be your reward.* He wondered who he was trying to convince.

He checked his emails and found one from a woman called Maxine Price, an editorial assistant at *Woman's Life* magazine, asking if he would like to feature in an article entitled 'The Good Man Guide'? The piece, scheduled to appear in their December issue, would showcase men involved in charity work. Maxine explained they'd had to drop one of their chosen men due to allegations of sexual harassment. How would Julian like to take his place?

According to Maxine, her mum, a fan of the Heart of the Nation Awards, had suggested him.

Invigorated by the flattering offer, he replied straight away to accept and passed on his phone number to Maxine as she'd requested. Wait until he told Olivia. His wife had spent most of the day upstairs on her phone. Business with David the accountant, she'd told him, and she had to speak to a charity director about an application to the Pearson Foundation.

He hurried indoors, feeling grounded and purposeful for the first time in weeks. At the top of the stairs, he found their bedroom door closed. He could hear Olivia moving around the room, the soles of her Birkenstocks clipping the tiles.

'I'm sure you could make good use of the money,' she said.

Julian hovered in the hallway, uncertain whether to interrupt.

'Fine. That's my limit, though.' Olivia paused. 'Yes, two separate bank transfers.'

Leaving her to her phone call, he trudged downstairs. He couldn't help feeling resentful at the thought of another charity getting a considerable donation from his wife. If only she wasn't so focused on giving all her money away. What was the point of her having so much if she wouldn't let herself enjoy it?

Tempted by the guest room's open door, he slipped inside and sat on the bed. He couldn't resist picking up Gabriel's pillow and pressing it to his chest. Olivia's footsteps paced above his head. What *was* the point of her having so much if she felt guilty about it? If it had become a burden to her. What *was* the point?

36

The following day, Julian and Olivia left Gabriel alone in the villa and drove to Sóller. After parking the Fiat in a shady side street, they took the wooden tram down to Port de Sóller, where Olivia had booked them in for lunch at Kingfisher, a popular seafood restaurant overlooking the bustling harbour. Under the shade of a pristine white parasol, they ate oysters and grilled prawns and sipped a crisp, dry Sauvignon Blanc.

'This really is the life,' Olivia said, licking garlic butter from her fingers.

'It is,' agreed Julian, although he wished he was at the villa with Gabriel. He bit into a prawn but tasted only the ashy flavour of Gabriel's mouth. He held the glass of Sauvignon beneath his nose but detected only the citrusy scent of Gabriel's freshly washed hair.

He tried to concentrate as his wife shared her memories of childhood visits to the port and trips out on the yacht her father used to moor there. At least he had her back on side. His news about the magazine article had won her over.

'We really did have so much fun on that boat,' she said.

'Sounds idyllic.' He stared at his wife's stylish cat-eye sunglasses and realised they didn't suit her cheery, round visage at all.

When Olivia's mobile rang, she excused herself and walked a little way along the promenade to take the call. A few minutes into it, she looked back his way and blew him a kiss. He blew her one back. He deserved to be in the 'Good Man Guide' she'd told him. That's what he was, a good man. As he sipped his wine, he couldn't help thinking about the man he'd replaced. The man no longer deemed to be good. A fall from grace could happen to anyone at any time, he thought. He realised the amicable, generous divorce he'd fantasised about yesterday would never happen. If he left Olivia for Gabriel, no one would think well of him. Not because he was leaving his wife for a man; most people wouldn't care about that any more. He would look bad for leaving a good, respectable person for a younger, less respectable one. He would look bad for exchanging a selfless life of charitable work for a selfish life of freedom and pleasure.

'Sorry, darling,' Olivia said when she returned.

'Business?'

'Isn't it always?'

After lunch, they wandered hand-in-hand along the promenade, stopping to buy gelato, which they ate on a bench overlooking the sea. This really *was* the life, Julian told himself. This *was* the life.

Olivia's good mood endured. She didn't seem annoyed when they returned home to find Gabriel asleep in a chair on the top terrace, an empty bottle of expensive Shiraz on the table in front of him. Later, over a light omelette supper, she even encouraged him to open another. Her kindness kindled Julian's guilt, and, once they were in bed, he pulled her towards him and placed a line of kisses from her neck to her navel. When his lips ventured to the prickly regrowth of her pubic hair, she pulled his head up.

'Come here,' she said, 'let me play with you.'

It took her a while to coax him from flaccidity, but she wouldn't give up. Julian gasped as her wide, dry palms pumped him to the brink of pain. Hurting him in her enthusiastic attempt to bring him pleasure. Too scared of offending her by asking her to stop, he bit his lower lip and pictured Gabriel sprawled out naked in the guest room below.

'That's it,' she said when his climax finally came. 'That's my little mouse.'

* * *

When Julian finished his swim the following morning, he hauled himself out of the pool just as Olivia appeared from the olive grove on her way back from her walk.

'Gorgeous out there,' she said, 'didn't see a soul.' She strode over and wrapped her arms around his dripping body.

'You'll get wet,' he said.

She flashed him a coy smile. 'Is that a promise?'

'Naughty.' Keen to avoid another zealous molestation, Julian kissed her nose and wriggled out of her embrace.

After breakfast, she inspected the paltry contents of the fridge and told Julian she needed to go into Deià to get some supplies.

'Shall I come in with you?' Julian said, eager to appear attentive. An anticipatory tingle ran along his spine when she refused his offer.

Gabriel was still asleep when the Fiat pulled out of the villa's driveway. Julian stood at the guest room door, marvelling as always at the younger man's smooth skin, taut abdomen and sizeable cock, already half-erect. Gabriel lay on his back, hair spread across one pillow and his injured foot resting on another. Julian bent over him, and, as he had done with his wife the previous night, kissed from neck to navel and then beyond. Gabriel stirred but did not stop him.

'That's it, big guy,' he said, his voice drowsy.

Julian took his time waking him up, savouring every moan that came from Gabriel's parted lips. Lost in the moment, he found the dizzying lightness he craved. It didn't take long for Gabriel to surrender himself with a startled cry.

'Come here,' Gabriel said, when he'd recovered. Julian accepted the invitation of the younger man's open arms and they lay together in the strange, heavy quiet that follows sex.

'So,' Gabriel said eventually. 'Did you think any more about stuff?'

'Stuff?'

'Me coming to London. Good plan, right?'

'Maybe.'

'Only maybe?'

'It's not that simple.' Julian propped himself up on one elbow. 'I can't afford to pay for you like that. I don't have that sort of money.'

'You seem to be doing pretty good to me.'

Julian sat up with his back to Gabriel. His neck flushed with shame when he confessed the truth about his salary from the Helen Griggs Awards. 'I make very little else apart from that,' he said. 'Olivia's the one with the money.'

Silence. Julian's throat constricted, trapping his breath. Gabriel's fingers tiptoed across his back.

'That's why you gotta get divorced, right?'

'That will take time. Unless we forget about any money and I leave now. Cut my losses and start again. With you.'

The idea excited him. He wouldn't tell Olivia about Gabriel. No need. He could say he'd never really recovered from Helen's death, and that he had rushed into their marriage too soon.

'Seriously?' Gabriel said. 'That sounds like a good idea to you?'

'Why not?'

'Man, I know what it's like to just get by. I won't live like that. I don't wanna have to steal and deal for the rest of my life. I want more for us. Don't you want more?'

'We could both get jobs. I'm sure we—'

'Hold on. Seriously? You've done your time, big guy. The world owes you one.'

'Then come to London and get a job for a while until I can sort things out. What's so bad about that? It will give you a purpose.'

'This is bullshit.' Gabriel sat up and shifted himself off the bed with no sign of any impediment from his bandaged foot. 'Total BS.' He picked up his swimming shorts from the floor and stepped into them.

'Gabriel, listen.'

'Screw you.' Gabriel grabbed his crutches and manoeuvred himself out of the room and into the hallway. Julian, paralysed with anxiety, stayed sitting on the bed, twisting the sheet in his hands. What was he going to do with Gabriel? How could he get him to understand?

He forced himself up and hurried through to the kitchen. The terrace doors were open. Gabriel sat with his injured foot up on the table, lighting a cigarette.

'Come on,' Julian said, sitting opposite him, 'be reasonable.'

Smoke trailed from Gabriel's nostrils. 'Me? I gotta be reasonable?'

'You've got to rejoin society at some point.'

'When you've lived outside it as long as I have, it's tough to get back in.'

'But not impossible.'

'I took a huge risk for you, man.' Gabriel shook his head. 'Huge.'

Julian shivered, despite the heat. 'What are you saying?'

Gabriel's cool blue eyes examined him. 'I'm saying I took a risk. You gotta take risks to get what you want, right?'

'Yes, but—'

'Like I said, I did what I had to do and you did what you had to do. Now it's time, man. It's time for us to get what we deserve.'

'Darling.' Olivia's voice floated out to the terrace. 'I'm back.' Seconds later, Julian detected the clacking sound of her progress across the kitchen tiles.

'Hello, my love,' he said when she burst onto the terrace, a wide smile on her face. She stepped clear of the doors and made a sweeping gesture with her right arm, like a magician presenting the crescendo of some trick.

A slender figure in a strappy black sundress stepped through the doors.

'Look who I bumped into,' Olivia said.

'Nina.' Gabriel swung his leg down from the table. 'Well, how about that?'

37

'Why did you invite her here?' Julian asked, as he filled the bottom half of the coffee pot with water.

'Why not?' Olivia arranged the four slices of almond cake she'd brought back from Deià on a serving plate. 'When I told her about Gabriel's accident, she seemed concerned. I thought she might as well come and see him.'

'Did she approach you or did you approach her?' Julian said.

'We bumped into each other on the street. I told you.'

Laughter burst in from the terrace. Gabriel's laughter. Julian had expected more awkwardness from both him and Nina. After all, they hadn't seen each other since the night at La Residencia, and Gabriel had shown no interest in keeping in touch with her.

'I thought she was leaving Mallorca?' he said, snatching up a mug from the draining board and scouring it with a tea towel.

'She is. Not sure when. She said she'd decided to come back to Deià for a few days.' Olivia opened a wooden drawer and produced four silver cake forks.

'If Gabriel had wanted to see her again, they'd have kept in touch,' he said.

'You heard what he told her just now. If she'd given him her number, he would have called her.'

An excuse Nina had dismissed with a knowing smile.

'She's very beautiful, isn't she?' Olivia said.

Julian shrugged. 'In an obvious way.'

When he returned to the terrace with the coffee pot, mugs and jug of milk on a tray, he found Nina sitting with Gabriel's bandaged foot in her lap. Her cupped palms hovered over his ankle.

'She's giving me some Reiki healing,' Gabriel said. 'How about that?'

The pair looked too at ease in each other's company for Julian's liking. Too familiar. He placed the tray on the table.

'Coffee, Nina?' he said.

'That would be great,' she said, traces of her German accent audible in her substitution of z for th and v for w. She was striking, thought Julian. He couldn't deny that. Even her partially shaved head, plentiful ear piercings and tattoo couldn't obscure her conventional beauty. Pale olive skin, amber, feline eyes and long, graceful limbs.

As he poured the coffee, Olivia materialised with another tray. She handed out blue ceramic side plates with matching napkins and the gleaming silver forks.

'Wow,' Gabriel said when she placed the cake at the centre of the table. 'Too much, seriously. Nina, didn't I tell you these guys were the best?'

'You did, for sure.' She lifted her hands from his ankle and brushed her palms together, as if removing some invisible substance. 'That's enough for now.'

'Like, I swear my ankle feels better already,' Gabriel said. 'Truly.'

'Don't be a dick.' Nina made no attempt to remove his foot from her lap, and Gabriel appeared happy to leave it there.

'Right, everyone,' Olivia said. 'Tuck in.'

Nina accepted the coffee and cake without a thank you. Julian imagined she was the kind of young woman used to being waited on. Used to her looks getting her preferential treatment. She had on the same style of oversized sunglasses worn by Olivia; her narrow face much better suited to them.

'So, Nina,' Olivia said, 'you were saying Deià had inspired a new story for you?'

Always the perfect hostess, thought Julian. Showing interest in her guest, keeping the conversation going.

'For sure,' Nina said, 'that's why I came back.'

'Let me guess, it's a story about a hot young American guy, right?' said Gabriel.

Nina rolled her eyes. 'It really is not.'

'And what about your travel plans?' Olivia said. 'When are you next heading off?'

'Sixteen days. I'm counting them, for sure.' Nina sipped her coffee but left her cake untouched. 'I've decided to go to Chile.'

'Awesome,' Gabriel said, through a mouthful of cake.

'My Opa, my grandfather, died six months ago and I inherited a little money,' Nina said. 'Enough to take some time out and travel.'

'Why Chile?' Julian asked, his mood lifting at the news of her impending departure.

'My mother spent time there before she died.'

'You lost your mom?' Gabriel said. 'That's harsh.'

Nina shrugged. 'There's this cool artistic community not far from Santiago. I'd like to hang out there for a while and work out what I want to do next.'

'Sounds like a wonderful adventure,' Olivia said. 'I went to Chile in 93. Loved it.'

'Good to travel while you can,' Julian said. 'Not everyone gets the chance.'

No one noticed the self-pity in his voice.

'Yeah, it's cool,' Nina said. 'I packed up all my stuff and sent most of it back to Berlin. Now I just got my rucksack and I can hang out and enjoy Mallorca until I go.'

'Where you staying?' Gabriel asked.

'A little place in the village with its own roof terrace. Basic but very cute.' Her slender hands rested on Gabriel's shin. 'You want to see it?'

Gabriel smiled. 'Love to.'

Julian's stomach clenched at Gabriel's suggestive tone.

'Good idea, Gabriel,' Olivia said. 'Have a change of scene.'

'I have my jeep here,' Nina said. 'We can take a drive and then eat lunch at mine?'

Gabriel clapped his hands together. 'Let's do it.'

38

Late morning. Julian pushed off from the shallow end of the pool. Kick, pull, breathe. Kick, pull, breathe. Speedy breaststroke for ten lengths before pausing in the shallow end to catch his breath. As his heart rate settled, he plucked several rogue pinecones from the cold green water and threw them onto the side of the pool.

Two dragonflies, entwined, skimmed the water's surface before darting upwards. The same pair he'd seen at the start of the holiday? He still couldn't tell if they were fighting or flirting.

Two sleepless nights had passed for Julian since Gabriel had left for a drive with Nina. As he and Olivia had waved goodbye to the young couple from the front door, Nina had revved up the engine of her silver open-top jeep and a screech of tyres had accompanied her exit through the gates. When they hadn't returned by early evening, Julian had expressed concern. What if something had happened? What if they'd had an accident? Olivia had smiled and said she doubted they'd even bothered going for a drive. Not long afterwards, Julian had answered the landline to find Gabriel on the other end. He'd pretended not to care when Gabriel announced his intention to spend the night at Nina's, a pretence

Gabriel picked up on right away. *I'm only doing this for us, big guy. Trust me.*

Julian turned onto his back and floated towards the centre of the pool, the water lapping at his ears. *Trust me.* If Gabriel had intended to improve relations with Olivia, he'd succeeded, thought Julian. Olivia seemed delighted to have her husband to herself, but to Julian, Gabriel's absence felt like a punishment. An enforced period of isolation for him to think about what might lay ahead.

I took a huge risk for you, man.

Gabriel's words taunted him. Had he imagined the hint of threat they concealed? The water beneath him cooled as he drifted towards the deep end. Gabriel would gain nothing from betraying their secret, but Julian resented him for weaponising the past. Over the past couple of days, aching for the release only Gabriel could give, he'd begun to despise the younger man. The way any addict despises the focus of the addiction.

His anger had seeped out the previous evening, as he and Olivia had sipped crystal flutes of Cava on the top terrace before dinner. Olivia was reading him an article from her phone about a women's collective in Mumbai that rescued and housed victims of sex-trafficking, but he couldn't shake an image of Nina and Gabriel curled up in bed together, Nina reading aloud erotic fiction by that writer she professed to admire, or, worse still, reading out some of her own efforts at the genre. Amateur, solipsistic efforts, Julian had thought. She'd seemed to him exactly the kind of young woman who would write about her own experience and expect everyone else to find it fascinating.

'He doesn't even have a toothbrush,' he'd said.

Olivia had looked up from her phone, confused.

'Gabriel,' he said. 'He doesn't have a toothbrush with him.'

'I doubt he's concerned about a toothbrush.'

'He hasn't phoned to say whether he's coming back tonight.'

'Why should he? We're not his parents.'

'It's bad manners. It's disrespectful to us as his hosts.'

'He's behaving exactly as a good-looking young man like him would behave.' Olivia's eyes had narrowed. 'I wouldn't expect anything else from a character like Gabriel.'

Julian exited the pool via the metal ladder at the deep end, shedding water as he padded out of the shade of the tall pines. With a sigh, he noted the rockery wall had collapsed again. So much for his handyman efforts. Too rattled to deal with it now, he pulled a sunbed into the sun's glare and flung himself down on his back. The moisture on his skin evaporated in the heat. He knew he should apply more suntan lotion, but he had an urge to burn himself, to have some visible sign of his inner turmoil to show Gabriel when he returned.

It's time for us to get what we deserve.

Julian put on his sunglasses and gazed at the blue and cloudless sky. The eye that never closed. He had given a lot of thought to how he and Gabriel could get what they deserved. At night, in bed, with Olivia asleep beside him, he'd wrestled with the impossibility of his situation. He thought it unlikely that divorcing his wife would bring any substantial financial gain. Rather, he would end up cutting off his access to his current lifestyle. He'd considered researching divorce law online or contacting a solicitor to get an opinion, but he didn't wish to leave a trail for his wife or anyone else to discover. If Gabriel could wait a few years, he might stand a better chance of compensation, but how could he support Gabriel in the meantime? He could max out his credit card, but what then? He'd considered taking a bigger salary from the Helen Griggs Awards, but that would have to be approved by all the trustees, Olivia included, and she would want to know why he needed more money and what he needed it for. As for the funds his charity held in its bank account, he could take none of it. All outgoings had to be approved by the trustees, and either David or Arnold would soon spot any discrepancy in the accounts. He'd even considered submitting a fake application for money from a fictional cause but had soon dismissed the idea. He and the board of trustees always subjected all applicants to a thorough vetting process.

A low droning noise near his left ear startled him. 'Christ.' He sat up and swatted away a large wasp. Blood drained from his head. The persistent insect darted back and landed on his shin. He flicked it away and got to his feet, groggy with heat. He needed to sit in the shade and drink something cold. He needed to sleep but suspected he wouldn't be able to until Gabriel returned.

Covering his head with his towel, he made his way across the flagstones. Halfway up the rocky steps to the villa, he heard Olivia's voice coming from the top terrace and stopped to listen.

'I appreciate your advice, David,' she said, 'but I know what I'm doing.'

A dog barked in the distance, as if trying to warn Olivia of his presence.

'It is my money,' she said. What came next, Julian didn't catch. His wife's voice faded, and he guessed she'd returned indoors.

My money.

'That accountant of yours giving you hassle?' he asked, when he found Olivia carving up the stale end of a baguette in the kitchen. 'I overheard you talking,' he added when she frowned in response.

'He's trying to put me off an investment I want to make.' The baguette splintered into crumbs beneath her assault. 'He's very risk averse.'

'Sometimes you have to take risks to get what you want,' Julian said. 'Right?'

Olivia nodded thoughtfully. 'Yes, darling. Sometimes you do.'

* * *

At around 5.30 p.m., they drove to Deià. Olivia had found out about an event at the shop of a local ceramic artist. Free drinks and a chance to buy some of the pottery at a reduced price. Julian had no desire to go but, for Olivia's sake, he faked enthusiasm about seeking out new serving bowls for the villa.

'Gabriel should have left us a phone number,' he said, as Olivia reversed the Fiat into a space in the car park near La Residencia. 'We could have picked him up while we're here.'

'If he wanted us to fetch him, he would call.' Olivia switched off the engine.

'He'd better not ring later asking for a lift,' Julian said. 'Why should we run around after him?'

They strolled into the village, Julian's deck shoes pinching his toes. He'd worn them as an insult to Gabriel, along with his drab, beige chinos, a white shirt and his resurrected Panama. The Rolex sat weighty on his wrist.

Deià had yet to come alive for the evening. They passed villas with shuttered windows, and Julian imagined people waking from long siestas behind them. That made him think of Gabriel and Nina, and his uneasy stomach churned. He glanced at the buildings clinging to the hillside opposite and below, at the numerous roof terraces on display. He had the oddest feeling he might glimpse himself on one of them, Negroni in hand and Gabriel by his side.

Olivia led him away from the high street, down a set of rough-hewn steps. They passed the entrances to numerous small villas and apartments, all packed close together in the heart of the village. A narrow path led to a wider one. Olivia stopped in front of a two-storey villa covered in red bougainvillea. The placard outside featured a blue pottery fish and the words *Ceramics by Anton*.

Olivia linked her arm in his. 'Let's go shopping.'

Anton's busy store occupied an airy space on the ground floor of the villa. Walls of exposed golden brick. Dark wooden beams overhead. Large glass doors opened out onto a terrace and the sea sparkled in the distance. Bowls and plates and cups jostled for space on long trestle tables. Vases and olive oil dispensers sat on thick wooden shelves. Classical music played at a soothing volume in the background.

Anton looked much as Julian had imagined – a bearded hippy in his sixties with long grey hair and dry, callused feet displayed in Jesus sandals. Baggy linen pants and a crumpled, round-necked linen shirt. He welcomed them in a soft, well-spoken voice and encouraged them to help themselves to a drink.

'Do let me know if you have any questions,' he said.

Julian fetched two peach Bellinis from a table by the open glass doors. 'Bit warm,' he said to Olivia, after taking his first sip.

'Never complain about a free drink, darling.' Olivia glanced around the room. 'Quite a crowd.'

Julian nodded. Middle-aged couples mostly, browsing for holiday mementoes. Some of the local artistic community too, he guessed. A tall, Nordic-looking woman with flowing blonde hair and paint-spattered dungarees and a younger Spanish man with long dreadlocks and black discs in his elongated earlobes.

'Look,' Olivia said, 'isn't that the woman from the Residencia?'

'What woman?'

'The one whose husband was in the wheelchair.'

Julian followed Olivia's gaze. A stately woman with ash-blonde hair was turning over a yellow ceramic plate in her veiny hands. 'Yes,' he said. 'I think that's her.' He guessed her to be in her mid-seventies, although she was well-maintained, her lean frame clothed in a long floral skirt and a white blouse. A string of pearls decorated her slender neck. Julian could imagine her taking Pilates classes and having regular facials.

Olivia turned her attention to the display of bowls on the trestle table in front of them. 'These are lovely.' She tapped the rim of a large white bowl decorated with vivid lemons. 'What about this to keep fruit in?'

'Very nice. Yes.'

'Or this one?' She pointed to the bowl beside it. Oranges instead of lemons.

'Either. I don't mind.'

'Can you at least try to show some interest?' Olivia's Birkenstocks clicked against the terracotta tiles as she stalked off to another table. Julian sighed. If Gabriel hadn't turned up in his life again, he might be enjoying this experience. Instead, he felt pressured to make choices about a life he was no longer sure he wanted.

He found Olivia studying a display of tiles, each one painted with a shoal of iridescent fish. He kissed the back of her neck.

'The lemon bowl,' he said. 'It matches the lemon trees in the garden.'

She pressed herself against him. A gesture of forgiveness. 'What about some of these tiles for the bathroom back home?' she said. 'We can get them sent over.'

'A few might look nice.'

'I'm not sure. You take a proper look and see if you can picture them in situ.'

'Am I fit for a decision of such magnitude?'

'It's your home too, darling.' She clinked her glass against his. 'I'm off to investigate the plates.'

Julian drained the last of his warm, flat Bellini and gazed at the dazzling leaping fish. Would they suit the en suite in the townhouse? He thought of the bathroom's stripped wooden floor, the imposing claw-foot bath and the ornate, gilt-framed mirror above the sink. The first time Olivia had taken him to her grand Bloomsbury home, the size of it had overwhelmed him. Later, alone, he'd browsed property websites and looked at similar houses for sale in the area. One such townhouse was on the market for over five million pounds.

He glanced up and saw Olivia chatting to the woman from the hotel. Libby was right, he thought, his wife couldn't resist a lame duck. He looked down at the tiles, in case she waved him over to join her. The leaping fish blurred in front of his eyes. He imagined himself back in the house in Bloomsbury, standing in their en suite bathroom. He tried to picture the piscine tiles around the sink or on the wall beside the bath but failed. He saw himself leaving the bathroom and stepping into the empty bedroom. The bed he shared with Olivia was neatly made, the silver brocade cushions artfully arranged on top of the pillows. He moved from the bedroom to the landing. Stood and listened. Not a sound. He was all alone. He smiled.

39

We did it! The Wellstood Foundation paid up... the full amount. I've
forwarded the original email and they'll send on an official confirmation
letter next week. Let's schedule a chat soon. I know you'll be delighted.
This is going to be such a boost for us and we can get cracking on that
ever-growing wish list soon as.
Best, Mike.

Julian swatted away the fly crawling across his laptop screen and
scrolled down to read the Wellstood Foundation's email.

We are pleased to confirm a grant of £200,000 to the Helen Griggs
Awards.

Two hundred thousand pounds. Julian removed his reading
glasses and tossed them onto the table. Two hundred thousand.
Instead of delight at the success of his application, he felt frustrated
at the thought of a bank account full of money he could not touch.

The sounds of his wife preparing lunch floated out from the
kitchen to the top terrace. Knife hitting chopping board, the gush of

the kitchen tap. She was singing along to the eighties radio station. 'Let's Dance' by David Bowie.

He stared with watery eyes at the view before him. Another stifling day. A single cloud marked the sky – a thin, white, knobbly streak. It reminded him of a spinal X-ray. The one Helen's consultant had showed him soon after the accident.

Two hundred thousand pounds.

A hot hand of heat pressed against his chest. The heat became Helen's hand, pinning him in place. He realised she had trapped him in death, just as she had in life. He would spend the rest of his years doing good things in her name. Always rewarding others instead of himself.

Slap slap, slap slap. Olivia appeared and placed a plate in front of him. Mozzarella and tomato salad garnished with fresh basil. She set down a plate for herself then bustled back to the kitchen to fetch bread and a jug of cold water.

'Christ, it's hot,' she said when she returned. 'Thirty-six degrees.' She sat down and poured them both a glass of water. 'Help yourself to bread.'

Julian shut his laptop and pushed it aside. 'We got the Wellstood grant.'

Olivia gasped. 'That's wonderful. Helen would be so proud.'

His dead wife's hand pressed harder against his chest. He clawed at his T-shirt as if to dislodge it.

'You'll be able to give Mike some more hours for a start,' Olivia said, 'which will free you up to network and promote. Oh, and when we get home you'll have to meet that freelance fundraiser who did some work for me a few years ago. She's a gem.'

Julian nodded. A brown bird landed beside his plate and risked a peck at one of the soft white discs of cheese before flying off again. He picked up his cutlery and tackled a thick slice of tomato.

'I had a text from Sheila while I was in the kitchen,' Olivia said.

'Sheila?'

'The woman from the Residencia. The one who was in Anton's shop.'

'Oh. Yes.'

'I wanted to introduce you to her, but you'd disappeared.'

'I went outside to look at the view.'

Unable to stop picturing himself alone in the vast townhouse, Julian had grabbed another warm Bellini and escaped into the grounds outside the shop.

'You really should meet her. She's trying to set up a carers' support group in High Wycombe and she'd love some advice.' Olivia cocked her head. 'Is that the buzzer?'

'I'll go and see,' he said, glad for an excuse to escape.

When he lifted the entryphone receiver, he heard the thumping beat of dance music.

'Hello?' he said.

'Hey, big guy, I'm home. D'ya miss me?'

* * *

'I'm telling you guys, Miss Nina Diaz here is a goddam miracle worker. My ankle's almost good as new.'

Gabriel kissed Nina, right in the heart of one of her red roses. She laughed and wriggled in his lap, her short black dress riding up her thighs.

'Are you sure you're comfortable there, Nina?' Julian gestured around the table. 'We've got plenty of chairs.'

'Can you put your full weight on your foot now?' Olivia said, topping up everyone's glasses with the fresh lemonade she'd produced when Gabriel and Nina returned.

'Sometimes,' Gabriel said.

'He still needs the crutches for a little while, for sure,' said Nina.

'Not for long, babe.' Gabriel wrapped his arms around Nina's waist. 'Thanks to you.'

'Well, you both look as though you've had a lovely time,' Olivia said.

Julian couldn't agree. He thought the pair of them looked hollow-eyed from lack of sleep, and he doubted they'd eaten a proper meal for days.

'Is your place comfortable, Nina?' Olivia asked.

'It was okay. You know, not like here. With this view.'

'It's too awesome, right?' Gabriel said.

'Okay.' Julian stood up. 'If you'll excuse me, I've got an important work call to make.'

'Mike?' Olivia said.

'Yes.'

'Julian had wonderful news this morning.' Olivia pressed her hands together. 'He's managed to get a very large grant for the Helen Griggs Awards.'

'Well, ain't that something?' Gabriel smiled at him. 'Nice work, my friend.'

Julian nodded and stalked off. Upstairs, he flung himself on the bed and took slow, deep breaths. When that failed to calm him, he went to the bathroom and splashed his face and neck with cold water. He called Mike's mobile but the call went through to voicemail. After faking a celebratory message, he decided to wait upstairs and make his absence felt.

Twenty minutes later, he returned to the top terrace to find Olivia and Nina clinking their glasses of lemonade together. 'Have I missed something?' he asked.

Olivia pulled out a chair for him and he sat down. 'I've asked them both to stay,' she said.

'Only if this is okay with you, Julian?' Nina said, as if she expected him to object. Gabriel shot him an apologetic look.

'Nina tried to get a few more days at her place,' Olivia said, 'but it was already booked out.'

'Everywhere is booked out,' Nina said.

Olivia nodded. 'Deià always is this time of year.'

'I thought maybe Gabriel would come to Palma with me, but he didn't want to abandon his friends.'

'And you can't live without me, right?' Gabriel nuzzled Nina's neck.

'You are such an asshole,' she said, laughing.

'It's not long until they both head off,' Olivia said.

'Eleven days only, for sure,' said Nina.

'Both head off?' Julian's shoulders tensed. Were they heading off together?

'When Nina leaves for Chile, I'll go to Ibiza,' Gabriel said. 'I got in touch with my buddy there. I can still get a little work before I head back to the States.'

'Sounds like you've got it all sorted,' Julian said.

'Just make yourself at home, Nina,' Olivia said. 'Julian and I insist.'

* * *

He didn't get a chance to speak to Gabriel alone until later that afternoon. After a post-lunch siesta with Gabriel, Nina returned to the top terrace, where Julian and Olivia sat reading. When she told them Gabriel was still sleeping and that she was going for a swim, Olivia volunteered to join her.

'I'll stay here with my book,' Julian said.

'It must be good,' Olivia said, 'you've been glued to it for ages.'

'It's really got me gripped.' He'd only managed a few pages of his spy thriller before his thoughts had roamed to Gabriel. What was he playing at? Did he really intend to leave for Ibiza? Julian had spent the rest of the afternoon pretending to read, his eyes roving side to side across the prose without taking in the words.

When Olivia and Nina set off for their swim, he dashed to the guest room. He found the shutters closed and the overhead fan stirring air saturated with sweat and sex. Gabriel groaned when he switched on the bedside light.

'Dude, seriously, I gotta get some sleep.'

'Nina tiring you out, is she?' It was then he noticed the discarded, knotted condom on the floor beside the bed. 'For God's sake.' He stormed into the bathroom, tore off a piece of toilet paper and used it to pick up the evidence of Gabriel's pleasure.

After disposing of the condom in the bathroom wastebasket, he returned to find Gabriel sitting up in bed, lazily scratching his smooth chest.

'Don't be mad, big guy,' Gabriel said. 'None of this was my idea.'

'Oh, really?'

'Seriously, I never asked her to come looking for me. I thought, okay, a few days of fun, get me out of Olivia's hair for a while, but her staying here was not on the agenda.'

'Well, it is now.'

'I thought she was heading back to Palma. I made it clear I was gonna stay and hang out with you. She just came out with it and asked Olivia. What was I supposed to do? I can't help it if she's into me.'

Julian noticed another rucksack leaning against the wall next to Gabriel's. Two free spirits together. 'Maybe the two of you should head off into the sunset?'

'Are you crazy?'

'I mean, what have you and I got in common? Really?'

'How can you say that?' Gabriel held out his arms and Julian, unable to resist, fell into them. 'No one makes me feel safe like you do, big guy. No one.'

Julian's lips sought out Gabriel's with a desperation that frightened him.

'I'm not going anywhere,' Gabriel said when they parted, 'you gotta trust me.'

'I do,' he said. He did. He stared into Gabriel's wide blue eyes. Who else had ever done more for him? *I took a huge risk for you.* Yes, he thought, Gabriel had taken a risk for him no one else ever would. That's all Gabriel had wanted to remind him of. The bond between them.

'So, this grant money,' Gabriel said, 'how much we talkin' about?' He whistled when Julian told him. 'Two hundred grand. Can you get at it?'

Julian shook his head. 'Not a chance.' His finger traced a circle around Gabriel's navel. 'I've been going over everything, looking at the finances from every angle but I can't take any substantial amount without getting caught.'

'She's got you sewn up tight, that's for sure.'

Julian hesitated. 'There's something else. Something I need to tell you.' He explained about the pre-nuptial agreement he'd signed. 'I'm sorry,' he said, 'I should have told you.'

A simmering silence grew between them.

'It's okay,' Gabriel said eventually. 'I guess I shouldn't be surprised. She's just the type to do something like that.' His hand caressed the back of Julian's neck. 'Pity, though.'

Julian's neck tingled. 'I don't know what else I can do.'

Gabriel smiled. 'Really?'

'It's an impossible situation.'

'Don't worry, big guy. You'll figure it out.'

40

'Didn't you hear them?' he asked Olivia when she woke the morning after Nina's arrival.

'Who?' she said, still befuddled by sleep.

Julian pointed at the floor. 'They were at it nearly all night.' The din of Gabriel and Nina's ceaseless fucking had obscured the normal nocturnal soundtrack of the frogs. Nina, it turned out, lapsed into German and Spanish at moments of sexual release, and Julian had endured streams of loud, unintelligible language from her, along with groans and yelps from Gabriel.

'I took half a sleeping tablet,' Olivia said. 'Didn't hear a thing.'

'Well, no doubt the two of them will sleep all day.'

Olivia threw back the sheet. 'You are a grumpy mouse this morning.' She got up and ambled into the bathroom, leaving the door open.

'We should go for a drive,' Julian said, over the gush of her pissing. 'You and me. What about lunch in Sóller?' He wanted to be away from the house for a while. Away from Gabriel and Miss Nina Diaz. Diaz? He was sure she'd said her father was German.

Olivia flushed the toilet. He heard a brief splash of water as she washed her hands, followed by the bristly scrub and energetic spit of her cleaning her teeth.

'It's going to reach thirty-eight degrees by lunchtime, darling,' she said as she padded back into the room. 'Let's relax by the pool.'

Julian sighed. 'I suppose we'll have to feed them as well?'

'We've got plenty in.' Olivia slipped on her bra and knickers and sorted through the pile of clothes on the chair until she'd found a pair of shorts and a T-shirt.

'It was a bit rude, don't you think? Her asking to stay like that?'

Olivia stepped into her shorts. 'Like what?'

'She's got a cheek. I wouldn't just invite myself to stay at someone's house.'

'I assumed it was Gabriel's idea.' Olivia zipped up her shorts and pulled on her T-shirt. 'Off for my walk. See you later.'

As soon as she left the room, Julian grabbed his phone from the bedside table. He switched it on and typed *Nina Diaz* into the search engine. A long list of entries and images appeared. He found her Instagram account, but it was set to private.

As if he'd summoned her, a soft peal of her laughter sneaked up from the guest room. Seconds later, Gabriel joined in. Julian hauled himself out of bed. He stamped hard across the terracotta tiles on his way to the bathroom, but the laughter continued.

* * *

'Is the music disturbing you, big guy?' Gabriel said. 'If it is, we can turn it off.'

Julian glared at the small speaker attached to Nina's phone. The trancey, repetitive dance music emerging from it had triggered a mild pulsing at his temples.

'I don't think he's a fan,' Olivia said. She reached across from her sunbed and nudged him in the ribs. 'It's chillout music, darling. Quite relaxing once you get into it.'

'I'm sure.' He shifted to the other side of his sunbed, out of Olivia's reach, but that only brought him closer to Nina and Gabriel. The two of them had pushed their sunbeds together and lay on their backs in the shade of an umbrella, Nina's miniscule black bikini barely covering her lithe body. She'd draped one of her long legs over Gabriel's, as if to claim him. Julian couldn't decide if the turmoil in his guts was caused by their showy intimacy or the punishing heat. Mid-afternoon and the temperature hadn't dropped since lunchtime.

'Have another beer.' Olivia reached into the ice bucket on the floor beside her and pulled out a stubby green bottle. She clipped off the lid with a bottle opener and handed it to him.

He wanted to refuse but needed the insulating, beery fuzz that had started to envelop him. He rested his book on his stomach and took the bottle. 'Thanks.'

'Another drink, you two?' Olivia said. 'We're on holiday, after all.'

Gabriel gave her a thumbs up. 'You betcha.'

Olivia passed Julian two more bottles. As he handed them over, Gabriel's fingers brushed against his, igniting the longing he was doing his best to ignore.

'You asshole.' Nina slapped Gabriel as he pressed one of the cold dripping bottles against her flat, bronzed stomach. Gabriel smothered her protest with a long, lingering kiss.

'Olivia, thank you for all this,' Nina said, when Gabriel released her and handed her a beer. 'Later we will go into Deià and get some wine and I was thinking maybe we could pick up some pizzas for dinner?'

'That would be lovely,' Olivia said, 'I don't think any of us will be in the mood for cooking tonight.' She sipped her beer and gave a contented sigh. She seemed to be enjoying her guests, thought Julian. Maybe because she knew they would be leaving soon.

I'm not going anywhere.

'Be gentle with me, babe,' Gabriel said. With a sideways glance, Julian watched Nina massage Gabriel's injured foot with one of her own. Gabriel had removed the bandage that morning. His left foot sported a yellow bruise beneath the ankle bone and looked paler than his right, but it appeared to have healed well. Julian had watched him walk from the villa to the pool with no obvious difficulty.

Minutes passed. The heat claimed them. Nina gave up on her massage, and Gabriel turned on his side, his wings facing Julian.

'Gotta close my eyes, babe.'

Olivia returned to her book, pausing every now and then to fan herself with her wide-brimmed hat. Nina produced a black note-book from her black beach bag and began to write. Julian's gaze lingered on her pert, full breasts. The bikini's tiny triangles of black fabric barely covered them. When he imagined taking one of her nipples in his mouth he felt a sudden, irritating surge of desire. He looked away. He would never have succeeded with a girl like Nina when he was Gabriel's age.

'What are you working on?' he asked when she stopped for a sip of beer.

'Nothing, really. Fragments of stories. Maybe one day I might make them into a novel but I have a lot to learn, for sure.'

'Ah, yes.' Julian nodded. 'Getting a full-length manuscript finished is quite the challenge. I certainly found it hard going at times.'

'Your memoir. Yes. I read a little of Gabriel's copy last night.'

'Oh. Right.' He waited for her to comment further, to compliment him on his work, but she set pen to paper again and became lost in ideas of her own.

Julian, annoyed by her bad manners, closed his eyes. So what if she hadn't liked it? He fixed a smile to his face, determined not to show she had got to him. The heat caressed his eyelids. He heard Gabriel breathing beside him and tuned in to his inhalations and exhalations, until the two of them were in synch. His mind wandered and took him to the townhouse in Bloomsbury, to the bedroom with the silver brocade cushions. He lay on the bed, his body curled around Gabriel's. The two of them, alone, cocooned from the world. No one and nothing to worry about.

A loud splash forced his eyes open. Nina stood by the pool, looking down into the water. Gabriel's blonde head broke through the surface.

'Awesome. Get in here, babe.'

Nina strutted to the deep end and entered the water with a running dive.

'You were out cold,' Olivia said.

'Only for a few minutes.' Julian rubbed his gritty eyes.

'At least half an hour, darling.'

She was right. The sun had moved and, along with it, the reach of the umbrella's shade. Julian's right foot lay exposed to the sunlight, his skin already stinging. He pulled it back to safety.

'Come on in, you guys,' Gabriel said, wading through the water with Nina clinging to his back.

'I'm fine,' Julian said. He wished Gabriel would take more care with his ankle. He shouldn't be putting so much weight on it.

Gabriel ducked Nina and brought her up again.

'Major asshole,' she said, torn between laughing and coughing.

'Don't mind if I do.' Olivia removed her reading glasses and put them on the sunbed, along with her book and hat. She walked up to the pool, plucking her swimming costume from between her buttocks as she navigated the hot flagstones. She climbed down the metal ladder at the shallow end, gasping as her body entered the cold water.

'Wanna race?' Gabriel asked Nina.

'What is the point? You'll win, for sure.'

'I'll race you,' Olivia said. 'Front crawl?'

'It's on, lady,' Gabriel said. 'Two lengths?'

'Make it three.'

'I'll give you some room.' Nina climbed out of the pool, water cascading off her.

'You do the starting orders, babe.' Gabriel took up his position in the shallow end next to Olivia.

Julian sat up as Nina told them to be on their marks.

'Get set, go,' Nina said.

Julian had never seen his wife swim front crawl before. Her speed surprised him. Gabriel took an easy lead in the first length but halfway through the second he lifted his head to see Olivia beside him.

'Go, Olivia,' Nina said.

Gabriel clinched it with a spurt of speed on the third lap, but Olivia wasn't far behind.

'Damn, that was close.' Gabriel shook water out of his ears.

'You nearly got your ass kicked, for sure,' said Nina, before lying down on the poolside to dry off in the sun.

'Well done, my love,' Julian said, waving at his panting wife.

'Don't worry,' she said, 'I'll get him next time.'

'Not bad for an old girl,' Gabriel said.

Olivia's husky laughter echoed across the pool. 'Cheeky bugger.' She splashed him, and he splashed her back. She held her hands up, as if calling a truce. Gabriel surged out of the water, placed both hands on top of Olivia's head and pushed her under.

You'll figure it out, big guy.

Gabriel looked in his direction, lifted one hand and waved.

'No,' Julian whispered.

When Gabriel released her, Olivia burst through the surface with a joyous whoop. When she retaliated, Gabriel raised both hands in surrender and let her submerge him until the tips of his fingers vanished.

* * *

They ate dinner on the top terrace just after 9 p.m. The mountains had lost their fiery glow, and all that remained of sunset was a coral band stretching across the horizon. Above it, layers of dusky grey merged into the encroaching darkness. Three white church candles lit up the table. The cooler night air contained the scents of hot baked earth, rosemary and lavender from the nearby terracotta pots and fresh basil from the pizzas Olivia had sliced up and laid out on serving dishes.

'Damn, this is seriously good,' Gabriel said, cramming a third slice into his mouth.

'For sure.' Nina paused to lick grease from her fingers, and the pair of them laughed at some joke Julian couldn't fathom.

'Sa Vito's has always done wonderful pizza,' Olivia said. 'Good idea of yours, Nina.'

Gabriel and Nina had sped off in the jeep around 6.30 p.m. and hadn't returned with dinner until almost half-past eight. According to Gabriel, they'd had a look round a few art galleries and enjoyed an aperitif before collecting the pizzas. Only one aperitif, wondered Julian? They were very giggly when they returned, and Gabriel had bloodshot eyes. Not that he should judge, thought Julian. He had been drinking heavily since 7 p.m. Chilled white wine followed by plenty of local red. The alcohol, combined with the effects of the day's heat, had left his limbs heavy and his head muddled. He didn't care. He intended to drink as much as possible so he could pass out as soon as he got to bed.

'The pizzas were Gabriel's treat,' Nina said.

My treat, thought Julian. When Gabriel had sought him out earlier and asked for some cash, Julian had handed over 100 euros.

He reached for a new bottle of red, opened it and topped up everyone's glasses. The two women sat at either end of the table with their chairs turned towards the view. He had Gabriel on one side of him and Olivia on the other.

'More pizza, darling?' Olivia said. 'This one with anchovies is gorgeous.'

He took a slice, despite having one unfinished on his plate. Gabriel and Nina dived in and grabbed another piece. Anyone would think they hadn't eaten for days, he thought.

'Olivia, I was reading online earlier about your foundation.' Nina wiped her chin with a napkin. 'It sounds amazing. It must be a lot of work, no?'

'It can be,' Olivia said, 'but it's so rewarding. My father was an unapologetic capitalist, but he did believe in charity and he supported a lot of causes. I wanted to carry that legacy on.'

'That's really cool.'

Julian wished Nina would stop flattering his wife. Perhaps she hoped the Pearson Foundation might provide her with some money. A donation from the Wannabe Writers Fund.

'Well, I'm not sure I've ever been cool, but thank you.' Olivia pushed the plate of seafood pizza towards the two guests. Gabriel picked up two slices. 'Tell us about your father, Nina,' Olivia said. 'Does he still live in Berlin?'

Nina nodded. 'He is an art historian there. He has a new wife and two sons so he is busy with them.' She twisted the stem of her wine glass back and forth. 'I don't see him much. When my mother died, I took her surname. She felt more like my family, for sure.'

Gabriel reached out and tucked a coil of Nina's dark hair behind her ear. The girl's trivial tale of family strife failed to move Julian. She hardly deserved his pity.

'The curse of the father,' Olivia said. 'Don't get me wrong, I adored Daddy, but he was a complex man. A good man, but also weak.'

Julian flinched as his wife's fingers brushed the thick strap of the Rolex.

'He liked women and women liked him,' Olivia said, 'which wasn't easy for my mother. When I was in my teens, he took up with a Playgirl bunny for a while. My mother got a private detective onto him, but when the detective presented her with the evidence she refused to look at it.' Olivia took a gulp of wine. 'I don't blame her. Sometimes it's easier not to know.'

'No.' Nina wagged a finger at her. 'Always better to know, for sure.'

Julian looked down at the Rolex. The pristine face glinted at him, a watchful eye. His father-in-law's eye, looking him over. One adulterer to another. 'You're safe on that score, my love,' he said. 'You are the only woman in my life.'

'That I know, darling,' she said.

'See, babe,' said Gabriel, 'that's true love, right there.' He drained his glass and held it out to Julian for a refill.

'You were married before, though, Olivia?' Nina said. 'Sorry, the German part of me is a bit direct.'

'Twice,' Olivia said. 'Thanks to my father I had a thing for love-able rogues.'

'Third time lucky,' said Nina.

'Some people might feel cynical with two marriages behind them.' Olivia rested her head on Julian's shoulder. 'But I'll always believe there are good men out there.'

* * *

After they'd finished eating, Nina and Gabriel insisted on clearing away the table.

'She's done wonders for his manners,' Olivia said to Julian once they were alone. 'He's much better behaved since meeting her.'

'He's only trying to impress her,' said Julian, the wine making him sullen.

Their guests reappeared, hand in hand.

'We're going for a smoke, Olivia,' Nina said.

'Okay. Watch where you're going down there.'

'You can have a cigarette here,' Julian said but the pair of them had already stepped out onto the grass, the torch on Nina's phone lighting their way.

'They're not smoking cigarettes,' Olivia said.

'Sorry?'

'They're off to smoke the indigenous crops they bought from some guy in Deià.'

'Really?'

'For goodness' sake, darling, did you not see they were totally stoned?'

'No. And they can't do that here. It's illegal.'

'Oh, lighten up. Nina asked me first, to see if I minded. I told them they could smoke in the olive grove.'

Julian's chest ached. The olive grove belonged to him and Gabriel.

'What's the point of them even spending time together?' he said. 'They're both leaving soon.'

'That's the way these young people are.'

'It's hardly going to turn into something serious.'

'I don't think Gabriel's capable of being serious about anyone,' she said. 'Do you?'

He didn't answer.

'I envy them in some ways,' Olivia continued. 'They don't seem obsessed with distracting notions of romance, or destiny, or the perfect partner.'

Nor did they understand the notion of commitment, he thought. The idea of being responsible for another human being. Of caring for someone in sickness and in health.

A door creaked deep inside him, setting off a flutter of panic.

'They might seem free,' he said, 'but it's not that simple, is it? People need people, don't they? How can we live a full and meaningful life if we only care about ourselves?'

Olivia smiled. 'You're right. It's good to hear you say that, little mouse.'

She didn't understand, he thought. She'd interpreted his questions as rhetorical, but he wanted her to answer them. He no longer felt sure that he could.

41

The following day passed in much the same way, the high temperatures making a day trip an unpleasant proposition. At dinner that night, seeing a drop of five degrees forecast for the next day, Olivia suggested they go to Sóller in the morning to look at the art gallery in the train station. Julian expected his two young guests to oversleep or to back out at the last moment, but they turned up on time to breakfast and were ready to leave at 10 a.m.

'This is such a treat,' Olivia said, as she swung herself into the back seat of the open-top jeep. 'Not having to drive for once.'

'Olivia, you are shotgun,' Nina said. 'Boys in the back.'

'Sorry, boys.' Olivia moved to the passenger seat. Julian stepped up into the jeep and put his seat belt on.

'Get ready for an awesome ride, big guy.' Gabriel clambered in beside him, sunlight bouncing off his mirrored glasses.

'Shouldn't you take your crutches?' Julian said. 'In case your ankle gets tired.'

'I'm all good.' Gabriel slapped the side of the jeep. 'Let's go, babe.'

Nina drove as fast as the busy mountain road would let her, the jeep clinging to the hairpin bends and lurching with every touch of the brakes. With one hand, Julian clutched onto the frame of the jeep, with the other, he pinned his pork-pie hat to his head.

'Isn't this fun?' Olivia said. Julian, already nauseous, nodded, not wanting Nina to see his discomfort. When Nina overtook a dawdling Honda Jazz, Julian waited for his wife to criticise the girl's risky driving, but instead Olivia flung her arms overhead, as if on a rollercoaster.

As they passed over an uneven section of tarmac, Julian bounced from side to side. Gabriel linked an arm through his.

'I got you, man.'

Julian's discomfort ebbed away. He clung on to Gabriel until the road evened out, squeezing the younger man's elbow before releasing him.

When they reached Sóller, Olivia guided Nina to a side street near the train station. They parked the jeep and climbed out, Julian's legs rubbery beneath him.

They walked to the train station, Nina and Gabriel with their arms wrapped around each other's waists. Julian followed behind, Olivia's sweaty hand clutching his.

'I'm excited for this,' Nina said, as they followed the signs for the Sala Miró and the Sala Picasso. 'I can't believe I've been in Mallorca all this time and haven't made it here.'

'It's a lovely little gallery,' Olivia said. 'Picasso and Miró were great friends so it's perfect to exhibit them together here.'

'When I was a child,' said Nina, 'my father took me every week to see art.'

'Can't say my old man did the same,' Gabriel said. 'Those military guys weren't really into art, isn't that right, buddy?'

'Mine certainly wasn't.' Julian smiled at Gabriel, glad to be reminded of what they had in common.

'Let's do Miró first,' Olivia said.

'Cool,' said Nina, 'I think he might be my favourite Surrealist.'

Behind the safety of his sunglasses, Julian rolled his eyes.

The Sala Miró contained several rooms with grey walls and low ceilings. Shallow ramps connected the split levels of each room. Julian noted the good disability access, a habit he wished he could shake.

'Miró's wife was Mallorcan,' Olivia told him. 'He moved here in his fifties and never left.'

'That's right.' Nina led them to the nearest wall of screen prints. 'You can really see how the colours of the island influenced his work.'

Julian could see only an egg-shaped blotch of red paint on a piece of white paper.

'He loved disrupting the visual elements of traditional painting,' Olivia said.

Nina nodded. 'The guy was radical. For sure, there wouldn't even be abstract expressionism without him.'

The two women moved through to the next room.

'Seriously,' Gabriel said to Julian, 'what is this shit?' He pointed to a picture made up of white splotches of paint on a murky green background. 'Looks like something a kid would do.'

'Nina would probably tell us he was a master at recreating the childlike.'

Gabriel smiled. 'Yeah, she probably would.' He pressed a hand into the small of Julian's back. 'Let's split and leave them to it. Get a little you and me time.'

The heat from Gabriel's hand spread up and down Julian's spine.

'Maybe we can stop and get a little cash out too?' Gabriel said. 'I'm all out, and I don't wanna look bad in front of Nina.'

Julian nodded, his craving for Gabriel's attention too great to refuse him the money.

They moved through to the next room and attached themselves to their women, each faking his admiration of the artworks on display. When they came out of the Sala Miró into the courtyard that led to the Picasso exhibition, Gabriel bent down to rub his ankle.

'If you guys don't mind, I'm gonna miss this one out.' He grimaced as he straightened up. 'I'll go to the bank and wait for you in the square. Coffees are on me.'

'I'll keep you company,' Julian said.

Nina glanced at Olivia.

'Shame to miss the Picasso ceramics,' Olivia said, 'they're really special.'

'We can always come back another time.' Julian pushed his hat firmly down on his head, as if the gesture decided the matter.

He and Gabriel strolled out of the courtyard, Gabriel hampered by a limp that vanished as soon as they reached the small, shady square outside the train station. On the Avinguda des Born, Julian stopped at the first cashpoint they came to.

'How about a drink?' Gabriel said, as Julian punched in his pin code. 'I'll get us a table at that joint over there.'

By the time Julian had withdrawn his maximum daily allowance of 350 euros, Gabriel had secured them an outside table at the café bar opposite the bank.

'I ordered us beers with bourbon chasers,' he said when Julian sat down beside him.

'Bit early for that, isn't it?' Julian said, not because he cared but because he felt obliged to point the fact out. When the drinks arrived, he swallowed half of the ice-cold beer in one long gulp. They weren't the only ones drinking. The bar looked like a place for locals rather than tourists. Four grizzled old men sat at the table beside them, sipping on glasses of cognac and playing cards. Two young Spanish women sat behind them, smoking and savouring glasses of white wine.

He took out his wallet and gave Gabriel 250 euros.

'Thanks, man.' After slipping the cash into his back pocket, Gabriel took a swig of beer. 'So, how's it going? You come up with any neat fundraising ideas yet?'

'Keep your voice down.'

'Relax, big guy. No one's listening.' Gabriel lit a Marlboro Light and let out a contented sigh along with his first, smoky exhale.

'What's the rush, anyway?' Julian said. 'You're far too busy with Nina to be giving our situation much thought.'

'I'm supposed to be leaving in a week. That's the rush.'

'Seems like you'll be glad to get away from me.'

'Don't be like that.' Gabriel placed a hand on Julian's thigh. Julian glanced at the next table. One of the older men was looking at him with ill-concealed disgust, his thick silver eyebrows knitted together.

'Stop it.' Julian pushed Gabriel's hand away.

'Hey, I'm taking one for the team here. Let's not forget that.'

'You're enjoying yourself. Don't deny it.'

'What do you think it's like for me? Do you ever think about that? Watching you with Olivia every day.'

Julian didn't know if he believed Gabriel's display of jealousy. He wanted to. He needed to.

'You think it's easy for me, having to see the way she treats you?' Gabriel said.

'Olivia's a very loving wife.'

'Oh, come on. What are you to her? Really? You're like some kinda token good guy she can dress up and take to charity balls. What are you getting out of it?'

Julian knocked back his bourbon, welcoming the numbing

scorch as it slipped down his throat. 'We have a very happy and comfortable life.'

'And boy, do you have to work for it. What kind of partnership is that? Seriously.'

A loud blast of a high-pitched horn distracted them. The wooden tram from Port de Sóller turned into the street and trundled towards them.

'What if something happens to her?' Gabriel said, his voice low beneath the tram's clatter.

'What?'

'What if something happens to her? You could give years of your life to this woman and then bam, she's dead and you're out on your ass again with nada.'

The tram drew level with them. The crush of tourists inside swayed side to side. A young dark-haired boy hung out of one of the windows, waving.

Julian waved back. 'That wouldn't happen.'

'Why not?'

Julian kept waving, as did the boy. How old was he, Julian wondered? Five, maybe six? So young, so innocent.

Gabriel crushed out his cigarette. 'You're in her will, aren't you?'

The tram pulled away. Julian leaned forward in his seat, trying to keep the boy in sight, but, with another blast of the horn, the tram curved around the corner of the street and disappeared.

'Am I right?' Gabriel said.

'She's left me the house in London. Maybe a little extra.'

'The house?' Gabriel's eyes widened. 'Holy shit.'

His hand shaking, Julian reached for his beer. It slipped and landed on the ground without breaking. Frothy liquid seeped from its neck as it rolled side to side.

Gabriel picked it up. As he passed it to Julian, their eyes locked.

'That's enough,' Julian said in a low voice.

'What? You never even thought about it?'

'No. Of course not. Never.'

42

£5,000,000.00

Julian stared at the notepad in front of him and the figure he had scrawled at the centre of the blank page. The zeroes danced before his eyes, merging together and separating again.

'I think it's worth considering that meal-sharing project down in Bristol.' Mike's earnest voice on the other end of the phone brought Julian back to the present. To the cream sofa in the living room where he sat with the notepad on his knee and his mobile clamped to his ear.

'Yes,' he said, 'that was an interesting proposal.' He pressed his ballpoint into the paper and scribbled over the numbers until he could no longer see them.

'And I loved the application by that yoga teacher in Newcastle,' Mike said, 'the one who wanted to offer subsidised places for carers. That's the kind of project a little of the grant money would go a long way with.'

'I agree. Plenty to choose from.'

Five million pounds. Give or take. The value of the house in

Bloomsbury plus whatever extra provisions Olivia had alluded to when she'd mentioned her will to him. This notional figure had kept him awake most of the night. Why had she told him about the will? Why wouldn't she? He was her husband. Her loving husband.

After his phone call to Mike, Julian stayed in the living room. Late morning sun streamed through the open windows. He could hear splashes and squeals coming from the pool, where Olivia and her guests had decamped to after breakfast.

Yesterday, in Sóller, he'd made it very clear to Gabriel that he would not discuss Olivia and her will any further. Gabriel had responded with a knowing smile that infuriated him. *Whatever, big guy.*

Five million pounds. Julian could not stop thinking about the money. The money that did not yet exist and did not really belong to him, but the more he thought about it, the more it seemed like his destiny. His right.

His mobile rang. Mike again? He checked the screen but didn't recognise the number.

'Hello?'

'Julian? Julian Griggs?'

'Yes.'

'This is Max. Maxine, from *Woman's Life* magazine.'

'Ah, yes. Hello.' He sat up straight. 'How can I help you?'

In a cheerful West Yorkshire accent, Maxine informed him that the 'Good Man Guide' article would now run in the October issue, rather than the December one. 'We felt it fitted better there,' she said. 'It's such a great piece and you're going to love what the writer's putting together about you.'

'All good, I hope.' He stood up and strutted across to the window, his reading glasses dangling from one hand.

'You wouldn't be in the article otherwise.'

'Very true.'

Maxine explained that the change in schedule meant she needed to get a picture of him to run with the piece. Could he make himself available for a photo shoot?

'I'm actually on holiday at my villa in Mallorca just now,' he said.

'What if I organise a local photographer to come and get the shots we need? We could send someone to the villa.'

'I'm sure that would be fine,' he said, his tone casual, as if he received requests for photo shoots on a regular basis.

'Great. I'll get onto it.'

'I'll make sure he or she gets my good side.'

'Bless you,' Maxine said. 'Your story's incredible, Julian. Heartbreaking but uplifting at the same time. Our readers love that.'

'You have to make the best of things.'

'If you don't mind me asking, how do you cope not knowing who killed Helen? That must be so hard.'

Julian gazed out at the unruffled blue sea, the cloudless sky. 'Life doesn't always give us all the answers.'

'If it were me, I'd be dead bitter.'

The sound of Gabriel's laughter swooped up from the pool. 'Love helps,' he said.

'That reminds me, do you think we can get a picture of you with Olivia?'

'I'll ask her.'

'Great.'

Over lunch, he announced the impending photo shoot to the others.

'That's wonderful, darling,' Olivia said. 'When is it happening?'

'Soon, I imagine. Whoever they send will come here. If that's okay with you?'

'Of course.' Olivia offered a basket of bread to Gabriel, who took a slice of seeded rye and passed the basket to Nina.

'What is this article about?' Nina asked.

'It's just a little thing,' Julian said.

'He's being modest.' Olivia cut herself a soft wedge of goat's cheese. 'It's for a major magazine.' As she handed round the cheese platter, she explained the idea behind 'The Good Man Guide'.

'I'm really a very private person, Nina,' Julian said. 'I don't enjoy all this nonsense, but it comes with the territory when you're running a charity. It's my responsibility to raise awareness. One of my responsibilities.'

'What did I tell you, babe?' Gabriel said. 'This guy here is a goddam saint.' He regarded Julian with a cool stare that made Julian's right foot tap against the warm tiles.

'He seems to be, for sure,' said Nina.

Julian twitched in his seat as one of Gabriel's bare feet pressed down on his jiggling one. He could feel the veins in Gabriel's arch, veins swollen with the heat.

'Maxine did say it would be great to get a picture of the two of us together,' Julian said to Olivia. 'Only if you're okay with that.'

Olivia hesitated. 'That's not really my thing.'

'You should totally do it,' Nina said, 'the two of you are a team.'

Julian freed his foot from Gabriel. 'Yes,' he said, 'we are.'

* * *

After finishing lunch, they sat and sipped glasses of iced tea. The intense heat of the morning and early afternoon had dissipated and a faint hint of breeze came in from the sea.

'Let's go to the beach for a few hours,' Olivia said. 'It'll be lovely down there now.'

'Sounds good to me,' Gabriel said. 'Babe?'

Nina shrugged. 'Whatever. We can go in the jeep.'

'I might walk down,' Julian said.

'At this time?' Olivia said. 'You'll be terribly hot.'

'I need to stretch my legs.' He turned to Gabriel. 'Fancy joining me? Give that ankle of yours a test drive.' He needed to get Gabriel alone and explain he couldn't just walk away from his life. 'We can cut through the olive grove and join the coastal path.' He needed to make him understand. To make him see.

'Okay, big guy,' Gabriel said, 'why not?'

'You ladies could drive down and we'll meet you there,' Julian said.

'Unless you want to walk as well, Nina?' asked Olivia. 'The views are glorious going that way.'

'It would be nice to see, for sure,' Nina said.

Julian swallowed his frustration. No point being annoyed with Olivia, he told himself. She was only trying to be a good hostess.

'I'll drive the Fiat down,' Olivia said. 'I'm sure we can all cram in on the way back.'

* * *

The three of them set off forty minutes later, leaving Olivia to pack the Fiat with their beach bags, the umbrella and a cooler box filled with beers and bottles of water. Gabriel and Nina traipsed hand-in-hand across the grass, separating on the rocky steps to the pool terrace only to cling to each other again. Julian trailed behind, a small rucksack slung over one shoulder. He'd dressed in long shorts, socks and trainers and a long-sleeved shirt. Olivia had rubbed sun cream on the back of his neck and insisted he wear his Panama hat for greater protection. The walk would only take around an hour, but the sun still had a bite to it.

Gabriel and Nina waited for him at the entrance to the olive grove. Neither had dressed appropriately for the walk, in his opinion. Gabriel had espadrilles on and Nina a flimsy pair of black plimsolls. Good job he'd put a large bottle of water in his bag, he thought. His irresponsible companions had brought nothing with them.

As they negotiated the narrow path that snaked between the olive trees, Julian tormented himself with an image of Nina with her back against a gnarled trunk, her legs around Gabriel's waist. He perked up when Gabriel turned around and tossed him a smile.

They descended the dusty terraces, past the curling pods of the carob trees. When Julian tripped over a dead branch, Nina glanced behind her before carrying on without a word. Sporadic bursts of birdsong punctured the hot, silent air, as if to announce they were still there. Still watching.

At the point where the path curved to the right, Gabriel stopped.

'This way, big guy?' he said.

Julian nodded. 'Just follow it round.'

The tall shrubs on one side, the smooth grey boulders on the other. Julian's breath, tight and shallow in his upper chest. Glimpses of the sea through the greenery.

'Whoa,' Gabriel said as they emerged from the shield of the shrubs onto the wider, exposed stretch of path. 'Awesome.'

'Very cool.' Nina dropped Gabriel's hand and ventured closer to the edge of the cliff.

The three of them stood in silence, admiring the expanse of sea and sky. From below came the sound of waves thrashing rocks.

'I can see why Olivia loves this view,' Nina said.

'She does.' Julian fanned himself with his hat. 'She walks this way every morning.'

'Every morning?' Gabriel said.

'Yes.' Julian kept his eyes trained on the horizon.

'Check out that rockfall.' Nina pointed to a pile of rock fragments and scree in the valley further along the path. 'This coastline is unstable, for sure.' She peered at the water below. 'Plenty of ways a person could have an accident around here.'

Julian glanced at Gabriel. The younger man was staring at him, an enticing smile spreading across his face.

'True that, babe,' Gabriel said, stepping closer to the edge. 'A girl should be real careful round these parts.'

Nina screamed as Gabriel wrapped his arms around her waist and picked her up.

'Put me down, asshole,' she said, but Gabriel swung her from side to side. Julian's heart thrashed in his chest as he watched Nina's legs hover over the abyss.

'Quit it.' Nina's arms flailed around, landing ineffectual slaps and punches.

'Put her down,' Julian said. He glanced around. No sign of anyone on the path below or in the pine trees behind him.

'Jeez, you guys.' Gabriel stepped back from the edge. 'As if I'd drop her.' When he let Nina go, she punched him in the chest.

'Arschloch,' she said.

'Hear that, big guy?' Gabriel said. 'I got a girlfriend capable of insulting me in two languages.'

'Estúpido,' Nina said.

'Make that three.' Gabriel pulled her towards him. 'Come on, babe. I'm sorry. I was just fooling around.' He kissed her neck. 'Come on.'

'Next time you will be the one going in the sea.' She gave his face a light slap before planting a passionate kiss on his lips.

They walked on with their arms wrapped around each other. Julian crept on shaking legs towards the cliff edge and glanced down. Black rocks, slick as seals. Water fretting and foaming. Crouching down, he picked up a shard of pink rock and hurled it into the air. He watched it drop for as long as he could, but lost sight of it before it met the sea.

43

Kick, pull, breathe. His lungs full, Julian submerged his head in the cool green water of the swimming pool. Kick, pull, breathe. With every stroke, he tried and failed to erase Olivia from his mind. She'd left for her walk five minutes ago. Where would she be now? He pictured her making her way down the terraces, her feet negotiating tree roots and fallen branches.

Kick, pull, breathe. Kick, pull, breathe. Two days had passed since his walk with Gabriel and Nina. In that time, Nina had added Gabriel to the jeep's insurance, and yesterday Gabriel had driven her to Porto Cristo on the east coast to visit the so-called Dragon's Caves. Julian had welcomed the break from his lover. He needed to think straight. When Gabriel and Nina had arrived back just before ten last night, they'd gone straight to bed. Julian and Olivia had followed soon afterwards. When Julian had reached for his wife, she'd hesitated and pointed to her lower lip. She might be getting a cold sore, she'd told him. The sun often brought them out. Might be nothing, but she didn't want to risk passing it on.

Kick, pull, breathe. He imagined himself at his wife's side as she passed the tall shrubs and the smooth grey rocks. Now they emerged onto the wide path to be stunned by sea and sky. Olivia at the cliff edge, peering down. Him close behind her.

Kick, pull, breathe. A jump cut to him stumbling from the olive grove onto the pool terrace, directing pointless calls for help at the empty villa.

At the deep end, he stood up, his breath coming in fast, painful gasps. He hoisted himself out of the pool and sat with his feet in the water while he recovered.

'Pull yourself together,' he muttered. He had a busy day ahead. An important one. Karl Meyer, a freelance photographer from Palma, was arriving at 11 a.m. to take his picture for the 'Good Man Guide' article.

He shook his head, scattering water everywhere, hoping to dislodge the thoughts he told himself Gabriel had put there.

* * *

He was in the kitchen slicing a sourdough loaf for breakfast when he heard the doors to the terrace open.

'In here, my love,' he said. 'How was the walk?'

'My love? I'm flattered, big guy.'

Julian spun round, the bread knife gripped in his hand. Gabriel climbed the steps into the kitchen, face glowing, his hair tied in a top knot. His white T-shirt clung to his toned torso, soaked with sweat.

'What are you doing up?' Julian said.

Gabriel leaned against a nearby worktop. 'Decided I'd go for a walk.'

Julian's stomach flipped. 'Where?'

'You know where.'

Julian stared at Gabriel's dusty espadrilles. 'Where's Olivia?'

'You know where she is.'

'Oh, God.' The backs of Julian's knees buckled. 'No.'

'Relax.' Gabriel picked up a bottle of orange juice from the worktop. 'It'll be fine.'

'Fine? Jesus Christ.'

'Chill out, man.' Gabriel swigged straight from the bottle.

'You pushed her off the cliff?' The knife shook in Julian's hand. His mind whirred, unable to take in the enormity of Gabriel's actions.

'Yup.'

Underneath his mounting panic, Julian detected a familiar sensation. The click of the door opening deep inside him.

'Morning, darling.' Olivia strode through the terrace doors, into the dining room and up the steps to the kitchen.

The knife fell from Julian's hand. He bent to pick it up, a shocked cry stuck in his throat. 'It's you,' he said.

'Who else?' Her face was beetroot red from exertion and large damp patches stained the underarms of her T-shirt. Julian glared at Gabriel, who shrugged and took another swig of juice.

'Nice walk?' Gabriel said.

'Very pleasant.'

'See anyone?'

'Not a soul. I never do.' Olivia picked up a discarded local newspaper and fanned her face with it. 'You're up early,' she said to Gabriel.

'Nina had me doing yoga in the garden,' he said. 'She's still out there, doing corpse posture or something.'

'Good for you,' Olivia said.

Julian laid down the bread knife, not trusting his trembling hands. Gabriel and Nina must have gone out into the garden while he was upstairs getting changed after his swim.

'Right,' Olivia said. 'I'm off for a shower. I'll leave you boys to sort breakfast out.'

'You got it, boss,' said Gabriel.

'Have you chosen your outfit for the photographer?' Olivia asked Julian.

'Not yet.'

'Well, let's get breakfast done as soon as possible so we've got plenty of time to get ready.' She swept out of the kitchen, humming to herself.

As soon as Julian heard her clattering up the stairs, he turned to Gabriel. 'I can't believe you did that.'

Gabriel laughed. 'I totally got you, big guy. Like, totally.'

'It's not funny.'

Nina sauntered through the terrace doors, dressed in black leggings and a clinging black vest. 'Hey, Julian,' she said as she bounded up the steps into the kitchen.

'Morning.' He opened the fridge door and stared at the contents inside, unable to focus. Yoghurt, where was the yoghurt?

'Wanna take a shower, babe?' Gabriel said.

'For sure.' Nina headed for the door that led to the hallway. 'Come soap me up.'

Before following her, Gabriel sidled close to Julian and kissed his shoulder.

'It would be easy, big guy. That's all I'm saying.'

* * *

Karl Meyer arrived twenty minutes late, techno music blaring from his red open-top MG as he drove through the villa gates. Julian and Olivia greeted him in the courtyard.

'Nice car,' Julian said as they shook hands.

'Thanks,' Karl said, 'she's a knockout, isn't she?'

Karl was just the type to carry off a sports car, thought Julian. In his late thirties with a head of thick, blonde hair, he had an air of the playboy about him.

Olivia led them through to the top terrace where Gabriel and Nina sat. Introductions were made over coffee. Gabriel and Karl did the kind of fist bump greeting Julian associated with men much hipper than himself. Olivia, as always, made her guest the centre of attention. Topping up his coffee, asking questions. Karl, it turned out, came from Münster. He and Nina enjoyed a few exchanges in their native language.

'We Germans are all over this island,' Karl said.

'Have you done work for *Woman's Life* before?' Julian asked.

Karl shook his head. Nina said something in German Julian couldn't understand, but he recognised the words 'Woman's Life' and he picked up her derogatory tone. Whatever she said made Karl laugh.

After coffee, Karl unpacked an impressive-looking camera and a set of lenses from his equipment bag and wandered out onto the grass to squint at the sun and assess where he wanted to take his first set of pictures.

'You don't have to stay and watch,' Julian said to Gabriel and Nina. 'Feel free to go for a swim. Do your own thing.'

'I wouldn't miss this, my friend,' Gabriel said.

Julian ignored him, his stomach still churning from Gabriel's earlier prank.

Karl carried a chair from the terrace and placed it on the grass. 'This will be nice,' he said. 'The mountains and the villa behind you.'

Sweat broke out on Julian's forehead as Olivia fussed with his hair. She'd chosen his outfit – beige trousers, white linen shirt and the smart brown loafers. At the last minute, he removed the Rolex and handed it to her. 'Might look a bit crass,' he said.

'Oh.' Her cheeks flushed. 'I suppose it might.' She had on the jade-green dress she'd worn for his birthday party. 'Do you think the diamond earrings are a bit much?'

'No,' Nina said, 'you look kick-ass in them.'

Julian sat on the chair as instructed by Karl and posed for some preliminary shots. The sun beat down on his head, and he had to keep stopping to wipe his face with a handkerchief.

'We won't be too long out here,' Karl said. He edged closer, the fat lens of his camera expanding and contracting. 'That's great. Look at me.' After a while, he stopped and checked the images he'd taken. 'Great place you've got here, by the way.'

'Yes,' Julian said, 'we like it.' He didn't have a place at all. Not really. None of it belonged to him, whatever impression Karl's photographs might give.

He twisted in his seat and saw Gabriel on the terrace, feet up on the table.

It would be easy, big guy.

Easy. How could it be easy? What if Gabriel had gone through with it that morning? He couldn't bear to think about the consequences.

After a while, Karl suggested they move location. 'Perfect,' he said when they showed him the pool terrace. Olivia, Nina and Gabriel took shelter on the sunbeds beneath the umbrellas. Julian sat at the wrought-iron table and posed for a series of pictures using the props he'd chosen. Reading glasses on, pen in hand, staring at his notebook in an imitation of working. After all, as he'd told Maxine on the phone, his work was his life.

Karl changed the lens on his camera and prowled around Julian, instructing him to shift position every now and then.

'Looking good, big guy,' Gabriel said.

Julian raised his notebook and gazed at the blank page, uncomfortable with the camera's scrutiny. As the sun pressed down on the top of his head, he thought of Helen. He was only sitting here because of her. He was doing this for her. The heat morphed once more into her hand, pinning him in place.

He saw the indent of his previous scribbling on the blank page before him. The numbers he had tried to obliterate rose up before his eyes.

£5,000,000.00

What would have happened if Gabriel had made good on his joke this morning? Would the police be here now, interviewing the two of them up on the top terrace? *So sorry for your loss, but we must ask you a few questions.* Could Gabriel have conjured a plausible alibi?

'Okay, Olivia. Let's get a few shots with you,' Karl said. Olivia, obeying the photographer's instructions, stood behind Julian with her hands resting on his shoulders. Julian laid his notebook and glasses on the table and crossed one leg over the other.

'The Good Man Guide, huh?' Karl said, bending down on one knee and angling his lens upwards. 'I don't think you will see me in that any time soon.'

'Me neither, buddy,' Gabriel said from his sunbed.

Nina laughed. 'No, you definitely won't see this asshole in there.'

'Hope you are proud of him, Olivia,' Karl said.

'I am.' She kissed the top of Julian's head. 'Very much so.'

Julian did his best to smile. Olivia's hands on his shoulders. Pinning him in place. He fought a desire to shake them off. He looked across to the sunbed where Gabriel sat, watching him. Julian couldn't see the eyes behind the mirrored sunglasses, but he could feel the disdain radiating from them.

It would be easy, big guy.

An act like that would not be easy at all, he thought. An act like that would take careful planning.

44

Julian gazed at the canopy of leaves above his head. 'I don't know why we had to come. It's already too hot.'

'What's with you this morning?' Olivia said. 'You're so grumpy.'

The two of them were sitting on a stone bench beneath a giant fig tree, drinking takeaway coffee. Palma cathedral loomed nearby. Tourists packed the courtyard in front of it, taking photographs of the ancient building.

'I've never seen it so busy,' Julian said. The air around him carried the stink of horse dung from the horses and carts that had lined up nearby to ferry visitors around the capital's landmarks. 'Look at those poor creatures. Bloody criminal working them in this heat.'

'Honestly, darling. Cheer up.'

He didn't want to cheer up. He'd endured a sleepless night and would have preferred to stay at the villa, but last night at dinner, Olivia and Nina had suggested a trip to Palma. They wanted to visit the Miró museum in the outskirts of the town to see where the artist had lived and worked.

'It's not as if you've got to come to the museum with us.' Olivia sipped her coffee. 'Once they've finished in the cathedral, Nina and I will go and do our thing and you and Gabriel can go and do yours.'

He didn't want to be alone with Gabriel. After yesterday's photo shoot, Gabriel and Nina had driven down to the beach while he and Olivia had gone to the supermarket near Sóller for supplies. The rest of the day had passed with no opportunity for them to talk. Before leaving the villa that morning, Julian had once again dressed himself in the clothes Olivia preferred, even subjecting himself to the uncomfortable deck shoes and the Panama hat. As if the outfit provided some kind of armour.

He checked his Rolex. 'They've been in there ages.'

'We could have gone in with them.'

'What's the point when it's so busy? Not my idea of fun.' He swigged his coffee and his heart raced in response to the caffeine. An unpleasant sensation, one he'd experienced frequently over the past few days. He suspected his blood pressure had shot up.

He looked at the low wall where he and Gabriel had sat and enjoyed the dawn after his stag night. The place where he had asked Gabriel to stay. If he could go back in time, would he revoke that invitation?

'Maybe I should come to the museum with you?' he said.

'No. This is for art appreciators only.'

'I appreciate art. Just not when it looks like a child did it.'

Olivia smiled. 'I think we'll keep it as a girls' trip.'

'I'm surprised you want to spend time with Nina. It's not as if you've got much in common. What do you even talk about?'

'You men, of course. What else?' She laughed her husky laugh. 'I'm teasing. Nina's an interesting character. The other day she was asking me about investments.'

'Investments?'

'Seems this inheritance from her grandfather is more substantial than she's been letting on.'

Julian's shoulders tensed. 'How substantial is it?'

'I don't know. And don't say anything. She hasn't spoken to anyone about it yet.'

'Not even Gabriel?'

'Good Lord, I think he's the last person she would mention it to.'

'Talk of the devil.'

Gabriel and Nina wandered across the courtyard towards them. Gabriel had one hand tucked in the pocket of his slouchy jeans. Julian imagined the peek of hipbone that would be visible if Gabriel lifted up his T-shirt.

'Hey, you guys,' Gabriel said when they reached the bench. 'Pretty cool in there.'

'It's a wonder, isn't it?' Olivia stood up. 'Right, boys, sorry to rush off but we should find a taxi and get going if we want to avoid the crowds at the museum.'

'For sure,' Nina said. 'What about you two? What will you do with yourselves?'

'Don't worry, babe,' Gabriel said, 'I've got it all planned out.'

* * *

The room on the third floor of the backpacker hostel had white walls, a small double bed with white sheets and an en suite shower room so small the door touched the toilet bowl when open. Julian glanced around him with distaste. Loud, aggressive rap music thumped through the floor. The window, although shut, let in the noise from the busy old town street outside – the whine of passing mopeds and chatter and laughter from a nearby café. Julian placed his backpack on a tiled floor begging to be swept.

'I bet the sheets aren't clean,' he said. 'Aren't these places usually full of bedbugs?'

'Who knows?' Gabriel leaned against a bare white wall, an amused expression on his face.

'I shouldn't be here.'

After Olivia and Nina had left for the museum, Gabriel had instructed Julian to follow him. Julian had obeyed, trailing in silence through the narrow old town streets until they reached the entrance of the World Traveller Hostel. Gabriel had negotiated the use of the room with the young Spanish girl on reception and Julian had paid. He could have protested at any point. He could have walked away.

'I mean it,' he said, 'I shouldn't be here.'

Gabriel peeled off his T-shirt and dropped it on the floor. 'So, leave.'

It took only three steps for Julian to cover the distance between them. His weight pressed Gabriel to the wall. When their lips met in a vicious kiss, he clamped Gabriel's tongue between his teeth. Gabriel, unable to move, let out a stifled groan. Julian unbuttoned Gabriel's jeans and found the younger man naked beneath them. When he released Gabriel's tongue, Gabriel turned to face the wall, making an offering of himself Julian could not resist.

Afterwards they lay on the bed, glistening with sweat, the overhead fan stirring the room's warm, musky air. Gabriel's head rested on Julian's chest. Julian, sated, weightless, stroked Gabriel's wings.

'Tell you what, big guy, you wouldn't win a place in any Good Man Guide right now.'

'I guess not.' Julian sighed. 'When I'm around you, I can't help myself.'

Gabriel rolled away from him and sat up. 'That was bullshit with that photographer yesterday. A total sham.'

'That's the reality of my life. I have responsibilities. Important work to do.'

'You've done your bit for the greater good. What about a little Julian time?'

'That's who I am. My role in life.'

'That's not the real you. No one knows the real you. Not like I do.'

'It's not that simple.'

'Olivia doesn't know you. Can you imagine if she did?'

Julian's cooling sweat tingled on his skin. 'Who would tell her?'

'I'm just saying, is that love? Really?'

'It's a life. A good life. One with meaning and value.'

Gabriel slid back to him and nuzzled his neck. 'What happened to being free? You could be. We could be.' His hand reached between Julian's legs. 'I've seen that house, man. We're talking a lot of zeroes for that piece of real estate. Right?'

'I don't know. I've never looked into it.'

'Listen, man.' Gabriel lay with his face close to Julian's. 'The universe wants this for us. I feel it. Why else would it give us this opportunity? Why else would it make it so easy?'

'Stop saying easy. How on earth would it be easy?'

'Come on, you've seen that place. The path, the cliff. As far as the police are concerned, she's out walking alone, she slips, she falls. Tragic accident. How they gonna prove otherwise? It's gotta be the cleanest way to do this kind of thing.'

Julian stared into Gabriel's cool blue eyes. 'I could never do that to her. Never.'

'I know, big guy.' Gabriel stroked his cheek. 'I know *you* couldn't.'

Outside, a moped sped past, horn blaring.

'Having two wives die on me might be seen as a bit careless.'

'We'll make sure you got a good alibi. Just like last time.'

'This isn't like last time.'

'I know. Way less complicated, right? No break-in to pull off. Less chance of leaving any clues.'

'I'm not talking about that. I'm talking about the fact Olivia is a perfectly healthy woman.'

'We did a good thing for Helen, right? But even good deeds have consequences. If we wanna be free, we gotta follow through on what we started.'

'Stop. Stop talking.' Julian pulled away and sat on the edge of the bed with his back to Gabriel. He needed to think. He couldn't think straight with Gabriel going on at him.

'Are you even serious about me?' Gabriel said. 'About us?'

'Yes. Of course. I just—'

'I get it, you need a little time.' Gabriel knelt behind him and ensnared him in a hug. 'But whatever we decide to do, we need some cash, right?'

'Cash?'

'In three days, I gotta leave, man, whether we do this or not. So, either I need some cash to lie low for a while or to keep me going until you figure something else out.'

'You know I don't have access to very much.'

'Sure you do.' Gabriel reached down and tapped the face of Julian's Rolex.

Julian stared at the watch, horrified. 'No. No way. Olivia would be devastated.'

'It's a collector's item. We could get a good price for it.'

Julian thought of his prior research. Watches like his could fetch tens of thousands of pounds. 'No.'

Gabriel's arms gripped him tight. 'Are you serious about me? Are you?'

'Yes. Yes, but I—'

'Then do it, big guy. Sell the goddam watch.'

* * *

Forty-five minutes later, Julian stood outside a food kiosk on the Plaça del Mercat. Cars and buses zipped past. He looked across the road at the entrance to Joyeria Morales, an upmarket jewellery shop. After he and Gabriel had showered in the hostel room, he'd lent Gabriel his phone to search online for a store that sold vintage watches. They'd hurried to Joyeria Morales, and Gabriel had instructed him to wait nearby.

Julian checked his phone and found a new text message from Olivia.

Museum fab. Having coffee then will head back into town. xx

He glanced at his bare wrist, the evidence of his deceit. She would be so upset when he told her he'd lost it. She'd think him so careless.

Gabriel emerged from the shop and waved him over. Julian waited for a gap in the traffic and darted across the road.

'Well?' he said.

'They wouldn't take it. Said they needed a certificate of authentication or something.'

'Of course.' He didn't doubt Olivia would have the certificate somewhere. At home in Bloomsbury, filed away with the rest of her meticulous paperwork. 'Well, that's that, then.'

'Not so fast, my friend.' Gabriel held up a business card. *Angélica's Antiques. 118 Carrer dels Oms.* 'The guy in there said Angélica is a little more flexible about paperwork.'

* * *

Carrer dels Oms was a busy pedestrianised street not far from the Plaça Major. Shabby three- and four-storey buildings rose either side of the precinct, many of the windows with 'For Rent' signs plastered across them. Angélica's Antiques was located next to a shop selling cheap sunglasses and Mallorcan memorabilia. The cluttered display in the antique shop window included a tin bath and several tall vases.

Julian hovered near the entrance, waiting for Gabriel, who'd entered the shop fifteen minutes ago. He glanced again at his phone and his last text exchange with Olivia.

In taxi. Where are you, darling?

Looking at some old church.

Mind if we look at a few shops before lunch?

Not at all. Text when ready to meet.

Nearby, a three-man band had set up to busk. Their infectious music, a blend of jazz and soul, had gathered a small crowd. The lead singer, a black man in a brightly coloured jumpsuit, sang lyrics in an African language that, to Julian, sounded dark and mournful.

He put a hand over his heart. He didn't like how fast it was beating. He was only selling a watch, he told himself, a watch he owned. These reassurances didn't stop him feeling like a thief.

Another fifteen minutes passed. The crowd in front of the band thinned and dispersed, but more passers-by soon paused to listen and a new audience formed. Surely, Julian thought, Gabriel's lengthy visit to the shop was a good sign? He hoped Gabriel would negotiate a decent price. He didn't expect the sale to fetch as much as an online auction, but surely they should get at least twenty thousand for it? Possibly twenty-five. The money would keep Gabriel quiet for a while. Buy him some time to think.

Eventually, a tinkling bell accompanied the opening of the door to Angélica's Antiques. Gabriel stepped out into the street, clutching a brown envelope. Behind him stood a curvaceous woman of late middle age with a wavy mane of bleached hair. Angélica, Julian assumed. She took hold of Gabriel's face and kissed him on both cheeks before retreating into the shop.

'Well?' Julian said when Gabriel sauntered up to him.

'Let's walk, big guy.' Gabriel wolf-whistled at the band as they walked past. The singer waved at them.

'You did it?' Julian said. 'You sold it?'

'Yup. She was some broad.'

'How much?' Julian swerved to avoid a hawker's blanket, strewn with fake Gucci handbags.

'Eight thousand, five hundred euros.'

'Is that all?'

'Might wanna stash this in your bag for now.' Gabriel held out the envelope. 'Give it to me when we get to the villa and I'll hide it.'

Julian put the envelope in his backpack. 'Those watches sell for forty grand online.'

'Doesn't work like that when you don't have the certificate and stuff. I haggled with her, but that's as good as it got. Better than nothing, right?'

'That watch was invaluable to Olivia. She'll be furious when I tell her I lost it.'

'You didn't lose it.'

'Didn't I?'

'No, dumbass. You got mugged.' Gabriel marched away. Julian, breathless and sweaty in the heat, hurried to catch up.

'Mugged?' he said.

'Yup. I got it all figured out. Walk with me.'

Gabriel led them to the top of the Carrer dels Oms, across the Plaça Major, and through a labyrinth of old town streets filled with expensive gift shops.

'Where are we going?' Julian said.

'You were mugged,' Gabriel said. 'Two guys came at you. Nothing you could do.'

Julian followed him down a series of narrow alleyways, tall colourful buildings hemming them in on either side. Arched wooden doors studded with metal hid the secrets of the courtyards behind them. Each time they turned into a new street, Gabriel either tutted at the people who passed them or scrutinised the windows above before shaking his head.

'Now, this is perfect,' he said as they stepped into a dark, empty street with no signs of life in the windows above. 'Totally.'

'For what?' Julian asked.

Gabriel turned to face him. 'Okay, let's do this quickly.'

'Do what?'

'Try not to scream.'

Julian didn't scream, but he did yelp like a wounded animal when Gabriel's coiled fist drove into his stomach.

'Jesus.' He stumbled and fell against the wall of the building behind him.

'Sorry, my friend. Truly.' Gabriel uncurled his fist and shook out his hand. 'Gotta make it look convincing.'

He stepped closer. Julian looked up and detected a vicious blankness in Gabriel's wide blue eyes.

'No.' He held up a hand to ward him off.

Gabriel curled his fingers into his palm and raised his fist again. 'Trust me.'

45

Julian flinched as Olivia pressed a freezer bag filled with ice against his left eye.

'Sorry, darling,' she said, 'I promise it will help.'

'Don't worry, big guy,' Gabriel said, 'it doesn't look as bad as all that.'

'I can assure you it feels bad.' Julian relieved Olivia of the ice and held it against the throbbing socket of his left eye. His right eye gave him a partial glimpse of the late afternoon view from the top terrace. The calm sea, the unblemished blue sky. He still had on the same clothes he'd worn to Palma that morning. Dark spots of blood soiled his white shirt. His nervous system still reverberated with the shock of the earlier violence.

'I still think we should have gone to the hospital and had you checked for concussion,' Olivia said.

'No need,' Julian said. 'Really.'

'I feel kinda responsible,' said Gabriel.

'No.' Nina, seated on Gabriel's lap, kissed his forehead. 'It wasn't your fault.'

'I should have had his back,' Gabriel said. 'I only stopped to look in that shop for like a minute. I didn't know he'd walked on so far.'

'It's not like you were in a dangerous part of town,' Olivia said. 'Getting mugged was very unfortunate.'

Julian pressed the ice against his skin with as much force as he could bear. After Gabriel had punched him for the second time, he'd collapsed to the ground with his arms over his face. Gabriel had apologised but insisted they needed to make the attack look convincing. How else would they get the police report they needed for an insurance claim? After Gabriel had hauled him to his feet, Julian listened to and repeated the facts of the story they would both tell. Two Spanish men had attacked him. Punched him and pushed him against the wall. One had held his wrist while the other pulled off the watch. At that point, Gabriel had appeared and joined the fray, scaring the two men off.

'The police officer I spoke to seemed surprised they'd attacked me,' Julian said, turning his one good eye on Gabriel. 'Apparently these types usually grab the watch and run.'

'Guess you were unlucky.' Gabriel shook a cigarette from his pack and lit it. Julian couldn't help admiring the younger man's coolness under pressure. And the plan had worked. Olivia couldn't be angry with him for being mugged.

'They sound like thugs to me,' Olivia said. 'The kind of men who would enjoy hurting someone. Did either of you get a good look at them?'

Julian shook his head. 'It all happened so fast.'

'I was too worried about my buddy here to remember much about them,' Gabriel said. 'We gave the police a description, but it was pretty vague.'

Olivia sighed. 'I doubt the police will do much. Muggings are quite common on the island, sadly. It usually happens in more touristy areas though. Magaluf, Palma Nova, places like that.'

Julian nodded. 'That's what Miguel said.'

Miguel, a young, disinterested police officer who spoke limited English, had interviewed him and Gabriel together in a windowless room with yellow walls at Palma police station. Julian, stricken with a rising panic and clutching the rucksack with over 8,000 euros in it, could barely concentrate as Miguel groped towards an understanding of the fictitious events. Gabriel, on the other hand, had showed no sign of being flustered.

'It might get in the local papers,' Olivia said, 'but that won't help.'

'The papers?' Julian glanced at Gabriel. 'What if the muggers tried to sell the watch? Wouldn't whoever they sold it to come forward?'

'Hardly, darling,' Olivia said. 'Fencing stolen goods is not uncommon here.'

'Won't the police go and ask at all the jewellery stores or something?'

'Are you kidding me, man?' Gabriel blew smoke at the gnarled vines overhead. 'That Miguel guy couldn't have cared less. Like, he said they'd look into it, but he didn't seem hopeful.'

'Sounds about right,' Olivia said, 'the police here aren't known for their efficiency.'

'I promise I'll follow it up,' Julian said to his wife. 'They can at least try to find it.'

'I won't be getting my hopes up.' Olivia wiped her damp hands on her kaftan. 'You should put some ice on your knuckles, Gabriel,' she said, 'they look quite swollen.'

Gabriel examined them. 'Nah, it's all good.' He'd insisted their narrative include him punching one of the muggers in his efforts to save Julian.

'You must have hit the guy really hard, for sure,' Nina said.

'Gave it my best shot, babe.'

'You certainly did.' Julian removed the ice from his face. After apologising for the attack, Gabriel had kissed him, long and hard. *I'll make it up to you, big guy.*

Nina suggested she and Gabriel drive into Deià to shop for dinner. 'I could make a pasta?' she said. 'Something soft for Julian to chew.'

'That would be very helpful,' Olivia said. 'Thank you.'

After their guests had left, Olivia refreshed the bag of ice and fetched Julian a whisky to settle his nerves.

'Drink this,' she said, 'you'll feel better.'

Julian sipped the whisky, relishing its reassuring burn at the back of his throat. 'I am sorry. I feel terrible.'

'It's not your fault.'

He pressed the bag of ice against his eye. 'At least the police gave us a crime report number. You shouldn't have any problem with the insurance.'

'It's not the money.'

'I know. I know how much the watch meant to you.'

'What if they'd seriously hurt you?'

'I'm fine.'

'I would have felt terrible.' She stared at his injured face. 'Poor little mouse.'

Her sympathy soothed him. He'd never been hit like that before. It had both frightened and reassured him, that glimpse of what Gabriel was capable of.

At one point, in the police station, as Miguel listened to Gabriel's fabricated description of the invented muggers, Julian had an urge to confess everything. To tell Miguel who Gabriel was and what he had done. Get the whole business over with, once and for all. The possibility gave him a surge of power that faded with the acknowledgement of Gabriel's equal and opposite power. Their past actions had joined them together, in a bond Julian both hoped and feared was unbreakable.

'I'll email the insurance company in the morning,' Olivia said, 'get the ball rolling.'

'Yes. Good idea.' He lifted the bag of ice from his eye, placed it on the table and settled back in his seat, keen to put the day's events behind him. Keen for the throbbing in his face to stop.

'It wouldn't have happened if you weren't with Gabriel,' she said.

'What?' Julian gripped the whisky tumbler as fear rippled through him. 'It wasn't his fault.'

'He's the type who attracts trouble.'

'He'll be gone soon.'

Olivia looked out to sea. 'That's true. He will be.'

'Then it'll be just the two of us again,' he said, telling her what he knew she wanted to hear.

When his wife turned her head, he saw tears shining in her eyes. Guilt washed over him as he thought of the envelope of cash hidden away somewhere in Gabriel's room. At least he'd bought himself some time, he reasoned. Time to think, and he'd done that for Olivia's sake. Yet as he imagined the envelope nestled at the bottom of Gabriel's rucksack, he couldn't help feeling the money was a down payment on something he wasn't sure he wanted any more.

He drained his whisky. It blazed a brave path down to his belly. 'Let's go away,' he said.

'Away? For a weekend somewhere?'

'Longer than that.'

'Caught wanderlust from our young guests, have you?'

'We could go anywhere we wanted. Travel the world for a while. Live on a remote island where no one can bother us.'

'What a lovely fantasy.'

'I mean it. What a life that would be.'

'No reality to deal with.'

'Exactly.'

'Just you and me in paradise every day.'

'Why not?'

'Who knows,' Olivia said with a weak smile, 'it might even work.'

'I know it would.' He stroked her cheek. 'We could make it happen.'

She edged away from his caress. 'You're not actually serious?'

'What's wrong with enjoying ourselves for a while? Haven't we earned it?'

'We're supposed to be enjoying ourselves now. This was meant to be our holiday.'

'Wouldn't it be nice just to please ourselves forever?'

'I'd be bored out of my mind. So would you. And charitable foundations do not run themselves.'

'We can get someone in to run yours for you. Same for the Helen Griggs Awards.'

'I thought your charity work meant everything to you.'

'It does.' Desperation crept into Julian's voice. 'I just—'

'You said you wanted to do something in Helen's name.'

'I do. I have.'

Olivia's clear grey eyes examined him. 'You would really give it all up? Abandon everything?'

Julian withered beneath her scrutiny. 'No. No, of course not.'

'Really?'

'No. I'm just... it's been a very trying day.'

Olivia nodded. 'Sorry, darling. I suppose you have been through the mill.'

'I'm exhausted.'

'I'm not surprised.'

'Ignore me,' Julian said, as despair seeped through him. 'I'm talking nonsense.'

Olivia grasped the empty tumbler and stood up. He thought he glimpsed tears in her eyes again, but she turned her head away from him.

'I'll get you another drink,' she said.

46

On the morning of Gabriel and Nina's last full day at the villa, Olivia rose at 7.30 and dressed in her walking clothes.

'You will get up, won't you?' she said. 'It's their last day.'

Julian had spent the previous day languishing in bed with the shutters closed. Olivia had tried several times to lure him out. He'd resisted, pointing out more than once that he had suffered a very vicious attack.

'I'll be up by breakfast,' he said.

'Don't forget we're going to the beach this morning.'

'Must we? I really don't think I should get any sun on my face.'

'You'll be fine. Just wear your hat and stay under the umbrella.'

Julian sighed. 'Fine.'

Olivia surveyed his injury. 'You didn't stand a chance, little mouse. Did you?'

After she left, Julian lay alone, the overhead fan spinning above him as sunlight tried to penetrate the room. He touched his tender eye socket with his fingertips. A current of fear and arousal ran through him.

Yesterday's bed-in had allowed him to avoid Gabriel. To avoid meeting his eyes and seeing the suggestion in them. In the afternoon, he'd taken one of Olivia's sleeping pills and had passed out until after midnight. He'd woken in the dark, his face aching. After that, sleep had eluded him.

He rolled out of bed and shuffled into the bathroom. In the mirror over the sink, he examined his left eye. The swelling had subsided, leaving a bruised black and yellow landscape behind. He lifted the toilet seat and relieved himself, his gaze drifting to the bathroom window. High in the sky, above a sun-dappled mountain flank, circled a large bird. The same eagle or hawk he'd seen on his first day at the villa, he wondered? This time he saw in it more menace than grace.

The mournful tolling of the bells in Deià church accompanied him as he returned to bed and slid beneath the sheet. The sunlight seeping into the room had grown brighter in his short absence. Tendrils of it reaching for him.

Olivia in the olive grove. Olivia stepping over tree roots and fallen branches.

From the guest room below came the sound of a toilet flushing. Murmuring voices drifted up through the floorboards, soon followed by Gabriel's laughter.

The universe wants this for us. I feel it.

Julian felt the pressure of evaporating time. An opportunity slipping away.

Nina let out a high-pitched moan that made him bury his head in his pillow. He thought about a life in which he lay in bed with Gabriel in the mornings. A life in which neither of them had to leave that bed to work. A life made up of nothing but pleasure.

He thought of Olivia on the cliff edge, staring out to sea.

* * *

By 10.30, Julian found himself alone on Cala de Deià beach, his body hunched over to fit beneath the shade of the umbrella, which Olivia had wedged between two large rocks. Sweat leaked out from beneath his Panama and trickled down his neck.

He shielded his eyes with his hand and scanned the sea for his wife. She was floating on her back, Nina and Gabriel treading water and chatting beside her. At breakfast that morning, Julian had endured his young guests pushing wedges of soft, fresh fig past each other's lips. Watched them share seedy, pulpy kisses between mouthfuls. Gabriel had managed to break away from Nina's embrace long enough to discuss their plans. Tomorrow, at lunchtime, they would leave for Palma and spend a night at a luxury boutique hotel in the old town. Nina's treat. When she left for her flight the next morning, Gabriel would have a day and night to himself before catching a flight to Ibiza on Sunday afternoon. He'd told them he didn't know what he would do with his last day. He'd said he was making a plan.

Julian watched as the outgoing tide pulled Olivia away from Gabriel and Nina. How strong were the currents along this coast, he wondered? How far could they carry a person? His attention shifted to the coastline, the sheer cliffs stretching off into the distance and, closer to the beach, the tall outcrop of rock on the right-hand side of the bay. Two teenage boys stood at the edge, looking down at the sea. They turned their backs and walked away, put off from jumping, Julian assumed, by the receding water.

The beach was already busy. A large cluster of bikini-clad girls sat on the concrete ramp beside Ca's Patró March restaurant. Every table at the Can Luc restaurant was full of people enjoying a late breakfast or morning coffee. In the shallows, three elderly men in tight Speedos doused their over-tanned bodies with handfuls of water as they chatted. Didn't they know how ridiculous they looked, thought Julian?

When he searched again for his wife, he saw her heading for the rocks on the far side of the bay with Nina. They were swimming breaststroke with their heads above water, chatting to one another. He wondered if Olivia was sharing investment advice again. Typical of her to take Nina under her wing and guide her. *Olivia loves a project.* He remembered Libby's words. Did his wife see him that way?

Further down the beach, Gabriel exited the water, smoothing his wet hair back from his face. Julian was not the only one looking. The bikini-clad girls had spotted him and turned their heads towards him in one synchronised motion, like sunflowers tracking the sun. Gabriel, oblivious to their admiration, strode across the stones without once losing his footing.

'We gotta talk, big guy,' Gabriel said when he reached the umbrella. 'We're running out of time.' He reached down, picked up his towel and draped it round his shoulders.

'We should forget the whole thing.' Julian glanced at all the people on the beach. Shut off from the world in the shabby hostel room, Gabriel's suggestion had seemed almost logical. Now, here, Julian found it preposterous. 'You'd never get away with it.'

'Chill. I got it all figured out.'

Olivia and Nina were heading back to shore. Julian watched as Olivia dived beneath the water. Thirty seconds later, she still hadn't surfaced. He kept his eyes on the sea until her head emerged and she continued swimming.

'Get up, buddy,' Gabriel said, 'we're gonna take a walk.'

Julian put on his sunglasses and crawled out from under the umbrella, clutching his hat. When Olivia and Nina reached the shallows, Gabriel let out a long whistle. When the two women looked up, he pointed along the beach and did an exaggerated marching mime. Nina gave a thumbs up.

Julian set off ahead of Gabriel, intending to take him to the far end of the beach, but the younger man soon overtook him and headed for the tall outcrop of rock on the right of the bay. Julian, struggling to keep up, had no choice but to follow.

'Can't we talk down here?' he said as Gabriel clambered over the boulders that led to the top of the rock, but Gabriel ignored him. By the time Julian reached the flat plateau, he was out of breath and soaked with sweat.

Gabriel stood at the edge, looking down at the sea. Julian hung back, but a sideways glance revealed the outgoing tide had exposed the tips of the rocks below.

'Sit with me, buddy.' Gabriel stepped back from the edge and lowered himself into a cross-legged position.

Julian sat beside him, legs outstretched. His left eye socket had started throbbing. He touched a fingertip to his bruised skin.

'Sorry about your face, big guy,' Gabriel said. 'Truly.'

'You didn't have to hit me quite so hard.'

'Worked, though, right? We got away with it.' Gabriel's splayed knee rested on Julian's thigh. 'That's what happens for me and you. Things work out for us.'

'So far.'

'This is the deal. Hear me out, buddy.'

'I'm not sure I want to.'

'Today's Wednesday, right? Nina leaves Friday morning and I got a ferry booked for Ibiza Sunday night.'

'You said you had a flight booked for Sunday afternoon.'

'As far as you know, that's true. Okay? That's the story. Now Friday, after Nina's gone, I'm gonna hire me a scooter, drive up the east coast a little then cut across and stay in Sóller for the night. Some of it, anyways. Middle of the night, I'll drive out and park up near the coastal road between here and Sóller. I'll hike along it and find where it joins the path to the villa. I'll hide out and when Olivia comes for her walk Saturday morning, I'll be there.'

Julian tuned in to the waves slapping against the rocks below.

'It'll be quick,' Gabriel said. 'She won't even know what's happening.'

Julian listened as Gabriel outlined the rest of his elaborate plan. 'It's too risky,' he said, 'too many things could go wrong.'

'Yeah, but seriously, man. Who's gonna suspect anything? I swear the police will think she slipped.'

'I'm a beneficiary in her will. The police are bound to suspect me. Not to mention her bloody lawyer.' He couldn't imagine Arnold not having his suspicions. Although, he remembered, Arnold had shared Olivia's morning constitutional many times. Arnold knew the walk formed part of Olivia's daily holiday routine, and he knew she usually walked alone.

'Don't worry. I thought about your alibi.' Gabriel explained that for his plan to work, Julian would have to take the bus into Deià while Olivia was out walking. Once in the village, he should buy breakfast supplies, maybe even stop somewhere for a coffee. People would have to see him there and remember him. 'You got that, big guy?' Gabriel said when he'd finished.

'Yes. That doesn't mean... I'm not going to even—'

'Relax,' Gabriel said, 'I got everything covered.'

'The police will find out we had guests staying. They might speak to you and Nina.'

'What's Nina gonna tell them? Only that Olivia used to go walking on her own every morning. As for me, I'll be gone. They might try and trace me, but they'll soon give up.'

Julian shuffled closer to the edge and peered down at the aqua froth of the sea and the cruel black rocks.

'I'm telling you, man, it'll be easy,' Gabriel said.

'Easy for you maybe. I've got a conscience.'

'You say that like it's a good thing.'

'For God's sake.' Julian removed his shades and wiped a sticky blend of sweat and sun cream from his eyes.

'Your wife's looking at us,' Gabriel said.

Olivia stood by the umbrella, her head turned in their direction. Julian waved and forced a smile he knew she couldn't see. Eventually, she returned his wave, one arm moving back and forth overhead, like a member of an airport ground crew guiding a plane to safety.

'She's a good woman,' he said. She looked small to him from this height. Small and far away.

'I won't do anything unless you give me the word, big guy.'

Julian experienced a shudder of déjà-vu.

Gabriel joined him at the edge of the rock and dangled his feet off. 'I need you to give me the word.'

'I can't.'

'Come on. Seriously?' A sulky expression settled over Gabriel's face. 'Maybe I should forget it all, huh? Consider my options.'

'What options?'

'Maybe I should follow Nina out to Chile?'

'Has she asked you?' Julian's stomach dipped. What if she'd told Gabriel the truth about her inheritance?

'No, but she can't get enough of me, right? Bet she'd have me along if I asked her.'

It didn't sound to Julian as though Nina had taken Gabriel into her confidence. How much had she inherited, he wondered? Enough to compete with his potential millions?

'Okay, listen.' Gabriel's legs kicked the rockface, dislodging a rattle of stones. 'How about this? Saturday morning, I'll be there waiting for her. If you don't want me to do it, you come with her. I see you together, I stay put and do nothing. If she's alone, it's game on.'

'This is insane.'

'It's up to you, big guy. Your call.'

'We'd never get away with it.'

Gabriel flung an arm round his shoulder. 'Look.' He pointed at the water below and the sharp snag of rocks jutting from it. 'Wanna jump?'

'No.' Julian squirmed in Gabriel's embrace. 'Of course not.'

'Why not?'

'The tide's too low. We could hit those rocks.'

'It'd be crazy to jump, right?' Gabriel released him and stood up. 'Only a real lucky guy could do that and get away with it.'

'Don't.'

Gabriel took several long paces back before running towards the edge and launching himself into the air with a howl.

A wild dive, arms and legs at all angles.

Julian peered over in time to see him hit the patch of water between two exposed rocks. He froze, unable to breathe. What if Gabriel failed to surface? A cry from the beach made him look up. Olivia and Nina stood by the shore, eyes trained on the water. The bikini girls were on their feet, pointing.

If Gabriel did not survive, he thought, wouldn't that set him free? Wouldn't that solve all his problems? He looked at the sturdy figure of his wife, the safety and solidity of the life that awaited him.

Seconds later, Gabriel's head emerged and Julian let out a noisy exhale. A piercing wolf-whistle came from the shore. Julian glanced up to see Nina with her fingers in the corners of her mouth. On the other side of the bay, the bikini girls applauded.

Gabriel cupped his hands around his mouth and called up to Julian. 'See, big guy. Easy.'

47

Friday morning. Julian sat in his boxer shorts on the bed in the empty guest room. In the sunlight spilling in through the half-open shutters, he looked around in vain for some sign of Gabriel's presence. The cleaner sent by the agency yesterday had devoted a large portion of her time to making the guest room and bathroom pristine. The scents of fresh bed linen, polish and cleaning fluids had obliterated all trace of his lover. As if Gabriel had never visited. As if none of it had ever happened.

He wondered what Gabriel would be doing now. Enjoying a final passionate tussle with Nina in their hotel room before she headed to the airport? How long would it be until Gabriel left the hotel and went to hire a scooter? This thought set Julian's pulse racing.

Yesterday morning, when the four of them had assembled in the villa's courtyard to say their goodbyes, Julian had caught his reflection in Gabriel's sunglasses. His drawn face and battered eye had startled him.

'Adiós, big guy,' Gabriel said as they'd merged together in a back-slapping hug. 'Till we meet again.'

Nina had given him a cool farewell embrace. 'It was interesting to meet you, for sure,' she said. She'd then gripped Olivia in a warm, lengthy hug.

'Good luck with your new start,' Olivia said.

'Good luck to you too,' Nina replied.

After Nina and Gabriel had driven away in the jeep, Julian and Olivia had returned to the top terrace for morning coffee. Gabriel's casual farewell had unsettled him. Gabriel was only acting out his part, thought Julian, but he couldn't help feeling as if he'd imagined it all. That Gabriel had never suggested they kill his wife.

'Here we are, then,' Olivia had said, 'just the two of us.'

The rest of the morning had almost convinced him life could carry on as it had before Gabriel's return. He'd passed the time answering emails, and he spoke to Mike about how to deal with inviting new applications for the awards. Olivia spent most of the morning upstairs on the phone. A short call to her accountant and then a longer one to Liberto at Casa Feliz.

'Were you getting him to sort out a plumber?' Julian had asked her at lunchtime.

'What?'

'Liberto. Is he getting a plumber to come and look at the boiler?'

'Oh. No. He's dealing with another query for me.'

Unnerved by the silent, empty guest room, Julian stood up and wandered into the en suite bathroom. The white tiled floor gleamed underfoot. Fresh towels hung ready on the metal rail attached to the door. Julian glanced around him. What was he looking for? Some tangible memento? A forgotten toothbrush, a stray blonde hair?

He returned to the bedroom and, on a hunch, opened the drawer of the bedside table. There, waiting for him, was Gabriel's battered copy of *On the Road*. When he touched the worn cover, a tingling sensation spread from the tips of his fingers up into his arm.

'Julian?' Olivia stood in the doorway, dressed in shorts and a T-shirt. 'If you want to come with me, you'd better get dressed.'

'Right. Yes.' He slammed the drawer shut. 'Won't be a minute.'

'What are you doing in here?'

'I remembered I lent Gabriel a shirt. I thought he might have left it behind.'

'Unlikely.' She smiled. 'Chop chop, darling. It's quarter to eight already.'

* * *

He followed his wife through the olive grove. Past the cluster of low, twisted trees where he and Gabriel had shared a number of illicit rendezvous. Lifting his feet over knotty roots in the dusty ground. Olivia marched ahead, confident and surefooted, her rucksack bouncing against her back.

He'd decided to accompany his wife so he could think more clearly about Gabriel's offer. Lying awake in the night, he'd felt no closer to a decision. Surely if he saw the scene of the potential crime with his own eyes, he would do the right thing? Surely he would accept the stupidity of the plan and prevent it from going ahead.

They picked their way down the terraces, past the carob trees with their curved black pods. What if, thought Julian, the fake driving licence Gabriel had purchased in India didn't fool any of the scooter hire companies in Palma? What if the plan fell apart at the beginning?

'It's going to be stinking hot today,' Olivia said as they turned onto the narrow path with the tall shrubs on one side and the smooth grey rocks on the other.

'When isn't it?' Julian lifted his Panama from his head and fanned his face.

Gabriel planned to stay at a hotel in Sóller that night. A respectable hotel with a manned reception. One where a member of staff would see him leave for dinner and see him return drunk and stumbling at around midnight. Gabriel wouldn't be drunk, of course, although he would have made a show of heavy drinking at a bar where he would be remembered. At the hotel, he would put the 'Do Not Disturb' sign on his door. The staff would think he'd passed out, but a few hours later he would sneak from the hotel unseen and make his way to where he had parked his scooter earlier in a quiet side street.

Through the shrubs on his left-hand side, Julian glimpsed the vivid cobalt sea. So many variables, he thought. What if Gabriel didn't escape the hotel unseen? What if he couldn't even find a hotel room? Everywhere was so busy at this time of year. Gabriel hadn't seemed at all concerned about these potential glitches, he recalled. Gabriel didn't believe the police would even investigate the possibility of foul play. Olivia's death would be an accident. A terrible, tragic accident.

'Here we are,' she said, as they emerged from the narrow path onto the wider one. The glare of the sun, the blue brilliance of the water. She wandered to the ragged cliff edge. 'I never tire of this view.'

Julian nodded. Tomorrow, this view might be the last his wife would ever enjoy. He glanced to the right and saw the coastal path to Sóller snaking around the cliffs. The path that would lead Gabriel to this spot before dawn. He glanced behind them at the tall wall of pine trees and the jumble of large grey rocks. Would Gabriel hide there? Ready to jump out when the time came.

So many variables. What about afterwards? Surely Gabriel might meet some keen early hikers on his way back up the coastal trail to pick up his scooter? Julian wished they could talk it all through again, but even if Gabriel did have a mobile phone, it would be foolish of him to call it.

'The sea's quite rough today,' Olivia said.

He joined her near the cliff edge and put an arm around her waist. Olivia leaned against him. He tried to remember if he'd been happy before Gabriel had appeared in his life again. Comfortable and content, yes, but happy? He wished Gabriel had stayed away. He thought about the envelope of cash Gabriel had stashed in his rucksack. Maybe Gabriel would disappear? Take the money and run. A foolish hope, he thought. Eight thousand euros wouldn't satisfy Gabriel. Not even close.

Far below him, waves pounded the rocks. Adrenaline surged through him. What if he pushed her right now? Wouldn't that be simpler? Cleaner? Once more, he saw himself rushing out of the olive grove, his cries of distress echoing around the villa's empty grounds. He stared at the vicious edges of the rocks below. Would they finish her instantly?

'Is something wrong?' Olivia said. 'You look terrible.'

He let go of her waist and stumbled back from the edge. 'Vertigo.' His shaking legs backed up his lie.

'Poor little mouse.'

He could never do it. No. He was not that kind of man. 'That's enough for today,' he said. 'Let's go back and get breakfast on.'

They turned and walked back the way they had come. Past the tall shrubs and the grey smooth rocks. Up onto the scrubby terraces. At least they had this night together, he thought. Time for him to remember what had brought them together. To rekindle his attraction.

'By the way,' Olivia said, when they paused to sip from her bottle of water, 'we're meeting Sheila for a drink tonight.'

'Who?'

'The woman from the Residencia. With the Parkinson's husband. Alex, his name is. They have a nurse with them, so Sheila can at least have the evening off.'

'You might have asked me first.'

'I thought you wanted to help people like her?'

'I do. It's just—'

'I was hoping you wouldn't mind.'

He wilted under her expectant gaze. 'Fine. We'll go.'

Olivia walked on. He trailed behind her, fighting mounting irritation.

'That was fun,' she said when they reached the pool terrace. 'Why don't you come with me tomorrow? We could walk all the way down to the beach.'

'Maybe,' he said. 'I'll see how I feel.'

* * *

The terrace bar at La Residencia looked exactly as Julian remembered it from his birthday gathering. The pianist at the white piano. The apron-clad waiters gliding between the tables. The fading sun casting a rose-gold haze over everything and making the terracotta tiles of the hotel roof glow. Julian and Olivia found Sheila at the same table Nina and Gabriel had occupied the night of Julian's birthday. An omen, thought Julian. He'd dressed in the navy linen trousers Gabriel had chosen for him, along with a black linen shirt and the black espadrilles. Olivia hadn't commented on the outfit, although he had made sure to compliment her on choosing her jade-green dress again.

Sheila gulped back the last of a martini as they approached.

'Forgive the early drinking,' she said in a refined Home Counties accent. 'Alex was a little trying this afternoon, so I thought I'd calm my nerves before you came.'

'No apology needed,' Julian said, 'we quite understand.' Either Sheila had a low alcohol tolerance, he thought, or she'd had more than one martini. A lock of her ashy blonde hair had escaped the silver clip at the back of her head and her long floral shirt dress had one too many buttons open, revealing the lace trim of a camisole.

'My goodness,' she said, as he claimed the seat Gabriel had once sat in, 'what happened to your eye?'

Between them, he and Olivia recounted the story of the mugging.

'I don't care about my eye,' he said, 'I just feel awful about the watch.'

'Nothing you could have done,' Sheila said. 'Lucky you weren't seriously hurt.'

'You never know,' Olivia said, 'I might get the watch back.'

His wife's false optimism made Julian feel even worse for selling it.

'Let's hope so, my dear,' Sheila said. 'Although I don't have much faith in the police here, I'm afraid.' She signalled a nearby waiter. 'Let me cheer you both up with a drink.'

She insisted on ordering an expensive bottle of Californian Chardonnay. 'I rarely drink Chardonnay,' she said as the waitress filled their glasses, 'but this one's exceptional.'

They clinked glasses before taking a sip. They all agreed the wine was complex, surprising, extraordinary. Julian wished he could appreciate it more. He'd spent the afternoon by the pool drinking one beer after another in the hope the alcohol might send him to sleep. It hadn't. Olivia's restlessness hadn't helped. She'd fidgeted on the sunbed next to his, opening and closing her book, constantly checking her phone.

'It's a shame Alex couldn't join us,' Julian said, as if Sheila's husband were as capable of swilling and swallowing the wine as they were. As if he would have joined in the conversation.

'I know, but he's had a bad day,' said Sheila. 'You know how it goes.'

'I do,' he said.

'Still, it's nice for me to meet some new people and let my hair down a bit.'

'Quite right,' Olivia said.

'We're so lucky we can afford a nurse,' Sheila said, her glass already almost empty. 'I don't know how I'd cope otherwise.'

She would have to endure a life of struggle, Julian thought. She would have to scrimp and save as he once had. She would succumb to overwhelming exhaustion.

'Have you had the same nurse for a while?' Olivia asked.

Julian drifted out of the conversation and stroked the side of his seat. It comforted him to think of Gabriel sitting there. He wondered where Gabriel might stay in Sóller. He remembered a nice hotel a few streets back from the Plaça de la Constitució, where he and Olivia had once eaten lunch. He pictured a room panelled with dark wood. A bed with crisp white sheets. Gabriel at the window, plotting a nocturnal escape route. An easy climb from the window onto the low roof of a nearby building, followed by a short jump to the ground.

'Isn't it, darling?' Olivia said, her hand brushing his arm.

'What?' he said.

'Sheila was just saying it's going to be a lovely sunset.'

The descending sun hung over the ocean, cushioned on a blaze of blood-orange sky.

'Shame it has to set at all,' Julian said, wishing he could pin the sun in place and put off the inevitable decision tomorrow would bring. His rattled nerves fizzed and seethed beneath his skin. When he reached to pick up his wine glass from the table, it slipped out of his hand and smashed on the flagstones.

'Sorry,' he said. 'I don't know what happened there.'

An apron-clad waiter appeared almost immediately with a dustpan and brush and swept away the debris.

'Maybe we should have a little something to eat?' Sheila suggested.

Olivia glared at Julian. 'Yes, maybe a bite would be a good idea.'

Sheila spoke to the waiter in Spanish. Before long, he reappeared with a sumptuous platter of cheese and charcuterie, another bottle of Chardonnay and a fresh glass for Julian. A glass the waiter only filled half-full for him.

'Do help yourself to food, Julian,' Sheila said, gesturing for the waiter to fill her glass to the brim.

Julian thanked her and piled a side plate with cured meat and cheese he had no desire to eat. As he tussled with a mouthful of Iberian ham, he wondered what Gabriel would do for dinner. Might he sit at one of the restaurants in the Plaça de la Constitució? A spot where plenty of people would see him. Julian thought of the envelope of cash and imagined Gabriel would treat himself to something special.

'This is delicious,' Olivia said. 'Isn't it, darling?'

Julian mumbled his agreement. Was he imagining it or did his wife have a look of suspicion on her face? As if she knew exactly what he was thinking.

'I have a confession to make, Julian,' Sheila said. 'I've been reading your memoir.'

'Oh.' Julian swallowed the rubbery, salty mouthful. 'Thank you.'

'I downloaded it. Our grandson got me an iPad last Christmas and I've never looked back.' She dabbed the corners of her mouth with a napkin. 'It's beautifully written. I found it very touching.'

'All the proceeds go to the Helen Griggs Awards,' Olivia said.

'I do admire everything you've done,' Sheila said to him. 'I don't think I could have sacrificed so much for others. Not at such a young age.'

He found himself resenting her praise. Did she think he'd enjoyed giving so much of himself to others? He hadn't done it through choice. What of all the other versions of him that might have existed? What about his hopes and dreams?

He reached for his wine. 'It's all about doing the right thing, I suppose.' As he sipped his drink, he wondered where Gabriel would choose to do his drinking later. In that bar full of locals they had visited that day in Sóller? He pictured Gabriel chatting away to whoever would listen. Offering to buy drinks for strangers.

The pianist launched into a rendition of 'Come Fly With Me'.

'Talking of doing the right thing,' Sheila said, 'I have an idea you may be able to help me with.' In a voice blurry with alcohol, she outlined her 'more than comfortable' financial situation. 'Alex did very well in the City,' she said, 'and what with his investments and pensions, I've been able to get the very best care and treatment for him.'

'Money makes a huge difference in these situations,' Olivia said.

'It really does,' said Julian, wondering how much difference five million pounds would make to his situation.

'I'd like to share some of our good fortune with others,' Sheila said. She outlined her idea of paying for other, less fortunate carers to have help from the private nursing agency she used. 'Even a few hours a week could make a great difference to someone.'

'That's a lovely idea,' Olivia said.

'Perhaps you could help?' Sheila asked Julian. 'Make it some kind of scheme through your charity.'

'He'd love to,' Olivia said. 'Wouldn't you, darling?'

He nodded, dampening his rising resentment with another swig of wine. He was tired of Olivia speaking for him. Tired of her taking advantage of his good nature.

The three of them clinked glasses to mark the conception of this new idea.

'I know none of us like to think about our old age,' Sheila said, 'but if you do need looking after at any stage, Olivia, you've picked the right man for the job.'

Julian smiled. The door deep inside him creaked on its hinges.

'That's the kind of man I was hoping for.' Olivia placed her glass on the table. 'Please excuse me. Must pop to the bathroom.' She rose from her chair and headed into the hotel.

'Now that it's just us,' Sheila said, leaning in towards Julian, 'I need to tell you something.'

'Okay.'

She pressed a finger to her lips. 'I couldn't say this to anyone else.'

'Please. Feel free to—'

'Some mornings, when I go in to see Alex, I hope I might find him dead.' Tears sprang to her eyes. 'Isn't that awful? Aren't I the world's worst person?'

'No.' Julian patted her arm. 'You're a good person dealing with a terrible situation.'

He thought of the moment he'd discovered Helen's dead body. Her bedroom had been a place of stillness, not of horror. Who would understand his relief at seeing her motionless in her bed? None of her usual twitches and spasms. No guttural moans. She'd looked peaceful. Her mouth had untwisted and settled into a shape Julian scarcely recognised. For the first time in many years, he'd had an urge to kiss it.

48

Julian sat up in bed with a gasp, his heart thundering. Olivia snored gently beside him, one of her strong freckled calves sticking out from beneath the sheet. The day he did not want to face had already begun, slivers of sunlight reaching for him through the shutters.

How had he fallen asleep? He hadn't expected to. For hours, he'd lain awake next to his slumbering wife, tracing Gabriel's journey in his mind. Imagining his staged drunken return to the hotel, his sober escape from it a few hours later. As the church bells in Deià had tolled in the distance, Julian had travelled with Gabriel along the dark mountain roads to where he had parked the scooter and then accessed the coastal path by foot. Together they had navigated the path to the point where it met another smaller trail. Together they'd followed that trail to the viewpoint on the cliff. Together they had melted away into the tall pine trees and taken shelter behind the tumble of grey rocks. He must have drifted off around then.

Stomach churning, Julian lay down again and nestled in behind his wife's warm, solid body. After a few minutes, she stirred.

'What time is it, little mouse?'

He twisted his head and checked his travel clock. 'Just after seven.'

'Good job you woke me. I might have slept through.'

He considered suggesting they go back to sleep. He considered holding her so tight she wouldn't be able to leave the bed.

When she threw back the sheet and edged out of bed, he didn't stop her. He listened to the thud of her feet on the tiles, the familiar gush as she relieved herself, the erratic splash of water from the taps and the punishing scrub and spit as she cleaned her teeth.

'Are you coming for a walk?' Olivia said when she came back into the bedroom.

Bile surged up the back of Julian's throat. He leapt out of bed and rushed to the bathroom. As he doubled over the toilet bowl, the contents of his stomach poured out.

'Poor little mouse,' Olivia said when he emerged from the bathroom. 'Too much to drink last night?'

'Maybe a little.' He watched Olivia step into her shorts. A perturbing blend of love and hatred gripped him.

'Sheila can certainly put it away,' Olivia said. 'Not that I'm judging. I don't suppose she gets to do that often.'

'No. When you're caring for someone, you have to take your chances when you can.' He picked up a T-shirt from the chair and dragged it over his head.

'Are you sure you want to come?' Olivia said. 'You still look a bit peaky.'

'I'm not sure,' he said as he pulled on his shorts. 'I'm not sure at all.'

He retreated to the bathroom again and splashed water over his pale face. He stared into the mirror, searching his eyes for some sort of sign.

That's when he noticed it. The small white feather lying on his right shoulder.

'Ready?' Olivia asked when he returned to the bedroom.

'I think I'll stay here,' he said.

'Oh. Okay.' She jammed her wide-brimmed hat onto her head. 'I'll get breakfast ready.'

'If you're sure, darling?'

He pressed the soft feather between his thumb and forefinger. 'Probably for the best.'

* * *

Julian stood at the bus stop a few metres from the junction of the villa's access road and the main road into Deià. He checked his phone: 8.10 a.m. His speedy walk up the access road had left him hot and breathless. He took his backpack off, pulled his brightly coloured tropical shirt away from his skin and waggled it to let in some air.

Not long to wait for the bus. He pushed aside a vision of Olivia making her way down the dusty terraces. Before she'd left for the walk, he'd reminded her to take her mobile. Five minutes after she'd left the villa, he sent her a text.

You did take your phone?

To his relief, a reply pinged back seconds later.

Yes. Stop fussing!

He sent her a line of smiley faces.

Enjoy. Going to take bus to Deià and get pastries. Do you have your keys?

Her reply was short and swift.

Thanks. No. Close terrace doors over.

After closing but not locking the terrace doors, he'd rushed upstairs, changed his top, put on his deck shoes and Panama hat and grabbed his wallet. Hurrying downstairs, he'd tried not to think about Olivia. Olivia with the tall shrubs on one side and the smooth grey rocks on the other. He could not afford to think about her. He had Gabriel's plan to focus on.

When the bus to Deià arrived, Julian climbed onboard. He forced a friendly exchange in his stilted Spanish with the recalcitrant driver, hoping his exuberance and his loud shirt would make him memorable. As he made his way down the bus, he smiled at his fellow passengers and tipped his Panama at an elderly Spanish lady who smiled back.

The bus, stuck behind a tourist coach and a long stream of cars, made slow progress towards the village. The driver muttered in Spanish and gesticulated at every car coming in the opposite direction. When the bus finally entered Deià, Julian got off at the stop opposite La Residencia. He glanced up the driveway to the main building and thought of Sheila with another monotonous day stretching out ahead of her. He checked the timetable on the wall of the bus shelter. Just over an hour until the first bus back. In an hour's time, his life would be transformed. His pulse thrummed and the backs of his knees went soft. He had to pull himself together. What had Gabriel told him? *You gotta believe your own story, big guy. You gotta act it out like that shit is real.*

He sauntered past the village car park, and, noticing the market stalls set up there, took a diversion. He purchased a litre of organic olive oil from a weathered Scottish woman with long white hair. She turned out to be from Edinburgh, and he lingered at the stall to reminisce with her about the city.

Afterwards, he continued on, following the narrow pavement down into the heart of the village. His arms swung at his sides, and he made sure to smile at anyone who walked past. He felt dislocated from himself. Not quite in his body.

Eager hikers marched past him. The usual weary knot of backpackers had gathered outside the post office, imbibing the first coffee and cigarette of the day. A young couple inspected the property adverts outside the estate agents. The gift shops had yet to open, but he had no doubt they would have a profitable day once the coaches full of eager day trippers from Palma arrived.

He went to the cashpoint in the bank's vestibule, took out 100 euros and kept the requested till receipt with its date and time of withdrawal. Next, he visited the grocery store, saying hello to the stout woman at the counter before browsing the cluttered aisles. He selected a jar of pesto and a packet of fusilli pasta for that night's dinner. Olivia's favourite.

He pictured the viewpoint on the cliff. The pine trees close behind. The pasta slipped from his grasp and hit the floor with a thud. It might all be over by now, he realised, as he bent down to retrieve the package.

A feathery lightness filled him as he stood up. He floated his way to the counter. Once there, he asked the woman for four ensaï-mades. 'My wife's favourite,' he explained as she put them in a box. She smiled and asked him what he had planned for the day. 'Nothing much,' he said. 'It's going to be a scorcher, so I expect we'll have a relaxing day by the pool.'

She nodded. 'Too hot for the beach today.'

Clutching his box of pastries, he headed for Sandrino's café and selected a table overlooking the street, where anyone could see him. A young waiter in long denim shorts took his order for a café con leche. When it arrived, Julian lifted the cup and spilled froth and coffee down the sides. He replaced the cup in the saucer.

His heart thrashed in his chest. A dull headache had started behind his eyes and his speeding pulse would not slow down. He picked up a copy of the *Mallorcan Daily Record* from a nearby table. He leafed through it as he waited for his coffee to cool, exuding the appearance of a man of leisure. On the third page, he came across an article that made his pulse race even faster.

Family of suicide teenager lose civil case against Mallorca's police force.

Olivia was right. The grieving family stood no chance against the incompetence of the police and the alleged corruption amongst the island's elite. A possible murder had gone unpunished. He thought of Gabriel hurling himself from the rock at the beach. The uncanny ability he had to get away with anything.

The church bell rang out, like an alarm or a warning. Julian gulped his coffee down, tucked a five euro note beneath the saucer and hurried from the café, making sure the waiter saw him leave.

'Got to catch the bus,' he said.

* * *

He picked the bus up outside the post office. Again, he made a point of chatting to the driver as he handed over his fare. He took a seat in the middle of the half-empty vehicle, smiling at everyone he walked past.

The bus chugged uphill. Despite the slow speed, Julian sensed time speeding up. The faces of the other passengers and the view outside his window blurred. As if his mind wanted to erase any recollection he might have of this journey. Even now, he did not remember much about the night of Helen's death. He recalled inviting Beverly to the flat before she left for her night out and presenting her with a box of Milk Tray to thank her for looking after Helen. His memory then jumped to his return home after the Young Carers disco. What had occurred between these memories he had gleaned from newspaper stories, from the police and from Kathy and the other carers he'd spent the evening with. Apparently, he had driven his Peugeot Horizon to Sighthill, picked up three child carers and driven them to the Carers First Centre. He'd then spent the next two hours serving refreshments and encouraging the shyer kids onto the dance floor. He'd even taken over the music for a while when the DJ went out to have a cigarette. No, he could not remember everything, but he could see a clear line between that night and this day. Between his first wife and his second. With Olivia gone, he would finally be free of Helen. He would never be free of Gabriel, he knew that, but at least Gabriel accepted him for who he was. With Gabriel, he could enjoy a much more pleasurable captivity.

When the bus approached the access road for Villa Soledad, Julian pressed the bell on the rail in front of him to alert the driver. The bus dwindled to a halt.

'Gracias, amigo,' Julian said to the driver as he alighted. The bus growled into gear and pulled away. As Julian watched it go, he thought about his mother, waving to him from the bus to Manchester as it departed, and he realised he had made a mistake. All these years, he'd thought her legacy was to turn him into a carer. To make him the opposite of her. Now he could see that by leaving she had hoped to teach him a valuable lesson. To win your freedom, you had to be strong and courageous. Sometimes you even had to hurt innocent people to get it.

* * *

Inside the villa's dim hallway, he kicked off the imprisoning deck shoes and allowed the cool tiles to soothe his hot, swollen feet. He stood still for a moment, savouring the silence that surrounded him.

'Olivia,' he called, although he knew she would not answer.

You gotta believe your own story, big guy.

She must have gone for a longer walk, he told himself. Maybe she walked a bit further along the coastal path towards Sóller, or down to Cala de Deià beach. He checked his phone. No new messages.

'Oh well.' He put his phone back in his pocket. 'She'll be back soon.'

He removed his hat and sunglasses and put them on the kitchen worktop, next to where he'd left his laptop. He flipped up the lid of the computer and opened his emails. He sent one to Mike, asking if he was awake and if they could do a quick video call soon to discuss a new idea he'd had for the Wellstood grant. Another email went to Maxine at *Woman's Life* magazine, asking if she'd heard yet about the publication date for the article. Both communications traceable to his laptop. Both indicating he was in the house when he would say he was. He also looked up the day's weather forecast and the *Guardian* website to check the news.

Where would Gabriel be now, he wondered. Had he made it back along the coastal path to Sóller unseen? How long would the walk take him?

His dry throat prompted him to fetch a glass of water and drain it in one long gulp. When to text his wife and ask where she was, he thought? Not yet. Too soon. He had to stick to the plan. He would make Olivia a delicious breakfast and lay it out on the table on the top terrace. Take a picture of it and put it on Twitter.

Not a bad spot to start the day. #blessed.

Stick to the plan. Just like last time. He remembered the quick and methodical way he had moved through the flat in Shawfair Street after discovering Helen's dead body, scanning each room in case Gabriel had left any clues that could identify him. He remembered the speed with which his brain had processed what was about to happen and how he'd stepped into the role of shocked and grieving husband with no hesitation. Never before had he congratulated himself on the way he'd handled the police and the pressure of the investigation. Guilt had prevented him from acknowledging his achievements. Not any more.

A refreshing waft of breeze made him look up. For the first time since his return, he noticed the terrace doors were open. Hadn't he closed them before he left? He stepped forward, his heart lurching when he noticed the wide-brimmed straw hat sitting on the dining table.

'Olivia?' he said.

He found her on the pool terrace, sitting at the wrought-iron table and looking at her phone.

'You're back?' he said.

'I've been back ages.'

'But you're back.' His head pounded as possibilities rushed through it. Had something happened to Gabriel? An accident? Had Gabriel tried to do the deed and failed? His breath caught in his throat as he pictured Olivia pushing Gabriel over the edge of the cliff. He scanned her face and arms for signs of a struggle. He couldn't see any, but her eyes were red and swollen, as if she'd been crying.

'Of course I'm back,' she said, an impatient edge to her voice. 'Where else would I be?'

'Did you... did you see anyone on the path?'

'No. I never do.'

Julian's phone buzzed in his pocket. He pulled it out and checked the screen, only to find an email from Mike. What did he expect? Gabriel didn't even have a mobile. He slid the phone back in his pocket.

'I can't put this off any longer,' Olivia said.

'What?'

'I've been wanting to talk to you for a while.' She gestured for him to join her at the table. He obeyed, too stunned to resist.

'Talk to me about what?' He stared at the distant sea. The sea his wife's body should have been floating in by now. He blinked against the harsh sunlight, wishing he'd remembered to put on his hat and sunglasses.

'I wanted to wait until I'd had a few things checked,' Olivia said.

Julian struggled to get his thoughts in order. What if Gabriel had encountered a temporary hitch in the plan but intended to try again? What if Gabriel had changed his mind about the whole thing and decided to disappear?

'I was waiting for Liberto to get back to me,' Olivia said.

'The guy from the property management agency?' He couldn't understand why she looked so serious about some issue with the villa.

'Liberto is a private detective. He runs a detective agency.'

'What?' Panic darted back and forth beneath Julian's ribcage. 'Why would you be in touch with a private detective?'

'Oh, come on, Julian.'

'I don't know what you're talking about.'

She tapped the screen of her phone and held it out to him. He saw a photograph of him and Gabriel, naked and entwined on one of the sunbeds.

'This isn't... I don't understand,' he said.

'The day I went to Palma to see Libby. Remember? Liberto sent one of his colleagues over to the house to see if she could collect some evidence for me.'

'The cleaner,' he said. The girl in the kitchen who had caught him naked.

Olivia nodded. 'I'd spotted you and Gabriel together by the pool one day, but I had to make sure.'

He looked at his wife through fresh eyes, unnerved by her craftiness. What else did she know?

'Had you slept with him before?' she asked. 'When you first met in Scotland.'

'No. God, no. I had no idea we... I didn't plan any of it.' A searing pain shot across his forehead. If Gabriel had executed their plan, would Liberto have come forward with information about the affair? That would only have proved him guilty of adultery, not murder, but the police would surely have investigated the supposed accident more rigorously? He wondered if Gabriel had somehow found out about the detective and decided at the last minute to stay away.

'I'm not sure I believe you,' Olivia said. 'The more I think about him bumping into us on the beach that day, the more I—'

'Olivia, please. Listen.' To what? What should he say? He needed to placate her until he could find out what had happened to Gabriel. 'I know there's no excuse for my behaviour, but it was a fling. A stupid, midlife crisis sort of thing.'

'That's what I thought. Initially. That's what I hoped.'

'It is. It was. He was very persuasive and I was flattered. I was vain and stupid and I'm sorry.'

'No, you're not.'

'I've explored that... that side of myself and it's over now.'

'Save it, Julian.'

'Oh, I see,' he said, his tone lofty and wounded, 'this is all because Gabriel is a man.'

'Don't be ridiculous.'

'Really, Olivia, you can't punish me for being attracted to men as well as women.'

'Man, woman, what difference does it make?' His wife's steely grey eyes unsettled him. 'You do realise he's gone?'

'Gone? What do you mean?'

'He took a flight to Chile early this morning.'

Julian's spirit slumped. 'He's gone away with Nina?' Of course, he thought. Sometimes the most obvious explanation was the right one.

'Nina's not in Chile.'

'She's not?' He wiped sweat from his face. 'I don't understand.'

'Gabriel thinks she's in Chile, but she's in Barcelona. Figuring out what to do with the money I paid her.' Olivia smiled. 'What's wrong, little mouse? You look confused.'

'What have you done?'

'It was only supposed to be for a night at first. I wanted to show you the kind of person Gabriel was. I've met his type before, and I knew he was out for what he could get.'

'What have you done?'

'It started the night of your birthday.'

Julian listened as, in a calm, clear voice, Olivia enlightened him. When Liberto had passed on the evidence of Julian and Gabriel's affair, she'd felt hurt and betrayed but had hoped the relationship would burn out when Gabriel left. To make sure, she'd formulated a plan to show Julian how untrustworthy Gabriel was. How unfaithful.

'I asked Liberto to help me,' she said, 'and he suggested Nina.'

Olivia explained Liberto sometimes used Nina as one of his honeytrap girls. A device for catching cheating husbands in the act. Suspicious wives paid well for this service, and Liberto had numerous girls on his books to help him provide it.

Stunned, Julian groped for an appropriate response. Unable to find one, he settled for indignation. 'She's a prostitute?' he said.

'A honeytrap girl is not a prostitute.'

'She slept with someone for money.'

'Don't try and turn this—'

'I doubt the other board members of Women Against Sex Slavery would approve of your behaviour.'

'Oh, come on. You can't compare Nina to a sex slave.'

'It's a fine line, in my opinion.'

'You're in no position to lecture me on hypocrisy.'

That, Julian could not disagree with.

'It was only meant to be for one night,' Olivia said. 'I just wanted you to see what Gabriel was really like. I thought maybe then we could get back to normal.'

He remembered now. Nina sashaying across the terrace at La Residencia. Gabriel's eyes alighting on her for the first time.

'And then Gabriel had his accident,' she said, 'if it even was an accident.'

The panic beneath Julian's ribs intensified. 'And you hired Nina again?'

Olivia nodded. 'I made her a generous offer. We started at 15,000 euros and she got me up to twenty. Enough for her to start a new life. She has debts to pay off and she wants to go and study writing. David made a fuss about the transfers to her bank account at first. He wanted to know what it was for.'

'Did you tell him?'

'No. I haven't said anything to Arnold yet, either. I'm mortified. I don't know how I could have got you so wrong.'

'You didn't,' he said, his denial a reflex reaction to her look of disappointment. 'You haven't.'

'I hope Gabriel's enjoying his flight. I doubt he'll get to travel first class again in a hurry.'

'He thinks Nina's going to meet him there?'

'He does, poor fool. On their last night in Palma, she told him the story we'd made up about her getting a large inheritance. She told him her flight to Santiago was full, but she offered to book him a flight leaving this morning so they could be together.'

Julian trembled as anger at Gabriel's weakness surged through him. He waited for anger to turn to hatred but instead it subsided to resignation. Who wouldn't choose a new life with a wealthy, attractive young woman rather than commit a risky murder for a middle-aged man with nothing to offer?

'Now you know who he really is,' Olivia said.

'He would never have gone if you hadn't put temptation in his way.'

'His choice says it all.'

'What's going to happen to him when he gets to Chile? Have you thought of that?'

'He'll survive. People like him always do.'

Julian thought of the 8,000 euros in cash Gabriel had taken with him. He pictured him in the bar of some plush hotel in Santiago, Negroni in hand, flattering some unsuspecting man or woman. With a hollow heart, he realised Gabriel would find another protector and benefactor, but he would never find another Gabriel.

'At first I just wanted you back,' Olivia said, 'that was all. If you were going to leave me, I didn't want it to be for someone like him.' Tears clustered in her eyes. 'He reminded me of Lars and all the other takers, and I didn't want to let him win.'

'You made sure of that.'

'Perhaps it did all get a bit out of hand.'

'Just a bit?'

'I thought you would see him for what he was and remember who you were.'

Who was he, Julian wondered? Did he know? Had he ever known?

'This is my third marriage.' Olivia wiped away tears. 'I really wanted it to work.'

Her unexpected show of vulnerability disarmed him. He looked at the idyllic villa and then at the magnificent sea view before him. Did he really want to give it all up? Gabriel had abandoned him and their plan. He had to consider his own future now. 'It could still work,' he said, 'we could get through this.'

'You sleeping with him isn't even the worst part.'

'What do you mean?'

'It's the betrayal that really hurts.' She scrolled through the pictures on her phone and, after taking a deep breath, turned the screen towards him.

Her father's Rolex. The vintage Sea Dweller.

'It was Nina who had her suspicions about the mugging,' Olivia said.

'What suspicions? What's she been saying?'

'I had no idea you were lying about it at first. Why would I? Even with all your behaviour up to then, I would never have suspected you of going that low.'

'Listen. Let me—'

'After the mugging, I was upset at the thought you could have been badly hurt. I even wondered, just for a moment, if I should forgive you.'

'Olivia. Let's take a time out and just—'

'Then Nina found an envelope of cash in Gabriel's belongings and guessed what the two of you had done. I wasn't convinced, but I asked Liberto to look into it. He spoke to one of the fences he knows, some woman in Palma, and he sent me this photo through this morning.'

'That's crazy. There could be any number of watches like that out there and who knows where Gabriel got the money from.'

'The woman gave a very clear description of the young man who sold it to her.'

Julian sensed the door deep inside him opening further,

tempting him. How cruel it would be to fail now, when he was so close.

'Once I've confirmed the watch belongs to me,' Olivia said, 'Liberto will buy it back on my behalf.'

Technically, he thought, the watch had belonged to him, but he refrained from pointing that out. His wife's words only proved she didn't think of him as an equal partner at all. What belonged to her would always belong to her alone.

Olivia sighed. 'It won't be cheap to get it back, but this isn't about money.'

Yes, it is, he thought. If Olivia had never discovered the affair and if Gabriel had gone through with the plan, he would be sitting here alone, a fortune waiting for him to claim it.

'I can understand you being blindsided by lust,' she said, 'or even being conned into helping him out financially.' She pointed to the watch. 'But this?'

A sour hatred rose within him. Through Olivia's scheming, she had unwittingly saved her own life, but she had intentionally derailed his. She had taken the future he deserved and she had taken Gabriel. Gabriel, who had wanted only to set him free.

'I used to think you were kind but weak,' she said. 'Now I'm wondering if you were ever kind at all.'

To his surprise, he had no desire to protest the insult. 'Maybe you're right,' he said, 'maybe I'm not the man you thought I was.' Relief flooded through him. He was tired of pretending to be someone he wasn't.

'If that's true, what's the point of us being married?'

'I honestly don't know.'

'I keep thinking maybe it was Helen.'

The sour hatred curdled on Julian's tongue. 'What about Helen?'

'Maybe the trauma of losing her like that changed you in some way? Maybe you'll never be able to love again. Not truly.'

When Julian slammed his fist on the table, Olivia recoiled.

'I'm sick of hearing about Helen,' he said. 'She's gone. I can't bring her back.'

They stared at each other, a dangerous silence blooming between them.

'I'm going to divorce you, Julian,' Olivia said, eventually. 'I'm going to ring Arnold and ask him to start the proceedings. We'll have it all done in no time.'

How arrogant she was, he thought, sitting there deciding his fate. As if he would let her kick him out and leave him with nothing. As if he would just take it like a good little mouse.

Without warning, he launched himself across the table, grabbed Olivia's phone and flung it behind him into the pool. It landed with a splashy plop.

'Julian?' Confusion clouded Olivia's face. 'What on earth do you think you're doing?'

He stood up, looming over her.

'You're scaring me.' She scraped back her chair and lurched to her feet. When he grabbed the table and tipped it over, she screamed and took a few steps back. Her fear amused him. She'd assumed she was in control. She'd assumed she'd seen the worst of him, but he'd surprised her. He'd surprised himself.

A dog barked in the distance. Olivia glanced behind her, as if trying to calculate how long it would take to run down to the nearest property. Her gaze flicked back. Too long, he thought. Villa Soledad. All the solitude and privacy money could buy.

'Julian, let's both... let's just calm down.'

'I'm perfectly calm,' he said, although his heart was pumping far too fast and another unholy burst of pain in his forehead made him flinch.

'Let's talk about this,' Olivia said.

He laughed. Olivia, with her plotting and planning. She thought she had everything covered, but she hadn't considered he might be willing to take his chances.

'Julian. Please.'

He watched her working out her escape route. Whether she went left or right, she still had to get past him. 'Come on,' he said, 'make your mind up.'

She darted to the right and he caught up to her in seconds, grabbing her by the waist and putting a hand over her mouth. As she struggled to free herself, he looked at the cool green water of the swimming pool and thought of Gabriel. Gabriel with his hands on Olivia's head, pushing her under the surface. Gabriel hadn't really abandoned him, he thought. Gabriel was here, guiding him as always.

You gotta take risks to get what you want, big guy.

He threw her in first and jumped in after her. As soon as she resurfaced, he grabbed her around the neck and dragged her to the deep end. To where he could stand but she could not.

The door inside him was wide open. With one hand on the back of her neck, he held her underwater. Air bubbles rose to the surface as she twisted and squirmed. He expected to feel as though he was crossing a line, but he didn't. He realised he had crossed that line a long time ago, but when? When he'd offered to pay for Gabriel's coffee in the café that day? When he'd stopped to pick Gabriel up at the side of the road?

Olivia kicked out, catching his knee and unbalancing him. She wriggled free of his grasp, one hand reaching for the side of the pool.

'No, we don't.' His arms circled her waist and he pulled her against him.

'Stop,' she said, her breathing ragged, 'you're not thinking straight.'

Her panic filled him with a sense of invincibility. He wondered if this was how it felt to be Gabriel. To not care. To be careless.

'Julian. Stop.'

Two dragonflies, entwined, darted across the surface of the pool. Fighting, he decided. They were definitely fighting. He forced his wife beneath the water again. She thrashed about and made a gurgling sound he found very unattractive. The more she fought, the lighter and freer he felt.

Her struggling ceased sooner than he'd anticipated. He'd expected more of a fight. As her limp body sagged in his grasp, he realised the extent of his own exhaustion. His breath came in laboured gasps, his heart flitted between beats with no sense of rhythm. His clothes lay soaked and heavy on his skin.

When he released her, Olivia sank to the bottom of the pool. A nearby pigeon let out a long, mournful coo. He backed away towards the shallow end, a fierce tingling spreading up and down his right arm. A vicious pain gripped his temples and made his vision blur. He closed his eyes.

A loud splash made him open them again. Olivia burst out of the water, gasping for air. He dived into a flurry of front crawl, but by the time he reached the deep end, he was too late. She had pulled herself out of the pool and bent double, hands on her knees.

'You really can hold your breath a long time, my love,' he said, moving towards the side of the pool.

'Stop.' Olivia turned to the rockery and grabbed one of the dislodged stones. 'Don't come any closer.'

The door inside him was not only wide open, he had stepped through it. There was no going back.

'No.' She held the smooth grey stone above her head as he edged closer.

He rubbed his tingling right arm. 'At some point you'll have to make a run for it, and when you do, I'll catch you.'

'Helen,' she said.

'What?'

'It was you.'

'I was doing my bit for the kids that night, you know that.'

'It was you. Somehow.'

He sighed. Always an obstacle. Always someone getting in his way. His father, Helen and now Olivia. Would he ever have a life of his own?

He lunged for the side of the pool. As soon as he reached it, Olivia screamed and threw the rock. It missed him by a few centimetres, and he fell back into the water. Olivia picked up another rock, jagged and yellow. When Julian struck out for the other side of the pool, she met him there, the rock held over her head.

'Fine,' she said, her body racked by violent shaking, 'tell me what you want. Is it money? I'll give you some. A lot. I promise.'

As if, he thought. She had no intention of giving him any money.

'What do you want?' she said.

What did he want? He wanted back all the wasted years of his life, but as that would never happen, he wanted to make the most of all the years ahead. When he opened his mouth to tell Olivia this, an unintelligible gnarl of words fell out.

'What?' She inched towards the pool. 'What did you say?'

He tried again but more jangled sounds spilled out of him.

'Stop trying to trick me,' she said. When he didn't reply, she peered at him, eyes narrowed. 'Your mouth looks funny. Sort of droopy.'

He tried to step closer, but the right side of his body wouldn't cooperate. Black fuzz obscured the edges of his vision as he listed to one side, like a ship about to sink.

Olivia crouched by the side of the pool. He saw her sideways, as if the world had tilted ninety degrees. Even her smile was sideways.

'Julian,' she said, 'I think you're having a stroke.'

MON

This time last year, Olivia Pearson was having her photograph taken with her husband, Julian Griggs, for an article in this magazine. We at Woman's Life had selected Julian, a hero to carers everywhere, to feature in our 'Good Man Guide'. As Olivia posed for those pictures, she could never have imagined that a week later, Julian would be dead. Now, in her own words, she tells us about the terrible day she lost her beloved husband and how it changed her life forever:

This time last year is a phrase I've used often since Julian died. This time last year we were enjoying Christmas at home in Bloomsbury. This time last year we were admiring the spring blossoms in Regent's Park. This time last year we had just arrived in Mallorca for a long holiday. A chance for us to really relax and spend some quality time together. This time last year, I left our villa for my morning walk along the coastal path, unaware I would never see my husband alive again.

Nothing about that morning indicated to me it would end in tragedy. We'd enjoyed a lovely evening out at the La Residencia hotel the night before and had woken up looking forward to another day of beautiful weather. I said I wanted to do a longer walk that morning, to go further along the coastal trail to Sóller, and we agreed to have a late breakfast when I got back. He did think about coming with me but changed his mind at the last minute. How often I've replayed that moment. How often I've wondered if a different choice might have saved him.

Not long after I'd set off, he sent me a text to check I had my phone with me. He was always looking out for me, making sure I was safe. He also told me he was going into Deià to buy some of my favourite pastries for breakfast. He really was such a thoughtful man. After the paramedics had driven his dead body away, I found myself in the kitchen, dazed and in shock, offering to make coffee for the two police officers who'd attended the incident. That's when I saw the box of pastries. That's when I allowed myself to break down for the first time.

It is as difficult now to think of the moment I found him as it was to recount what had happened to those police officers that day. When I first emerged onto our pool terrace from the olive grove, I was in a wonderful mood. I'd had a glorious walk and on the way back I'd stopped at my favourite viewpoint for a rest and a drink of water. I spent almost ten minutes there, sitting by the edge of the cliff, admiring the sea and the sky. I have been assured those ten minutes would not have made a difference to my husband's fate, but I can't help the guilt that comes over me from time to time.

At first, I couldn't understand why Julian's Panama hat was floating in the pool. I saw it from a distance, and then I noticed the novel he had been reading lying on one of the sunbeds, along with his sunglasses. I assumed he had come to wait for my return, as he often did in the mornings. But why was his hat in the water?

I hurried over to the pool, intending to fish it out, and that's when I saw his body, lying at the bottom. He was on his side, as if asleep. I opened my mouth to scream but nothing came out. Before I knew it, I'd dived fully clothed into the water. He was at the deep end, and every time I got him to the surface, he slipped from my grasp. He was so heavy, and his clothes weighed him down further. Eventually, I managed to swim with him to the shallow end, where I could stand. I was calling his name, shaking him, desperate for some sign of life. I needed help but realised I'd dived into the pool with my phone in my pocket. I tried various ways to lift Julian out of the pool, but he was just too heavy for me. I tried giving him mouth-to-mouth, but it was impossible to do that and keep him afloat at the same time. In the end, I had to make the terrible decision to leave him while I ran up to the villa to phone for help. I did my best to wedge him against the metal ladder, but when I returned he had slipped underwater again.

What had happened, I wondered, as I held him in my arms in the water, waiting for the paramedics to arrive? Had he slipped, hit his head and fallen into the pool? I could see no sign of a head injury. A heart attack, perhaps? Julian's post-mortem would later reveal he'd suffered a terrible stroke, severe enough to have rendered him brain-damaged and incapacitated, had he survived it. I would give anything for Julian to be here now, and I would have dedicated myself to looking after him, but I also cannot imagine him trapped in a wheelchair, unable to communicate. A carer by nature, I don't think he would have found it easy to let others care for him.

I don't know how much time passed before the paramedics and the police arrived. The paramedics worked as hard as they could, but it wasn't long before they had to admit defeat and pronounce Julian dead. I remember sitting on the side of the pool in my wet clothes, shivering, as they put his body on a stretcher. The police officers attending the scene were wonderful. They saw right away a tragic accident had occurred and treated me with such consideration. They even apologised for having to question me briefly about the events. I really cannot thank them enough.

Throughout this difficult year, the person I have turned to most often for help is my dead husband. As many of you will know, he suffered an appalling loss some years ago when his first wife, Helen, was murdered. Every time I find myself in a dark place, I remember the strength Julian showed after losing her. How he managed to deal with a horrific situation and still keep going. I told myself that if he could do it, so could I.

Yes, my late husband taught me so many valuable lessons. From him, I learned that it may not always be easy to do the right thing, but it is necessary. You may think of my husband as a victim of a tragic accident, but trust me when I say he was so much more. Every day, I have to come to terms with the fact that no one knew my husband like I did. No one knew the real Julian Griggs.

Anyone who knows about Julian's charity work does, however, know how important that part of his life was to him. He set up the Helen Griggs Awards for many reasons, most of all so he could salvage something worthwhile from his wife's death. Soon after his own demise, myself and the other trustees of the Pearson Foundation unanimously agreed to take over the Helen Griggs Awards and to keep Julian's good work going. Not in his name. He didn't care what the world thought of him, and he wouldn't thank me for any kind of memorial. No, I wanted to keep the charity going for Helen's sake. I wish I could give her justice, but, given the lack of evidence in her case, it seems unlikely anyone will ever be charged with her murder. But I can give her a voice. She deserves that much. In my own lifetime and beyond, I will make sure she is never forgotten.

ACKNOWLEDGMENTS

First thanks go to my agent, Charlie Brotherstone. His support for my writing, his perceptive feedback and his story instinct have been invaluable. Huge thanks to Tara Loder, my brilliant editor at Boldwood Books and to the whole Boldwood team. Your enthusiasm and hard work on behalf of *The Perfect Holiday* is truly appreciated.

This novel would never have come together without the guidance of Louise Dean and her wonderful writing courses at The Novelry. I'm so grateful for the support I've had from the Novelry crew and from my fellow writers there.

A few 'without whoms': Liz Barling, for brilliant plot suggestions and for insisting I change the ending! Lesley Glaister and Cherise Saywell for insightful readings and crucial comments. Maria Ramirez from Perth College, UHI for supporting me and so many other writers and for her help with my Spanish language queries.

So many people assisted with research for this novel, and I apologise to anyone I haven't had room to mention here. Thanks are due to the following: the carers who spoke to me so openly and honestly about their lives and responsibilities; Dr Mark Flynn and Dr Peter Copp; the staff at Victim Support Scotland; Stuart Gibbon from the Gib consultancy and Stewart Hay for help with police procedural queries. I'm also very grateful to the island of Mallorca for providing me with such a perfect setting for this story and to the people I spoke to on my visits there. Never has research been so enjoyable!

As always, big love and thanks to Dad, Susan, Charly and Billy for their love and support.

To Susie and Mary, love and gratitude for everything. Thanks for all the help and inspiration and, most of all, thanks for putting up with me and the writing journey!

MORE FROM T.J. EMERSON

We hope you enjoyed reading *The Perfect Holiday*. If you did, please leave a review.

If you'd like to gift a copy, this book is also available as an ebook, digital audio download and audiobook CD.

Sign up to T.J. Emerson's mailing list for news, competitions and updates on future books.

https://bit.ly/TJEmersonNews

ABOUT THE AUTHOR

T.J. Emerson's debut psychological thriller was published by Legend Press and received brilliant reviews. Her short stories and features have been widely published in anthologies and magazines, and she works as a literary consultant and writing tutor. She lives in Scotland.

Visit T.J. Emerson's Website:

http://www.traceyemerson.com/

Follow T.J. Emerson on social media:

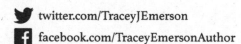

twitter.com/TraceyJEmerson

facebook.com/TraceyEmersonAuthor

ABOUT BOLDWOOD BOOKS

Boldwood Books is a fiction publishing company seeking out the best stories from around the world.

Find out more at www.boldwoodbooks.com

Sign up to the Book and Tonic newsletter for news, offers and competitions from Boldwood Books!

http://www.bit.ly/bookandtonic

We'd love to hear from you, follow us on social media:

 facebook.com/BookandTonic

 twitter.com/BoldwoodBooks

 instagram.com/BookandTonic